DROWN

A Novel

By
Albie Cullen

PUBLISH AMERICA

PublishAmerica
Baltimore

ISBN: 978-1-61582-696-4 (softcover)
ISBN: 978-1-4489-9586-8 (hardcover)
PUBLISHED BY PUBLISHAMERICA, LLLP
www.publishamerica.com
Baltimore

Printed in the United States of America

For My Mother, who continued to believe in me when nobody else did, including myself

Acknowledgments

Dad, Deirdre, Pete and Aidan without all of you there is none of this, Heather who inspired me to persevere with my writing as well as everything else, I love you, Jodi, a true friend to the very end, Tom and Shari for your incessant support, Jim, Joan and Danny whose unconditional and ongoing support saved me at the end (both times), Rich, guru and friend, Don whose advice was only good once I took it, Charlie, Megan, Mark, Spider, Kristoff, Jeff and everyone in Falmouth, thank you, Ira and Mary who always had a smile and a supportive word (not to mention a great beach house!), Jerry, the man behind the curtain, literally, who made dreams come true, Mary and June in Boston for the laughs, wisdom and support, Alim for your mediation skills, Steven Manchester for the initial edit and Heather for the re-edit-Thank you one and all, and finally John Wall although you are not around to see it published I know you are smiling for me somewhere—AFC

Chapter 1

The One-Two Lounge wasn't located on one of America's many boulevards of broken dreams. The *One-Two* was located on a dead end street in a dead end town and was a permanent, self-storage bin for broken dreams.

Billy Sunday, dressed as always in faded blue jeans and a worn out T-shirt, drove slowly down the dead end street. It was a typical suburban, residential street with two and three bedroom colonials situated on three-quarters of an acre each. Some of the houses looked brand new. Others could have used a coat of paint and someone to mow the lawn. There were no kids playing outside or family sedans parked in the driveways. Billy's twelve-year-old, red Toyota Corolla bounced up and down, as it slid in and out of the many potholes left in the wake of another harsh, New England winter. Both the early evening shadows and his exhausted mental state made his navigation of the potholes more difficult. Two years of constantly being on the run-both literally and figuratively-was beginning to exact a permanent toll.

The temperature this Thursday night felt almost as far from a New England winter as one could get. The air was warm, breezy and dry. On nights like these, it always seemed to Billy that there were a few more stars in the sky and the breeze smelled as if it carried a bouquet of intoxicating incense. Tonight, the weather made even the most hopeless of men able to forget their despair, if only for a few hours. The *One-Two* parking lot was crowded and the jukebox could be heard through the open door.

As he opened the car door, he hesitated. Like most places that remain embedded in one's memory, somehow avoiding the cleansing which time constantly provides, the *One—Two* contained, for Billy at least, memories that represented some of his best times as well as some of his worst times. After the non-stop trip that had been the last two years, he was back in search of the best memories. The memories he wanted to recapture always came back to Nacy. There are only a few natural forces in this world that can make a rational man go against his judgment: love and greed. To the best of his knowledge, Nacy didn't have a trust fund.

Against his better judgment, he headed up the creaky stairs to the lounge. He'd convinced himself that he was drawn by the laughter, the sound of the jukebox and the promise of a cold beer and the company of some old friends. Deep down, he knew the reality was that like most people, he was searching for something that had developed into a constant craving; something that would keep him grounded and centered. He was searching for a solution that would provide him the inner peace he craved-like everyone else-but seemed so elusive. It was not something that could be found in a bottle, a pill, or a powder, nor could it be delivered through a song, a book, or a mass. It was a missing intangible that could only be found in and provided by a special someone, or so was his way of thinking. That was the conclusion he'd come to believe after contemplating this dilemma for the better part of two years. If asked, he would convincingly deny this desire. He'd become the consummate bachelor and liked the idea of no strings attached. He'd played at love and sometimes lost, and sometimes won. More importantly, however, he'd learned to avoid the insatiable hold created by the longing for love for a certain special someone; the hold that had gripped all other mere mortals at one time or another, usually to that mortal's detriment.

Despite this outward persona, the constant traveling of the past two years had made him realize that he'd never even been introduced to love. The longing, which he had so successfully repressed through a state of denial for so long, was now unavoidable.

The *One-Two* was in effect a small, two storied, white house converted into a bar. From the outside, you could tell that it had once been a house by the black shutters that framed the two windows which faced the street. The stairs leading up to the glass entrance door didn't mimic the appearance of a residential home, they were an obvious addition. There was no sign outside to indicate exactly what type of establishment resided at this location. Nobody was really sure how long the *One-Two* had been there. At the last annual outing the invitations read, *Celebrating 20 years of affairs, divorces and addictions*. The theory as to whether the *One-Two* was actually responsible for these social ills depended on whom you asked.

If you asked most patrons, they'd insist that the ex-wife, as well as the pressures and ultimate boredom of a middle class life drove them to the *One-Two* which took it from there. If you spoke to the ex-wives, they'd say that their husbands detour to the *One-Two* after work was what led directly to the problems and ultimately the divorce. Billy figured it was like the chicken and the egg argument, and that both sides would just have to agree to disagree. Regardless of the actual cause-the separations, divorces and addictions provided a steady clientele for the thousands of lounges everywhere like the *One-Two*.

As Billy sauntered in, he could hear the unmistakable *CRACK* of a pool stick hitting its mark as somebody broke on the pool table to his left. Beyond the pool table, the bright, rotating lights at the base of the jukebox illuminated the pink and yellow plastic of the machine's cover. The angst of Sully, the lead singer of a band called *Godsmack*, emanated loudly from the CD presently spinning behind the plastic. *Godsmack* was a band that originated from the area, selling over a million records and just recently completed the *Ozzfest Tour*. As a result, everybody at the *One-Two* loved to lay claim to knowing the members of the band personally, particularly the lead singer, Sully.

Despite his long involvement in the music business, Billy had never heard of *Godsmack* before he came to frequent the *One-Two*. This was most likely due to the fact that FM radio, in his humble opinion, had become un-listenable. In spite of this, he liked the band. Their "sound" was a little heavy for his personal taste, but none-the-less it was melodic. On a night like tonight when you were ready to party, the music fueled both your physical energy and mental excitement. But after numerous hours, the bass drum was the last sound you wanted to accompany the unnatural pounding inside your head, provided free of charge by your hangover. A hangover so infamous that when your friends saw you the next day, they knew you had been at the *One-Two* the night before. It was a hard drinking, hard partying place-not for the faint of heart. As a more conservative classmate of his once said after partying at the *One-Two* (from which it had taken the classmate a week to recover), "The *One-Two* is strictly for professionals."

Beyond the jukebox were three small booths. The first booth was covered with beer bottles and ashtrays discarded by the pool players. The next two were empty. To the right of the booths was a horseshoe shaped bar that extended into the center of the room lined with bar stools. Nearly all twenty stools were filled with patrons and various neon beer lights hung on the wood paneled walls which illuminated the shiny pine topped bar. The place permeated a heavy odor of smoke and a blue haze wafted below the stained white ceiling. Billy strolled past the bathrooms on his right and walked to the bar. Despite the small size of the club, the bathrooms were almost always full, as patrons used the single stall bathrooms in order to transact various types of commerce.

When Billy had been initially introduced to the club three years ago, he'd joked that a passport should be required to enter the men's room. It was the only place he'd been other than Amsterdam where virtually anything and everything was available for a price.

As he made his way closer to the bar, he began to recognize a few of the faces. The bartender was a woman named Penny. She was an attractive woman with long brown hair and a body with curves in all the right places. She was easy on the eyes but had a surly personality and nearly every time she waited on you, you felt like she was doing you a favor. Despite this apparent professional shortcoming, she did it with a certain charm that appealed to the clientele. This explained why she'd been a bartender at the *One-Two* for years.

Across the bar was Ramie, a slight, good looking, Dominican who was one of the club's resident drug dealers. He always looked "smart." Nothing was ever out of place with his hair, clothes or overall look. Next to Ramie was his girlfriend, Mercedes, a striking, pale, long legged blonde who always dressed to show off her best features. Ramie and Mercedes rarely used drugs, they drank in moderation and were always very pleasant. To Ramie, sitting at the *One-Two* constituted his daily employment and he approached it in a very business like fashion. He and Mercedes smiled and waved at him from across the bar. They appeared genuinely happy to see him. He had always liked them and felt that the feeling was mutual. He figured musicians and drug dealers had much in common, their two professions seemed intertwined. The striking of the first musical note in all probability followed the ingestion of some form of narcotic. The best part was that if a musician or a drug dealer were the least bit successful, beautiful women surrounded them.

Next to Ramie and Mercedes sat Billy and Jimmy, two guys who worked second shift for the local gas company. They were still in their occupational blue jump suits, drinking shots of Sambuca followed by Budweiser chasers. He was introduced to these guys through his friend Danny. Danny, also a gas company employee, was responsible for his patronage at the *One-Two* and in due course, his introduction to Nacy. You wouldn't be able to find the *One-Two* unless a regular brought you, and the regulars were very discriminating on who they drew to their lair. Upon reflection, which he had a lot of time to do in his profession, he felt both Danny's invitation to the *One-Two* and his introduction to Nacy, was sometimes for the better and oftentimes for the worse. After two years without seeing or talking to her, Billy felt ready to try and reconnect and maybe re-establish their relationship. He was determined, at least in his exhausted state of mind.

Along with those that were familiar to him there were a couple of people at the bar he didn't recognize. The fact that he didn't know their names didn't mean he didn't know their story. He pulled up one of the few remaining vacant barstools and sat down next to Parker and William. They were two former telephone executives in their late forties who had already put in their twenty years of company time and were now retired with a healthy pension, a lifetime of health insurance and too much free time.

Billy had been good friends with Parker, but had not talked to him since he'd left town a couple of years ago.

"Look what the fuck the cat dragged in," Parker bellowed with a wide grin.

He quickly recognized that Parker was a few Miller Lights and a couple packs of Newport's into the evening. Seeing Parker again made him feel good and instantly at home. He immediately stuck out his hand, which Parker grasped with a firm grip and a slap on the back.

"Jesus, you actually look pretty good for an old bastard," admired Parker. He looked Billy up and down while still shaking his hand. "You know, my twenty year old kid's in a band at college. When you gonna grow up and get a real job?"

Billy was 35 years old-much older then his tattooed, multiple pierced contemporaries wailing away on MTV. The years had been kind to him, no lines on his face or grey hairs yet, despite his lifestyle. His sandy brown hair came down to and sometimes covered his eyes which were a cool slate blue. Many people told him his eyes were his best physical feature. If you spoke to some of his ex-girlfriends (of which there were many), they might say that his eyes were his only redeeming quality. He was of medium build, if slightly overweight, though he carried it well.

He was sensitive to his weight. Since turning thirty he suddenly began gaining weight despite the fact that he really hadn't changed his lifestyle. His favorite libation, beer, seemed to settle right in his gut. He resented the fact that he now had to pay attention to what he ate, when he ate it and how much booze he drank. He'd tried skipping the eating and sticking to the drinking, however, that didn't seem to be working on decreasing his girth. He also regretted that when he went out on the road now, he had to worry about having enough prescription stomach antacid, along with his recreational drugs. His weight and all the problems that went with it were just a couple of the things that he didn't like dealing with as he got older.

Parker's outburst prompted the rest of the patrons to look over, people who knew him or recognized him began saying hello or waved from across the bar. Penny came over with a cold Budweiser in hand and managed a slight upward turn of her lips this being her idea of a smile. As she placed the beer in front if him she said, "This one's on me."

Billy and Parker made small talk as they drank their beers. Billy was explaining to Parker what had transpired over the last couple of years since they'd seen each other. He'd been touring relentlessly in support of

12

the record which he'd recorded nearly two years ago and was just recently signed to a "major" record company.

"Like I have any idea what the hell you're talking about," remarked Parker. "Why don't you start at the beginning?"

"Feels like I've been starting at the beginning every two years." Billy could only laugh at that truth.

"Yeah, with every part of your fucking life, too," agreed Parker.

Wasn't that the truth, was his only thought.

"A lot of fresh starts and disappointing endings," Billy said, "Well, Parker you've heard the saying, it's always darkest before the dawn."

Parker responded, "Yeah, well it feels like it's been 4:00 am around here for years."

They continued talking, while Parker waved Penny over for a couple more beers. The conversation bounced back and forth between catching up on old friends and Billy's whereabouts these two years. Basically, he and his band had been criss-crossing the country.

"I bet you meet a lot of broads out there?" Parker asked.

"Yeah, perfect length of time for a relationship too," sighed Billy.

"What? About eighteen hours?" They both laughed at that.

"It's like somebody once told me," Parker said, "whenever you see a beautiful broad walking down the street, just remember one thing. There's a guy somewhere who's happy to get rid of her."

Parker concluded their analysis on relationships with this, "Just remember-if it floats, flies or fucks just lease it, don't buy it." This greatly amused them and they continued laughing. Penny, who'd obviously been eaves dropping, showed her disapproval with a scowl and turned her back and walked to the other end of the bar.

"I guess it will be a while before we get another drink?" laughed Billy.

"Yeah, this place doesn't change," said Parker. "We're looking at least one shift change now."

As they sat nursing their beers, Ramie came up to Billy from behind and rubbed his shoulders. "Yo, Billy, where you bin, man?"

"Hey, Ramie, I been playing with the band, man."

"Yeah, you come down and play some of that Marc Anthony shit for me and my girl?

13

"No, Ramie, you know I'm too white to play that shit. But I like that stuff, good rhythm."

"Yeah, we Dominicans got rhythm, you know?"

"I wish I did Ramie, but you know how it is with us fat, white Irish folk."

"Yeah, you do all right though, I seen you play. Listen, you want to see me?" That was Ramie's code for meeting him in the bathroom if you wanted to score some coke. He hadn't done any in a while but not because was trying to quit or anything. Over the years, he'd done more than his fair share to keep the Colombian economy rolling along. Most people nowadays denied doing coke, which one of his band mates correctly referred to as dummy dust. The fact was that there was more blow coming into this country than coffee. People were just more discreet or better liars, depending on how you looked at it or who you talked to. He figured it was like the so-called health kick in the early 1980's. Everybody told the pollsters they were eating healthy, while Oscar Mayer's hot dog sales rose to record levels.

Billy had played at an industry party in New York the night before and was now running on exhaust fumes. He was only able to grab a few hours of sleep before driving up to Boston earlier in the day. The two beers he'd had were beginning to hit him and he was feeling pretty good, feeling no pain. "Yeah, sure," he answered Ramie with a glimmer in his eye.

"Well, then meet me in my office." Ramie smiled and his white teeth glistened out from under his brown skin. Billy followed him into the bathroom without any hesitation.

"So, you doin' alright? You lookin' good," asked Ramie before Billy could answer. As Ramie spoke, he reached into his sock and picked out a baggie. The baggie was filled with a bunch of smaller baggies, each of which was filled with an ivory powder. "What can I do you-forty or sixty?" asked Ramie as he pulled out the different sized baggies. He sold only small bags of coke. The forty dollar bags weighed a half-gram of blow. The sixty dollar bags were supposedly a gram, but probably weighed closer to three-quarters. It really didn't matter to Billy because it was going to be gone in a few hours either way.

"I tell you what," said Ramie, "give me twenty and I give you a sixty. Consider it a little welcome home gift."

Billy handed him a twenty dollar bill and Ramie gave him the corner of a baggie with the plastic knotted at the top in return. He could never figure out how the dealers made the small knots so tight.

He put the top of the bag up to his mouth and with his two front teeth pulled on one side of the knot until it was loose. He untied the rest with his fingers. With his other hand, he reached into his back pocket and pulled out his wallet. Placing the open bag on the sink he then removed a credit card from his wallet. With one hand he picked up the bag, while he dipped the corner of the credit card in the bag with the other. As he lifted the small pile of white powder on the corner of the card up to his nostril he inhaled deeply. He quickly felt the familiar rush that ran through his sinuses and into his brain. It felt as though the chemical had the power to lift his heels right off the ground.

"Now, you doin' all right?" asked Ramie.

His response, as he looked sadly into the mirror was, "Yeah, now I'm doin' all right."

Chapter 2

Even attired in a traditional, gray business suit, you couldn't miss that Kelly Agis was an attractive woman. Her long athletic legs led to narrow hips, a flat stomach and there was something to be said for the way she filled out her fitted blouse. The tightness of her skirt only highlighted her backside, which the men she worked with in law enforcement unanimously decided was her best feature. Despite recently graduating with a master's in criminal justice, her facial features resembled that of a college sophomore. Her red hair was long and shiny, but she wore it up in a conservative twist when she was working. She epitomized what the modern women hoped to attain in her dress, her walk, and most of all her attitude. She strode through the vestibule of the upscale co-op building in Manhattan's Upper East Side and crossed the lobby floor which was covered with small, sand-hued tiles that reflected the soft light from above on this early, Friday morning. The attendant sitting behind the lobby desk simply pointed to the elevator when she approached him as he'd already seen Kelly flash her badge to the doorman-she hadn't been the first constable to pass through the lobby this morning.

Kelly took the elevator to the tenth floor and as soon as the doors opened she encountered two uniformed police officers standing guard. Both men nodded politely while the smaller one said, "Unit 310, down the hall."

Kelly snaked her way through the apartment hallway which was lined with both uniformed officers and detectives dressed in old, ratty sport coats. The door was open to Unit 310, thereby concealing the number, but the yellow police tape gave the crime scene away to anyone who happened upon it.

She ducked under the tape into the single room apartment. Three of its walls were a bright clean white while the fourth wall, which was facing Kelly, was all glass and revealed a stunning view of the East River. To her immediate right was a small alcove which looked to be a galley kitchen. There was a door opening from the left of the kitchen that she assumed led to a bathroom.

Jutting out from the middle of left wall was a queen-size bed that rested three feet off the ground with a huge headboard crafted out of perpendicular brass pipes. Whatever was lying amongst the linen on the bed had captivated everyone's undivided attention. Once in the room Kelly saw a striking woman lying on the bed with her hands lashed to the headboard. She appeared to be in her late thirties, if Kelly had to venture a guess. The woman's shoulder length hair was brown and obviously well maintained by a high price salon. She had striking dark brown eyes that actually looked black. Her sensual lips were painted with a bright, red lipstick that accented her stunning features. The dark circle that wove around her neck was the color of a purple horizon just after the sun has disappeared from view. Her small and firm breasts were bare. A black corset adorned her flat stomach and an inch below that was a black garter belt that was attached to two black silk, thigh high stockings which covered her long, shapely legs. Both her ankles were tied to the end posts of the brass baseboard rendering her legs in a spread-eagle position which left a clear view of her clean-shaven genitals.

Love and murder had one thing in common, Kelly though to herself, *both start with the discovery of a body.*

"Looks like somebody is a regular at Victoria's Secret," Kelly deadpanned.

"I finally meet a girl who knows how to have a good time and she's dead," responded Detective Jimmy Gerard. Jimmy was Kelly's partner. He was in his late fifties, just trying to play out the string in his last few years on the force before retirement. He'd been a New York, homicide detective for over twenty years. His lined, weathered face reflected the toll the job had taken on him. He had to admit that it felt a little strange being partnered with a young, attractive woman. Initially he was irritated when he learned of his new partner. It wasn't because he had a thing against women cops like so many others, but rather because he didn't need or want any temptation this close to the finish line. Maybe twenty years ago a little flirting or maybe more would be all right but in today's age of political correctness one wrong word or hand brush could cost you the whole shooting match: badge, gun, job, and pension. *What a pathetic time to be alive*, Jimmy thought, not for the first time.

His father had once told him he could resist everything but temptation. The truth of the matter, for him, was that he didn't find it any easier to resist it today than he did when he was younger. But due to his age, he wasn't as quick at giving in to his impulses. He reckoned the deterioration of his ability to spot and succumb to temptation had probably saved him a lot of trouble with Internal Affairs over the last decade, not to mention his pension. As it turned out, Kelly was completely capable and actually had a sense of humor, as opposed to the standard issue, "I'm here to avenge three centuries of oppression" attitude that most women cops seemed to carry with them these days. The more dates he went on in New York City confirmed this attitude and he felt it was beginning to be shared by all the women he encountered lately. He genuinely liked and respected her and enjoyed showing her the ropes. If he was honest with himself, he'd admit it had breathed new life into a job he seemed to have lost interest in over ten years ago.

"What do we have Jimmy?" Kelly asked.

"What you see is what you get, pretty much. We have one unidentified female, who I'd lay odds she was killed by strangulation. There is cocaine residue on the dresser and various sex toys and two prescription bottles over there on the nightstand. One of the bottles is labeled percocet and the other oxycontin.

"Has the M.E. been here yet?" asked Kelly as she looked around the room.

"He was here briefly. I think he went back to his office for some gear. I mean, do these guys think we're calling them over here for coffee?" asked Jimmy, sounding a little exasperated.

"Any time of death yet?"

"Not yet."

A uniform in the bathroom called out to them, "Detectives, you better come in here." They walked over to the bathroom not sure what to expect. In the spotless, white tile bathroom was a purse was lying on the sink. The three of them, Jimmy, Kelly and the uniform, had no possibility of fitting in the tiny bathroom together so Jimmy waved the uniform out.

"Two million dollars for a condo and you don't even have room enough to take a crap in comfort, for Christ sakes," Jimmy muttered as he walked into the bathroom. *Rich people get what they deserve*, he thought to himself. He grabbed the pencil from his small notebook and used it to carefully remove a wallet from the purse and opened it to reveal the driver's license.

"Belinda Caruso. Born December 12, 1965," he recited.

"Dead sometime this week prior to Friday morning," Kelly added.

As Jimmy stared at the picture on the license Kelly figured it was because this was one attractive woman and that was saying something in a city full of very attractive women.

Jimmy kept repeating to himself, "Belinda Caruso. Belinda Caruso. How do I know that name?" Suddenly he yelled, "Oh Fuck!"

"What?" Kelly responded, obviously startled by his outburst.

"You know who this fucking broad is?" Jimmy asked.

"If I knew, I would have already told you, you know, being a detective and all."

"She's married to some guy named Phil Caruso-he's the president of some big record company, always in the news. The Post is gonna go postal. They're gonna fucking love this one."

"I better put a call in to McBride and give her a head's up," said Kelly, as she pulled out her cell phone. She knew the District Attorney would want to be all over this one. "Then we better start talking to the neighbors before they start spreading rumors. There's no way we're going to be able to keep a lid on this one."

"I certainly don't need this at my fucking age," said Jimmy, almost to himself. He knew in his gut that this one wasn't going to end pretty, no matter how beautiful the victim had been.

Chapter 3

The offices of Artiste Records were located forty stories above Times Square. Phil Caruso was standing in his palatial office, yelling across the room into the speakerphone. "I don't fucking care if WXKL doesn't like the fucking record. I sent them two fucking acts for their Christmas Jingle, or whatever the hell that thing was called. If they ever want to see another one of our artists, or tickets we have to give away, they better play this fucking Dead Boys record," Phil continued to scream, "and I'm talking regular Goddamn, heavy, fucking, rotation. Are we fucking clear?!"

"Yes," said a meek male voice on the other end.

"And if you don't get this record on, I'll get a fucking promo man who can! Call Vell and light a fire under his ass. What am I paying all this Goddamn money in independent promotion for?" screamed Phil. By this point, his face was becoming flushed with anger. He picked up the handset and slammed it down. "Fuckin' PD's," he muttered, "they're all a bunch of whores." He lifted the phone over his head and tossed it. The recoil from the cord caused the phone to boomerang and strike him in the shoulder.

Phil Caruso, like most of his contemporaries, had risen to the position he was in as President of a major record company by hiding his incompetence with inaction. He'd learned how to exploit his handicap in today's age of political correctness. He was a midget or dwarf as they now preferred to be called. Though he would never admit it, even to himself, everyone knew his handicap had contributed significantly to his appointment as President. Place a handicapped guy as the head of the label and appear more sensitive to the artists (and the stockholders, if the company under performed). The apparent logic was: the artists feel better about getting screwed by a guy literally half the artists' size than say, a former limo driver (who, in fact, was also presently the President of another major label).

He'd started out in the mid seventies as a local promotion guy. Major labels had local promotion guys in every major city where there were airwaves. These guys worked with all of the radio stations and concert promoters within the market and would swing by the station with the new releases. When the artists were willing and able, they'd drop by the stations with the promo guys, making sure the stations had tickets, back stage passes, and anything else the station employees or in rare instances the station's listeners needed. In theory, they were responsible for getting the label's records played on the radio from morning till night. The object being to get the whole city singing the lyrics to the songs they were promoting.

Back in the 1970's, getting records played on the radio was too difficult for a total loser like Phil. Even though all you had to do was walk into the station with five records, a hooker, an eighth of an ounce of blow and some single malt scotch. By the time you got back in your car, all five records would have been added to the playlist and you'd be humming along with the last single as you pulled into your driveway. In Phil's case, he paid for a lot of hookers, bought a lot of blow, but still didn't get many records played. No one was singing his song.

In the early '80s, the game began to change a little bit. The stations started to rely on the so-called independent promoters. Independent promoters were a small group of middlemen who'd formed relationships with all of the program directors (or PD's) at the major market radio stations. The PD's were, and still are, responsible for what is being heard on any given station's playlist. (The stations only play a total of twenty or so songs which explains why the same songs are repeated every two hours). The PD's also began insisting that the labels go through the so-called independents if they wanted to get a record played, or "added" on the station. The independents started to charge a hefty fee for this service. In turn, the independents shared these fees, usually in the form of women and drugs, (people in the music business always seemed to have limited needs) with the PD's. It was often said that the independents couldn't always get a record on a station (although they usually could), but they could always keep a record off. If you were a record company trying to break a new artist without airplay, you were dead. As a result, the independent record promoters became the most influential people in the music business.

Even a moron like Phil had this figured out. He had every independent he could on a hefty weekly contract and he continued to keep them on the payroll regardless of whether the independent was working the stations in his market or not. His records were always added to the playlist immediately or "out of the box." The first week the record was out, it was being "worked" and the promo guys were making brownie points with the powers that be at corporate.

Toward the late '80s, the national media began to pick up on the role of independents in the music business. For obvious reasons, the independents had always preferred to work in the shadows of the bright lights of the music business. Soon after the media interest gained momentum, government interest came along in the form of the Justice Department. Given all the sudden interest in his present occupation, Phil decided that he'd had enough of promotion and became the Vice President of Artists & Repertoire.

A&R men were responsible for finding and cultivating the talent. It was a tough job with a high turnover. Sign one or two acts that "stiff" and you'd be gone. Even if you were to find a hit act, you'd run the risk of signing acts in a similar genre and if the kids' taste changed, which happened about every other month, you'd be screwed. Everybody would forget the hit act you were responsible for and just remember the five arena rock acts you signed, while everybody was now listening to heavy metal. Furthermore, if you were canned from an A&R gig, you were done in the music business. There were former A&R execs bartending throughout New York and LA.

If there was anything Phil was less qualified to do than promotion, it was A&R. As dumb as he was, at least he was smart enough to realize this fact. For ten years as an A&R executive, he never signed a single artist. He figured if he didn't sign anybody, he couldn't fail and his theory worked. If he received any pressure from above, which wasn't often, he would sign a band to a production agreement.

A production agreement was a deal that was just short of receiving a record contract. The label would agree to front the production costs of a few songs, referred to as "tracks" within the industry. In addition, the label would put the band up at a decent hotel and give them a little walking around money. After the tracks were done, the label would then decide whether the band warranted the financial commitment of a record deal. Phil never even passed any of the recorded tracks on for review. He simply told his superiors that there was nothing there and they bought it. In addition to providing Phil with job security, this was inherently unfair to the musicians he signed to these production deals. This was probably the only aspect of his experience that made him qualified to serve as a record company president; the ability to completely screw over artists, while maintaining a clear conscience.

After a brilliant A&R career without a single "stiff"-or a single signing, for that matter-Phil was promoted to Vice President of East Coast Operations. Two years after being appointed Vice President, the existing President stepped down after getting caught laying down with a group of female artists thereby leaving Phil the keys to the so-called presidential washroom.

After having thrown the phone, he gazed around his office and realized that the game was beginning to change again. All of the chrome that glittered from the coffee table, the couch, and the window casings-which served to frame colorful Times Square—suddenly seemed to be losing some of its shine.

Nobody seemed to care before that he was totally in over his head, however low that might actually literally be. Now, there was nowhere for him to be promoted to and people were starting to care. Those people happened to be the stockholders of his company. With Artiste's stock dropping due to its lack of sales since his indoctrination as the President, the stockholders were beginning to feel uneasy.

In the early '90's, as the economy began to turn around, large corporate entities began to comprehend a couple of things about record companies that these corporations were oblivious to before. Once deemed a shady businesses run by unsavory characters, the music industry was becoming a cash cow, creating twelve billion dollars annually in music sales alone. With the emergence of the internet and the digital age, music could be easily exploited through new and developing technologies. The music catalogues these companies owned became attractive content and licensing material for these same corporations. In turn, public corporations began buying up the major record companies and merging them into large conglomerates, or spinning them off into their own public entities. The latter was what was happening in the case of Artiste. Since Phil wasn't high enough in the executive food chain, Artiste went public and he failed to collect on the millions in cash that the stock options had provided the previous management team. It seemed the only thing he was accumulating was the aggravation involved when a public company's stock was sliding.

What became more alarming was that the drop in sales coincided with his appointment as the leader to take Artiste into the 21st century. He could only hope his handicap would buy him some time in this age of blind loyalty to political correctness. However, as the Board of Directors had informed him last week, if the stock price kept falling, both the Board and the stockholders would be calling for someone's head. With Phil's already being so close to the ground his melon was the first likely choice.

Phil sat back in his ergonomic chair and glanced around the office. Gold and platinum records adorned the walls of what he considered his sanctuary. What wasn't covered in chrome, glass or mahogany was covered in brown leather. *Christ*, he thought, *if I hocked the furniture alone, I could probably live on the proceeds for two years.* His next thought only served to further depress him, *unfortunately, it would probably only last Belinda one month, if she ever bothered to stay at home that long.*

Chapter 4

"It's Luke from Artiste on one...again!" Jonathan "Johnny" Vell's assistant yelled through the walls of the offices to his boss. Like most dysfunctional work environments, common courtesies weren't something anyone working for Vell respected. It was easier to yell across a room than to use the modern technology at hand and make use of call transfer-or walk the few feet into somebody's office to relay a message.

"I told him the Dead Boys ain't going on WXKL this week," Jonathan shrieked. The reality of the situation was that Jonathan didn't know the Dead Boys from the Dead Kennedy's from the Grateful Dead, but he wasn't going to let that stop him from collecting a $10,000 weekly retainer.

His assistant, who was only four feet away from him, yelled back, "Well, he's left fourteen messages and says he was promised two adds for supporting the WXKL Jingle Ball Christmas Concert, and if he doesn't get the Dead Boys added this week, 'XKL is done, as far as Artiste is concerned."

Jonathan didn't give a fuck about what he promised somebody last December. As far as he was concerned, the only thing that was guaranteed was that his rates were about to increase in a month. The inside trade magazine, Gavin, had named him *Alternative Promotion Man of the Year*. It was a mere coincidence that Gavin's Alternative Editor, Sammy Smoker, was Jonathan's best friend in the business. Another irony was the fact that Sammy was also on Johnny's payroll, to the tune of six figures annually. The music industry made Enron's dealings look like amateur hour.

Didn't these labels know that promises from the PD's, in exchange for acts, was like the good looking girl at the bar saying, "You buy my drinks and I'll give you a good time when we get home?" Assuming you're not too drunk by last call, it's unlikely that she'd share your definition of home or a good time, when two o'clock rolls around. "A fool and his money are soon parted," and Johnny feeling there were no bigger fools than the major record companies. Given the way they were run and the idiots running them, there was at least some truth in this evaluation.

Artiste hadn't produced a hit on the airwaves or anywhere else since Phil Caruso acquired the position of President and this was becoming a point of contention among everyone involved in the company. In fact, Artiste was running four months behind on the invoice's Johnny had been submitting. If it wasn't for the fact that Phil was a personal friend of Jerry Stone's, Jonathan's former boss, he wouldn't be dealing with Artiste at all and would be shopping around for another home to shop his wares. Jerry Stone, however, was still one of the most successful independent record promoters in the country and Jonathan knew enough not to screw with the Golden Goose. Every once in a while though, Jonathan would suffer a lapse of what little cognitive reasoning he possessed, and try to sign one of Jerry's radio stations directly. All of the radio stations Jonathan "worked" had been handed over to him by Jerry many years ago but were still ultimately controlled by Jerry himself. This was something he had come to greatly resent and often deny, but it was a well-known, undisputable truth throughout the industry.

"Luke said he's going to hold until you talk to him," His assistant shouted, not even caring if she was heard because she didn't even wait for a response before picking up another line.

"All right, all right," Jonathan muttered under his breath.

"Luke, my man, what's happening? How you doin'?" Jonathan boomed into the phone but with the most pleasant of tones.

"Jonathan, man, cut the crap. This is my ass here on the line. If this record doesn't air *this* week on 'XKL, Phil said I'm going to be the next thing to go and I really don't feel like hitting the pavement right now so please, help me out here!"

Jonathan didn't care too much for the local reps, but these guys were his liaison to the labels who signed his checks. Luke he was a decent enough guy and that was the highest opinion he'd held of anyone, other than himself, in a very long time.

"Listen, Luke, I've been begging Carter at 'XKL for an early add on this Dead Boys record, but you know how he can be when it comes to music."

Luke rattled off a multitude of data about the other major stations playing the record, the increase in overall spins this week and the upcoming local tour dates-all of which both Jonathan and Carter had heard from every local rep for years. Other than Jonathan's fee, the only real statistic that mattered was the record sales in the market. Unfortunately for Luke, in XKL's market, there were yet to be any sales.

"You're not hearing me Luke, the reality is that the Soundscans on this album are terrible." Soundscan, being a computer program created and run by Billboard Magazine, was the industry's bible. Basically, every record store had this technology at the sales counter so that when the bar code of a record scanned when sold, it was registered with Soundscan. This technology compiled weekly reports and then they sold those reports to the record companies. With this information, the record companies could tell how many CD's a given title had sold in the last week, last year, or since its original "street date," so long as the bar code was registered with Soundscan. Initially, the record companies thought this was a great promotional tool as it enabled them to finally force the PD's who didn't like a given record, to play that record, if the sales were significant. This tactic almost always worked, but what the labels didn't recognize was that Soundscan was also a boon to the artists. For once, artists were able to tell exactly how many CD's were sold and then able to check their corresponding royalty statements. Overnight, the day of record companies selling "platinum albums" (over 1,000,000 units) and accounting for "Gold" (over 500,000 units) sales were gone. It became a fact that wasn't sitting well with most of the record company's accounting departments.

"Johnny," Luke stated in a calm voice, so calm in fact that it was almost cause for concern. "Screw the Soundscan, screw 'XKL, screw Carter and screw you. You've been the Indie for 'XKL for years and if I tell my people you can't get my record to air when I absolutely *have* to have it, what good are you?" And with that Luke slammed down the phone.

The resulting sound the slamming of the phone made was in direct contrast to Luke's sedate voice and it startled Jonathan causing him to jump up out of his seat. He didn't like the threat, but the fact was that he couldn't dispute that Luke was right. Why pay 10 gee wizzes a week if you weren't getting anything in return.

Chapter 5

Everyone at the crime scene stopped and turned, as District Attorney Beth McBride marched into the room. "Detective Kelly Agis?" Beth commanded of the uniformed officer stationed at the door.

"In the bathroom, District Attorney," someone replied. Detectives and forensics investigators alike acknowledged Beth, as she made her way to the bathroom.

"Hey, Kell'."

"Hi, Beth."

Nobody had called her "Kell'" since she'd attended Williams College. In fact, Kelly felt somewhat embarrassed by the DA's use of her nickname, which was no longer used by even those classmates with whom she still kept in contact. Since Beth and Kelly had been classmates at Williams, old habits were obviously tough to break, even for District Attorney McBride.

At Williams, Beth had been all business and no pleasure. Kelly had heard rumors then, which had persisted ever since, that McBride's appetite for carnal pleasure came in the form of young, female co-eds. Despite Beth's public, heterosexual relationships, Kelly was inclined to take these rumors as fact. Her opinion was heavily influenced by one drunken night they'd spent "experimenting" at Williams College. Beth had blonde hair that she wore in a short bob, her steel blue eyes, thin red lips and well-toned body undeniably aroused sexual thoughts in those she encountered. Her attitude, however, made it clear that she liked being on top, regardless of the sex of the person who lay beneath her.

"I appreciate the heads up on this, Kell."

"Given Mrs. Caruso's frequent appearance in the gossip columns and her husband's not so favorable reviews in the business pages, my thought was that this case is sure to generate public interest."

"Yes, New York is a tough place to have PR problems, as they say. Let's make sure we don't have one on this case. Wouldn't you agree, Kelly?"

Kelly could only nod in agreement.

Jimmy Gerard found himself wedged between the sink and the bathtub the whole time Beth and Kelly had been renewing old acquaintances.

Jimmy and Beth weren't the best of friends by anyone's stretch of the imagination. This was a well-known fact that traveled throughout the Police Department. Whenever they happened to come across each other in public, neither one feigned any behavior that would dispel this fact.

Back when Beth was an Assistant District Attorney, Jimmy had been the lead Detective on a homicide she was prosecuting that centered on the high profile murder of a very young child. Jimmy believed the death was accidental and that the case warranted a manslaughter charge. Beth, seeing this as an opportunity to introduce herself to the public, felt the case warranted first degree murder charges. She was hoping this case would be the beginning of her march to the Presidency. Jimmy, being far from an idealist, didn't like envisioning the law much less justice or the lack thereof as being used for the advancement of a political career. During the trial, Beth didn't feel his testimony was compelling enough and blamed him for the final outcome. Jimmy had no problem apologizing for his delivery, but felt the truth of the matter didn't require the dramatics McBride so dearly sought from him. The jury came back with a verdict of second-degree murder yet the Judge immediately reduced the charges to manslaughter. For Jimmy, it was a hollow victory. Beth's attractive persona and Hollywood staged performance during the trial was apparently enough to get her elected to District Attorney. As luck would have it, it was appearing that Jimmy would once again be the lead detective on a case that she clearly envisioned as her ticket to the

Senate; Beth's next rung on her ladder to the highest seat in the land and arguably the world.

"What do we have here, Detective?" Beth asked Jimmy in a voice encased in ice.

"I'm assuming you've been made aware of the victim's identity? Based on the preliminaries, the Coroner is placing the time of death somewhere between late Wednesday evening and early Thursday morning. Rocket Science Records owns the apartment and I have someone researching their corporate accounts. The body has been removed for the autopsy and toxicology report. Based on the crime scene, as we found it, we expect the victim to test positive for alcohol and narcotics and that the cause of death appears to be asphyxiation by strangulation. No motive or suspect as of yet. Again, all of this is based on a *very* preliminary investigation."

This last remark was a clear shot at McBride. As Jimmy was reciting his initial conclusions, he could see McBride calculating the number of women's votes in her eyes.

The successful prosecution in the possible kinky sex crime and murder of a beautiful young wife of a prominent, entertainment executive was sure to have McBride reciting her victory speech, thought Jimmy.

After an awkward pause, McBride directed Kelly and Jimmy to interview the neighbors. "No uniforms, no pressure, but most of all, no fuck-ups," ordered the District Attorney.

"Yes, Ma'am'" said Kelly, as Jimmy was brushing past McBride on his way out the door.

Chapter 6

Even before Billy could open his eyes, which seemed to be sealed shut at the lids, he recognized the pounding in his head as all too familiar. He certainly hadn't missed mornings like this. After a night at the *One-Two*, your head felt like it had spent the night vigorously bouncing off a slab of concrete.

The sun was beaming through the bedroom windows directly into his eyes which he'd finally managed to tear open. As he turned over to avoid the sun, he had to quickly stop his momentum for he forgot he was sleeping in his parents' guestroom and he almost rolled himself right out of the twin bed and onto the floor.

He'd never been able to figure out how his sister, who'd been married for almost five years, still had a bedroom at their parent's house. Her room was furnished with a comfortable, queen-size canopy bed covered a goose down mattress and possessed all the amenities she grew up with- it was like she never left. Meanwhile, Billy, given his profession and inability to commit to anything, was the one who often ended up at his parent's home on a regular basis, yet he only warranted a thirty-year-old twin bed. Given his touchy relationship with his father, he assumed it was the best his mother could do instead giving him a fold out cot.

Billy Sunday wasn't always known as Billy Sunday. He'd been christened William "Billy" McCarthy in a middle class suburb just north of Boston. He was the only son and name-sake of a successful criminal defense attorney and an imaginative, sought after kitchen designer.

Education had always been the priority of the McCarthy household and neither he nor his sister had been allowed to watch television growing up. In addition to their required school work, they were also obligated to give weekly book reports at the Sunday dinner table. They had both been above average students. His sister, who'd applied herself toward her education, had been an exceptional student. While TV was forbidden, music was not. Almost as far back as Billy could remember he'd spent his days listening to rock and roll. From the moment his clock radio alarm went off in the morning-blaring the sounds of WXKL until he fell asleep with his walkman over his ears each night-he was continuously listening to music.

Having been accepted to one of the most prestigious boarding schools in the country, he was enrolled as a day student since it was located in the town he grew up in. He didn't have much in common with either the teachers or the students at the academy. The teachers acted, to him, as if they were infallible, due to their employment at such an esteemed institution. The students didn't pay much attention to the teachers, as most students were just passing the time at school until their trust funds kicked in. As a result, Billy spent most of his time hanging out with his childhood friends from his neighborhood. The professors at the academy felt he should move beyond his "townie" friends and anything else that wasn't solely associated with the school. These teachers even went so far as to verbally express these opinions to him. This only made him appreciate his "true" friends all the more, in particular, the boys who made up his first band. He found humor in the fact that these same educators later found themselves in serious legal trouble; pedophilia, child pornography, incest with a stepdaughter and statutory rape. These charges fueled his vindication in remaining faithful to his true friends.

Billy had no trouble admitting that he was a rebel without a clue during his academic career at this prep school. Nonetheless, he took a certain amount of satisfaction that his earliest detractors turned out to be the lowest forms of human scum. In his humble opinion, the academy was just another institution that justified its failure to address its shortcomings by touting what they believed to be their contributions to society. He couldn't deny the reality that what they considered their contributions turned out to be fairly notable; two United State's Presidents, three Nobel prize winners, a corporate officer in every Fortune 500 board room, and even a Super Bowl winning coach. (One of those Presidents would, however turn out to be the worst leader in US history, but hey that coach was more than alright). After graduation, he'd never returned to the school and rarely mentioned that he was a graduate.

He joined his first band when he was a sophomore at the academy. They called themselves Conspiracy and played mostly classic rock covers with a few originals mixed in. It was around this time that he began to lose interest in school and gain interest in sex, drugs and rock and roll-though not necessarily in that order. This coincided with the onset of the vocal disagreements with his father about his priorities, motivation and overall direction. His shift in priorities that began in his sophomore year also marked the advent of being thrown out of some of the best schools in the country. A fact in which he was most proud and often recited. He notably failed to mention that he had ultimately graduated from these schools and that these accomplishments were at the persistence of his father. His later successful graduations further epitomized what was most frustrating for those who loved him, particularly his father. Being very bright made it easy for him to achieve anything to which he applied himself, but despite this enviable intelligence and ability, he rarely applied himself to anything—including the music he loved. This continually frustrated everyone who came into contact with and/or tried to support him through his many endeavors. Unbeknownst to any of his friends, including his father, it frustrated him most of all. He was constantly trying to find the solution to this dilemma, but when unable to locate the answer, he often masked his frustrations with illicit chemicals that only served to further complicate this conundrum that plagued and forever haunted him.

As reality slowly descended upon him and replaced the fog of his hangover, he realized that his father was outside his window, mowing the lawn with his ride-on tractor. It sounded as if he was making one continual path directly below the window of the guest bedroom. *Is he trying to tell me something?* Was what ran through his mind as the noise that emanated through the window started to play on his already frayed nerve endings. When he dragged himself home in the wee hours of the morning he was hoping he would be able to avoid his old man. Unfortunately, his father was taking a rare Friday morning away from the office to take advantage of the belated spring weather and attend to some home maintenance. In reality, he and his father both knew he was trying to make his sleep as uncomfortable as possible. His dad didn't much care for his son's lifestyle, but most of all-his father couldn't tolerate anyone sleeping past sun-up. Billy had argued for years that sun-up was actually bedtime in his line of work. Since his father didn't consider what he did work, this argument continually fell on deaf ears. He figured that if his father was trying to irritate him it was a good sign because when his dad was really pissed at him, he wasn't interested in breaking his balls, he just simply chose to ignore him. Finally, after working up the fortitude to move, Billy searched for his sweatpants and a clean T-shirt.

Chapter 7

Jimmy was finding it hard to comprehend how many people appeared to be home during a weekday morning. Granted, Jimmy didn't have many co-workers or friends who lived on the Upper East Side, come to think of it, he didn't have any friends in this part of the city but still, he figured maybe one or two of these people had to actually work some kind of job for their money. Apparently, Jimmy was wrong.

In addition to the recently deceased Mrs. Caruso's unit, there were five additional apartments on the third floor. After "Commandant" McBride had left the crime scene, Kelly and Jimmy agreed it was probably best to begin interviewing the neighbors. The commotion created by the various crime scene technicians coming and going from the victim's apartment had most of the residents sticking their heads out from their doorways and into the hallway trying to assess the situation. While they were still showing signs of interest they knew the time for questioning potential witnesses was now.

The tenant's residing on the same floor as Mrs. Caruso appeared to lead comparable lives to one another. The similarities between the furnishings in their living quarters as well their own personal attributes served to accentuate their wealth. The first subject under their attention was a gentleman who introduced himself as Chad Pennysworth. Chad was dressed in Burberry beige dress slacks, a white Brioni dress shirt adorned with a pair of Tony Duquette gold frog cuff links and a tan cashmere sweater. On his wrist he wore a Rolex watch. Jimmy noticed his clothes cost more than he earned in a year of service protecting NYC. All he knew for sure was that they weren't the standard cotton found at The Gap or J. Crew. Chad's face was void of the lines and blemishes one acquires via stress and hard work. The most common trait between Mrs. Caruso and her neighbors was that they all looked airbrushed. Chad informed them that he was employed as an investment banker, in a long line of investment bankers. Glancing around his apartment, furnished with what appeared to be very expensive artwork, Jimmy concluded what he already knew-investment banking paid quite well. As Jimmy walked around the apartment looking at the family photos that were placed among the carefully collected antiques, he noticed that Chad was the spitting image of the previous two Chad Pennyworths, only younger.

Chad divulged that "Lindy" pretty much kept to herself. He found her pleasant and courteous when they crossed paths but that wasn't very often. Apparently, Lindy kept somewhat irregular hours. Chad noticed that she would come and go at odd times, either in the middle of the afternoon or late at night. She was almost always accompanied by younger, attractive men who were never to be seen more than once. In other words, Jimmy thought, *she had a revolving door policy on men!* He was quick to point out that the men didn't appear to be Wall Street types. When asked what he meant by this he told them that they usually had longer hair, wore jewelry and dressed in ripped jeans. *Artists or musicians,* is what Chad figured. When Kelly asked why he thought they were artists or musicians, he answered that despite their dress they appeared to be successful in that they were well-groomed and not hippies from the village. Lastly he noted that a few of the men looked familiar to him from various magazines or newspaper articles.

Chad was pretty sure that "Lindy" didn't live in the apartment. In addition to her strange hours, he never saw her with groceries or carrying any of the necessities required for day-to-day living. More importantly, he never once saw a delivery boy at her door, a sure sign of residency in New York City, unless they were delivering a fifth of expensive vodka.

Mrs. Clara Clementine Vanderbrook lived on the opposite side of Mrs. Caruso. Her story matched that of Mr. Pennysworth; not much interaction, strange men, and strange hours. In addition to answering the detective's questions, Mrs. Vanderbrook also offered her unsolicited opinion. Basically, Mrs. Caruso dressed like a tramp and kept the company of any number of strange men and apparently, she informed them, she spent most of her time in the apartment having "boisterous" sex. Jimmy somewhat expected Mrs. Vanderbrook's monologue given that she appeared to be a divorced socialite who obviously spent all her time and money on shopping for clothes. Every inch of her body looked like it had been surgically altered. All of this, and she was probably just going to sit around her apartment all day. Jimmy assumed she would welcome the company of any man which was why she spent so much time listening to Belinda Caruso's cries of passion from across the hall. While Chad and Clara were helpful, the tenant at the end of the hall provided the detectives with the first useful information in New York's most recent homicide.

Jimmy and Kelly knocked on the door of apartment 315, again. Their initial knocks a couple of minutes earlier drew no immediate response. As they were turning away from the door, they heard the first of what would turn out to be a series of deadbolts being unlocked. They had become used to this. After three clicks, the door finally opened but only a crack. Their natural instinct was to stick their head toward the opening and as they did they almost head butted each other, they then each withdrew, as half a face appeared in the doorway. The inch in the door opening allowed them to just make out what revealed to be a young gentleman with chiseled features and a well-defined, unshaven chin jutted out just underneath his soft pale lips. Kelly's line of vision drifted up from his freckled nose to his dark brown eye; only one eye, which seemed to have been just recently opened and was having trouble staying that way. His long brown, curly hair had that unmade bed look. Due to what Jimmy assumed was a very expensive haircut, the tenant's hair seemed to fit perfectly with his outfit; an outfit which consisted of at least one bare foot, one flannel pajama leg emblazoned with polar bears and a black T-shirt with a logo knitted on the right breast. Jimmy wondered why at the suggestion of the fairer sex he spent time on his own hair using several expensive treatments and gels, yet his hair never seemed to look as good as some guys who just rolled out of bed. The reality of his situation, he knew, but didn't want to acknowledge, was that he was missing one key, unobtainable ingredient: twenty years, give or take.

"What's up?" asked the half face.

"NYPD," they said in unison. The two detectives flashed their badges in front of the lone eye.

"Give me a minute," responded the half face, closing the door. They heard the recognizable sound of bare feet moving quickly about the hardwood floor followed by the unmistakable sound of dirty dishes being placed in the sink, beer cans being tossed in the trash, and furniture being straightened, all audible through the apartment door. After a couple of minutes, they heard the now familiar sound of the chain dragging across the top half of the door. "C'mon in."

Upon entering, their professional training reasoned that the other half of the body perfectly matched the half previously exposed by the partially opened door.

The apartment was similar to all the others they had been in as far as the ivory white walls and hardwood floors. This apartment, however, was twice the size. Being a "floor through," it ran from one end of the building to the other. Kelly and Jimmy sat down on a black leather couch facing the river. The view of the river was partially blocked by what appeared to be the door to the bedroom. To the right of what they assumed was the bedroom was a small galley kitchen which looked like it served little purpose other than as a receptacle for empty beer bottles.

The wall to Jimmy's right was lined with professionally framed and matted, autographed rock posters. The only band Jimmy had remotely recognized was The Grateful Dead. The poster was multi-colored shades of blue with a blue rose in the middle, and appeared to be a promotional poster for the Grateful Dead's New Year's Eve concert in 1972. It announced that the Grateful Dead were playing with an outfit called N.R.P.S. and the Blues Brothers. For a brief second, Jimmy recalled those days. Even though he was a cop, he would still hang out with a few of his high school and college friends. Back then they were smoking dope, dressing wild and going to great parties with their only interest being the pursuit of good-looking women. He hadn't become a cop because he wanted the façade of a card-carrying member of the Christian Right (which in Jimmy's opinion, they were neither) nor had he joined the police force because he came from a legacy of law enforcement. After graduating from Holy Cross, he'd been recruited by the FBI. Once he figured out that the bureaucracy of the FBI would only put him behind a desk in Washington for the majority of his career, he became interested in the challenges of high profile criminal cases and decided to leave justice and the law to the lawyers, however unfortunate that maybe for the rest of society.

Living in Brooklyn, he took and passed the NYPD police exam. Given the lack of individuals willing to dodge bullets on a daily basis, he quickly rose up through vice and after three years became a homicide detective. He was interested in catching the dangerous criminals who roamed the streets of New York, not easy marks like the hippies who smoked a couple of joints or the poor addicts trying to scrape up enough for a few jums a day. As a result, he had no problem fitting in at the parties down in the village; where else could a young cop get laid by so many good-looking, liberal minded women?

The young gentleman closed the door and walked over to where the detectives were seated. Still standing, he introduced himself as Andy Solomon as he shook both their hands. As he settled into the black leather recliner that matched the couch, the bedroom door behind him slowly began to open. Emerging through the bedroom doorway was one of the sexiest visions Jimmy had seen in a long, long time.

"Shit, if I was lying next to that every night, I'd be a late riser, too," Jimmy mumbled to himself. Still gawking, he thought, *Fuck that, at this point in my life I wouldn't bother to rise at all.* His pleasant daydream had been somewhat dampened by the literal interpretation of this last thought, knowing that if he was worrying about performing even in his dreams, then he really was getting old! In an effort to distract his thought process, he looked over at Kelly. From the look in her eyes, he thought she might have been having the same impure thoughts; thoughts that that didn't recede to just any distraction.

The girl was rubbing the sleep from her cobalt blue eyes, as she passed through the door way, into the room they were occupying. Her shoulder length, dirty blond hair had a rustled, after sex look to it. The white

'Entrain' T-shirt she wore clung to her small, firm breasts as her nipples strained against the fabric. The T-shirt relaxed as it draped over her slender hips, just barely long enough to conceal her crotch and the bottom curve of her ass. Two very toned and tanned legs supported the T-shirt.

"I swear, Officers she told me she was eighteen," joked Andy, as he saw both detectives looking at the vision walking through the doorway.

"Very funny, asshole," was the vision's response. She seemed oblivious to the presence of two strangers in the apartment, never mind the fact that they were the "authorities." After a few steps, Jimmy discerned that she simply didn't give a shit.

"Detectives, this is Dakota," said Andy by way of introduction. Dakota shot Andy a stern glance. Jimmy had been around long enough to know that Dakota was most likely her stage name. Jimmy and Kelly recognized her glance as one of complete disapproval. They introduced themselves as Dakota continued walking toward the kitchen paying no attention to them. "So, how can I help you?" asked Andy, sounding anxious and looking for the opportunity to correct his mistake by joking about Dakota's age. *There is something about guys and strippers*, Jimmy thought. Deep down, every guy wanted to have a stripper (or two) at least once in his lifetime. Stripper's being the sort of Holy Grail for the sleazy, depraved side of every man's sexual desires.

Kelly took the lead. "We'd like to ask you some questions about your neighbor down the hall, Mrs. Belinda Caruso."

"Mrs!" Andy responded, almost before Kelly could finish. Based on this reaction, Jimmy immediately assumed Andy was probably fucking Belinda, as well.

"Is she all right?" inquired Andy, regaining control of his emotions.

"Well, ah, no," said Kelly, hesitating slightly.

"She's dead," Jimmy said in answer to his question. After years on the job he'd learned that the simple truth was the best way to deliver bad news, regardless of how insensitive it sounded. Kelly was still sometimes struggling with the ability to be brutally frank.

"Dead? How?" asked Andy, sounding a little shaken.

"We haven't made that determination yet." said Kelly, resolute not to give him any details.

"Murdered?" mumbled Andy.

"Nobody said anything about murder," Jimmy replied.

"Would anyone like some green tea?" yelled Dakota from the galley kitchen. Jimmy assumed that she either hadn't heard their conversation, or she'd simply become accustomed to the violence that was a part of day-to-day life if you lived in New York City. Although in contrast to Jimmy Kelly found Dakota's indifference unusual, the Upper East Side wasn't often the site of many murders. After observing her for a minute, she concluded that her attitude wasn't due to a lack of concern, but rather a lack of awareness. Kelly couldn't blame her after just waking up from spending the night with a hunk like Andy, in a place like this. It would be all Kelly could do to manage making green tea.

"How well did you know Mrs. Caruso?" Jimmy asked, directing his question to Andy.

"I only knew her in passing," he said, sounding defensive. "I mean, when I saw her in the elevator or the hallway."

"How often was that?"

"Well...often, I guess...I mean, we seemed to keep the same hours," Andy seemed to be trying to digest what was happening. Ten minutes before, he was asleep, entangled with Dakota dreamily revisiting a night of wild sex. Now, as the fog in his head began to lift, he found himself being questioned in a murder investigation.

"Look, I'm a law student at NYU. Do I need a lawyer?" he asked.

"I don't know. Do you?"

Playing the good cop, Kelly stepped in, "It would appear you have an alibi." He glanced at Dakota, who was on her tiptoes, baring her perfect little ass, while reaching for the tea bags. *"On second thought maybe I will have some tea...but I should wait a few minutes,* thought Jimmy.

"We're just looking for some information here. We're not really interested in what extracurricular activities you enjoy while attending NYU Law." Having attended Williams, Kelly was aware of the moral clauses parents and grandparents often inserted in trust fund documents. It was clear that Dakota and some of the paraphernalia around Andy's apartment would violate such clauses. Upon hearing this Andy seemed to relax.

"What do you mean that you kept the same hours?" inquired Jimmy.

"Well, I would pass her in the hall or share the elevator with her. And this was usually late at night or mid-afternoon, not exactly the busiest time around here, considering who our neighbors are. You know what I mean?" Andy asked rhetorically, while tilting his head toward Mr. Pennysworth and Mrs. Vanderbrook's apartments.

"Are you aware if Mr. and Mrs. Caruso lived here together?" Kelly already knew the answer but figured that McBride wanted all the i's dotted and t's crossed on this one.

"No," Andy replied.

"How do you know that?" Jimmy asked.

"Well, for starters, I've never seen Mr. Caruso here or anywhere else, for that matter. In fact, if I only knew Belinda from this building, I wouldn't even think there was a Mr. Caruso," stated Andy. "And if I wasn't interested in the music business, I wouldn't even know what her Mr. Caruso looked like. Although, putting it together, it all makes sense to me now." Given his thought process and the lighting of his first cigarette of the day, it appeared Andy was now completely awake. Appearing to read the detectives minds, he continued, "Mrs. Caruso liked to entertain." Andy's left and right hands formed quotation marks, as he recited the word entertain.

"Yeah? Any idea who she was entertaining?" Jimmy was glad Andy was cooperative and knew where this was going, unlike the opinionated Mrs. Vanderbrook.

"Young guys, mostly. Musicians. Do you want names? Billy Brill, Darius Damon, a few others I recognized but don't know who they are."

"Whoa, whoa, whoa," They exclaimed in unison, while reaching for their pens and notebooks.

"All right, what are these guys names again?"

Going slowly, Andy reiterated, "Billy Brill, the lead singer of The Dead Boys. He's been around a lot lately. Darius Damon was the guitar player from the heavy metal band, Res Judicata. And there was an older dude who I'm pretty sure was also a singer. Then there was this business type…a promo guy."

"A what?" Jimmy asked.

Kelly looked at Jimmy and said, "I'll bring you up to date on the industry terminology later."

"He still thinks Neil Diamond is a rock star," Kelly confirmed to Andy and Dakota, who was still in the kitchen. They all shared a laugh at Jimmy's expense.

A little embarrassed by this, Jimmy asked angrily, "How about Wednesday night? Did you happen to see her with anybody then?"

"Brill came by in the afternoon and so did the suit. And then I heard that older singer dude when I came in late Wednesday night or Thursday morning I guess at about 2:00 am."

"How do you know who it was?" inquired Kelly.

"Cause the dude's been around for a while. He has a new band. Dakota likes them…loves them. Honey, what's the name of that dude's band that you like?"

"That narrows it down, honey," Dakota said sarcastically, emerging from the kitchen, sipping her green tea.

"The dude who was hanging out with Belinda Wednesday night…the guy you said you talked to…his band?"

Dakota hesitated for a brief second and shot Andy a glance before deciding to answer. It was if Andy were her attorney. "Oh, you mean, Drown." The thought seemed to bring a slight smile to her face.

"Yeah, that's it-Drown. Why can I never remember that?" asked Andy, as if to himself.

"Maybe I will have that tea after all," said Jimmy.

Chapter 8

"Drown yourself in the music. I guess that's how I came up with the name," Billy said in a rather tired, nasally voice. It was the result of snorting a gram of street coke, the last of which he finished just before picking up the phone.

"We're speaking with Billy Sunday, lead singer of Drown, who will be kicking off their spring and summer tour Sunday night at the Paradise in an exclusive W-X-K-L show. We'll be back with more from Billy right after these messages." Carter Lane's smooth radio voice resonated into the phone and across the airwaves.

"And we're off, back in three." Billy heard some computerized blips and beeps. He assumed that these were signals that the DJ was now off the air and the producer would be running the requisite three minutes of commercial spots.

"So, how you been Billy? Long time, man," Carter's calming voice conveyed sincerity.

Billy always found it amusing listening to radio jocks. Since he recognized their voices from the radio, it was as if he was listening to the radio when he heard them speak-even when he was speaking to them face to face. Since the voice never matched the persona he anticipated, it was to him as if the jocks were just that voice and not a real person.

"Good man, a little tired but hey-things could be worse." Billy had been acquainted with Carter a long time and respected the fact that he was still all about the music, which was saying something since radio in the 21st century had become anything but about music. Like the record business, large media conglomerates now owned the radio stations and everything was about the bottom line, not the artists and certainly not about the music that was played. Carter was doing him a solid by giving him airtime and promoting the show, especially since he and his band had essentially no airtime, at this level.

"Sounds like you're dragging a little?"

"Considering 10:00 am is the middle of the fucking night," retorted Billy. "I had a show in New York Wednesday night and drove home yesterday making a detour to hang with my homeboys."

"So, in other words, what your telling me is that after you played with your band you spent all Wednesday night fucking some groupie and then came home and probably fucked some broad who actually thinks you're a rock star."

Billy laughed at his monologue and said, "Yeah, that's about right."

"I don't know how you rock stars do it," exclaimed Carter. "In three, two and…" After a brief pause, Carter's voice boomed once again out into the airwaves. "W-X-K-L, Killa Radio, we're back and we're talking to Boston's own latest band to continue the trend set by Aerosmith, the Cars, and J. Geils, just to name a few. Billy Sunday is the lead singer and founding member of Drown. We've just been discussing their name and how it came to be, and actually, it's apropos of their style of music. If you haven't seen Drown, be sure to get your ass down to the Paradise Sunday night, cause the next time you see them will probably be at the Fleet Center. So, about the name…"

"Yeah so, well you know…" Billy's hangover was now exploding across his brain and effecting his ability to form a single thought. "Drowning is supposed to be peaceful, once you get over the panic and succumb. And I guess that's what our music is like-peaceful once you succumb. Either that, or you feel like drowning your sorrows after you hear us play." They laughed at the last comment.

"All right, I know that we're taxing what few brain cells you have left at this ungodly hour of 10:00 am," declared Carter. "However, you do realize that most people are actually working and not being paid to recover from a night of debauchery?"

"Debauchery? That's too big a word for me at this time of night," exclaimed Billy, jokingly.

"Means sex, drugs and rock and roll," Carter informed him.

"Don't be trying to ruin my pristine image," laughed Billy, "I can do that all on my own."

"Now, the new single from Boston's next great band. Here is *Betrayed* from Drown, exclusively on W-X-K-L, Killa radio." With that, Billy could hear the first few drumbeats of the first single from his album. "Thanks Billy, I have to run. We'll hang out Sunday."

"Yeah, that's cool," said Billy.

"See you Sunday," With that, Carter hung up.

Billy agonizingly arose from his prone position on the twin bed to which he'd returned after he awoke to the sounds of the lawn mower. He walked over to the desk and flipped the Sony, mini-stereo to WXKL turning it on the just in time to hear his own voice singing the lyrics to the mid-tempo rock music he had written. One thing he'd learned from his years associated with the music business was that no matter who you were, or how famous you were, you never tired of hearing your voice singing on the radio. Every time he heard his voice coming through the speakers of a sound system, it was like the first time all over again, that adrenaline rush always revisited. The older his career became he realized he couldn't escape the feeling like this might be his last hurrah. Billy listened to himself sing:

> "Red Grows the Rose that's never been picked.
> Hard Grows the Heart that keeps getting kicked.
> Innocent the Child that can't understand,
> Guilty the woman who won't stand by her man.

(Chorus)   "Always looking but simply refusing to see
> You keep taking more of what you don't really need
> Collecting and breaking all those pretty hearts
> Trying to begin at the end to avoid the pain from the start

"Lonely grows the man who gets left again and again.
Tired becomes the boy whose one night stands won't end.
Seductive the goddess that can't remain faithful,
Plagued goes her lover vowing to stay hateful.

"Always looking but simply refusing to see
You keep taking more of what you don't really need
Collecting and breaking all those pretty hearts
Trying to begin at the end to avoid the pain from the start

(Bridge) "You know you have to get to one before you get to two
But you just don't want to address all those things you
done and do

"Mesmerized is the man that can't let go of his obsession,
Suicidal the boy who doesn't drink off his depression.
Daisy sold out Gatsby and it's forever been the same,
Boy meets Girl, Girl Leaves Boy, some things will never
change

"Always looking but simply refusing to see
You keep taking more of what you don't really need
Collecting and breaking all those pretty hearts
Trying to begin at the end to avoid the pain from the start"

As Billy listened to his music he picked up on another common characteristic he'd heard was shared among other musicians. No matter how long he'd been doing this, no matter how many songs he'd recorded, it still made him uncomfortable listening to the sound of his voice without feeling the need to critique himself. The rush of adrenaline was always followed by the need to find fault in his accomplishments. His ability to listen to himself had become easier, over time, but he never reached a point where he'd become comfortable or able to sit back and listen with pride. As the song ended, his attention shifted to his surroundings as he viewed them from his horizontal position in the twin bed. The room was flooded with sunlight-something his red, watery eyes were presently battling. The curtains or window treatments were a deep blue and mushroom colored. *Curtains were something you purchased at Home Depot. Window treatments were curtains you paid an interior designer to purchase for you at Home Depot, thereby quadrupling the cost.* The window treatments matched the tan, grass cloth wallpaper. A large, mahogany armoire filled the room and he was surprised to notice that it still contained some of his old clothes which were hung inside neatly.

Even in his parent's home, he didn't feel like he was at home. His reality was that he was, in fact, homeless. Two years of constant touring meant his sleeping arrangements were a different floor, someone else's couch or a strange bed, if he was lucky, every night. He knew Wednesday night with Belinda had been a major mistake because all he was looking for was a warm bed accompanied by a warm body to help chase his demons away. But she had too much invested in him for her to consider him a one night stand. Occasionally, his sexual encounters on the road temporarily alleviated his sense of homelessness, but later on only left him feeling more alone. He was at the point in his life where casual sex only served as a further reminder of what he was really missing. He attributed these unhappy thoughts to crashing from the booze and coke the night before. *How could a guy with a song on the radio be unhappy?* Billy arose and placed a CD in the stereo that was on the desk next to the armoire. He lay back down. "I'll find me a wife who'll give me the steady life and not keep going off the rails." David Gray's pristine voice filled the guest room, as well as Billy's head, and he slipped back into a coma.

Chapter 9

Everyone who knew him had advised Phil against his marriage to Belinda. Clarence Weatherby, his attorney, had been the most vocal.

"Phil, if it has wheels or tits, eventually it's going to give you problems," Clarence quoted. "Belinda is like a limited edition Ferrari and she demands high fucking maintenance and I'm not sure you can afford her, at least in the long run. I know she loves the music business and that it's the basis of your relationship, but she really only loves the people who make the music," he continued, putting it as delicately as possible. "I just think a woman like that has an ulterior motive in moving from the people who make the music to the people who screw the people who make the music," Clarence concluded.

While Phil would agree that Belinda's motivation, in all probability, didn't have anything to do with true love, he figured that because she was moving up the food chain, and he was at the top, could be taken as a sign of maturity and a willingness to settle down…or up, as the case may be. Artists come and artists go, along with their fleeting fortunes but record company executives were indomitable, at least that's what he told himself. As he sat contemplating his state of affairs he noticed the chrome and glass that surrounded him in his office was beginning to dull as the late Friday afternoon sun began to set.

Phil's career, and what was left of his fortune, was disappearing as fast as the latest one hit wonder that had been signed to his label. If this Dead Boys record didn't happen soon, he knew he was as good as gone, which undoubtedly meant Belinda was as good as gone, too. It would come as no real surprise to him if she'd already had one foot out the door and was investigating her options. The ironic thing was that she was the one who convinced him to sign The Dead Boys in the first place. Billy Brill, the lead singer, was Belinda's second cousin or nephew or some shit or so she said. It didn't come as a shock to him that signing this act would turn out to be his downfall. His reflections on his inevitable demise were interrupted by the loud beep that came over his intercom.

"Mr. Caruso, there is a Detective Agis and Detective Gerard here to see you." His secretary informed him in a voice tinged with wonder.

He was reminded about one of Artiste's rap artists being arrested for threatening his producer at gun point. *Not what I need right now,* ran through his mind. This type of occurrence wasn't uncommon in his profession, given the size of the stars' egos in this business. However, most musicians didn't do it by putting a 9 millimeter handgun to the producer's head. When the rapper called, threatening to shoot the producer if his thirty thousand dollar advance for the single wasn't paid immediately, in cash, Phil's response was "Shoot him." Hey Phil had said the guy was a lousy producer. In his opinion, artists in this business were a necessary evil while producers were a dime a dozen. Unless, of course, the producer was Daniel Lanois (Bob Dylan, Rolling Stones) or Steve Lillywhite (U2, Dave Matthews) because then they were worth their weight in gold. There were rap producers that were known to steal whatever music was being rapped over and these producers were particularly disposable. One of his Business Affairs people, or record company attorneys, had mentioned that the police might want to speak with him and make sure the artist in question was gainfully employed by Artiste. However, none of the company lawyers had come up to his office for the meeting, which was unusual. He quickly checked his schedule and noticed he didn't have any appointments. Being late Friday afternoon, he'd left it open, like most Fridays. He paged his secretary and asked her to come in. When she entered, he motioned for her to close the door behind her. "I don't seem to have an appointment scheduled. Is this about that rap artist?" he asked.

"No, that's next week," she responded. "I don't have anything written down either. Perhaps I made a mistake and missed something?" she said, timidly.

Given his mood, he'd normally assume this to be the case and blast her for her incompetence. This explained why he went through assistants monthly. However, the fact that it was a Friday afternoon made him hesitate to accuse her. Like most record company executives, Friday afternoons might as well have been Sunday mornings as far as being available was concerned. As he stared absent-mindedly at his assistant, his initial thought was to turn them away. Then, he figured, what the hell? He had no idea where his wife was, The Dead Boys record was dying a slow, painful death *what the fuck else could possibly go wrong?* "Go ahead, send them in and hold my calls."

He gradually rose from behind his desk, as Kelly and Jimmy entered his office. The size and décor of Phil's office would have impressed most businessman, never mind civil servants, but working in New York City, Kelly and Jimmy had seen all the trappings of wealth before. Besides, Phil's office was a studio apartment in comparison to, say, a mutual fund manager's office. "Thank you for taking the time to see us," said the older detective.

Phil had no problem assuming this man was a detective given his clothes, dark blue chinos and a worn blue, Brooks Brother's blazer. *This guy is right out of central casting*, thought Phil. *Probably going to ask me if I know any of the producers of NYPD Blue when we're finished. He is not Sippowitz,* continued Phil's train of thought, *but who the fuck is? There are plenty of other parts.* This was the total extent of his thoughts on the detective, whatever his name was. He realized that the detective had failed to introduce himself, while holding out his hand.

His attention, but more perceptibly his gaze, had turned to Kelly. Like most self important, self centered men, he figured she would find that his undressing her with his eyes would be a turn on. *What the fuck?* Phil figured, *she probably has a demo and spent Sunday nights at amateur night down in the village like everybody else did.* However, if listening to her demo could get Phil a roll in the hay with this sexy law enforcement officer, it would certainly be worth it-particularly given her figure. He had no problem adding a cop to his list of conquests. The reality at hand was that Phil's conquests pretty much began and ended with Belinda. This was a fact his lawyer, his only real friend, was willing to point out on a regular basis. His not so expansive; not so impressive list of female conquests, however, had never stopped him from making a complete ass of himself, as he was presently doing in front of the detectives before him.

Immediately upon introducing himself to Phil, Jimmy noticed that subtlety was not the man's strong suit and he could tell that Phil's idea of "suave" was clearly pissing Kelly off. There were an unusually high number of sexual harassment suits in the music industry and Phil through his lack of couth could be their poster boy. The most recent lawsuit making the tabloids entailed a music exec who was fired for charging hookers to his company expense account while he was in Amsterdam. However, the fact that the now ex-label president saw nothing wrong with what he'd done had sealed his fate, once again proving that it usually isn't the crime, but the cover-up, that ticks people off the most. Notwithstanding, even if Phil were in the dark ages, he would have to be a total moron not to see that Kelly wasn't pleased with his idea of foreplay. Jimmy decided to waste little time getting to the point. "I'm afraid we have some bad news concerning your wife" he started, as Phil closed the double mahogany doors to his office and turned to face them. Phil's confident demeanor began to diminish, while the color in his face from his fake tan, started to vanish. "I'm sorry to say, she's been murdered." No matter how many countless times he'd delivered this line, it was something he hoped he would never grow accustomed to, the effect it had on a family member was always devastating.

Based on Kelly's experience, she allowed the proper amount of time to pass, approximately one minute, then feigned condolence and went right into questioning Phil. "I know this is a very difficult time, Mr. Caruso, but if you don't mind, we'd like to ask you a few questions?" The number of dead bodies Kelly had seen, in her few years on the force, had made her less emotional when dealing with the relatives of the deceased. And Caruso's leering had eliminated what little sympathy she may have felt, in this particular case.

Obviously, Phil's initial reaction was shock. But if honest, he really wasn't surprised, given Belinda's lifestyle. He'd figured a drug overdose was just one toke away.

Jimmy and Kelly could tell by his mannerisms that the initial shock was passing rather quickly. Almost immediately, Phil began to wonder whether Belinda's life insurance premium was up to date. However, he quickly brought himself back to reality and panic started to set in. He'd seen enough cop and tabloid TV shows to know that the husband was the primary suspect in the murder of a spouse-so much so, that it was practically the only lead the cops bothered to follow.

Clarence Weatherby had been right, Phil thought, *Belinda was a major mistake.* Had Clarence told him that she'd continue to haunt him from the grave, he might have actually listened. Phil's thoughts went back to Belinda, her body and her infectious smile. He didn't know much, but he knew enough to know that even had Clarence guaranteed him that Belinda would be Phil's ultimate downfall, it wouldn't have made one, little fucking bit of difference in the end. What a week... first The Dead Boys and now a dead wife. The Board of Directors was going to be less than thrilled. Most individuals first thought, in his position, would be to call their attorney. Phil's first reaction, however, was to call his broker and sell every bit of Artiste stock he owned. Once word of this was out the stock would be toilet paper and Phil wouldn't be able to afford a public defender-never mind Clarence Weatherby. "Fucking Belinda," he muttered to himself

Man, if you only knew, thought Jimmy, reading Phil's lips. Jimmy's experience had taught him to never take his eyes off a suspect, particularly this early in an investigation.

Chapter 10

Belinda Clairgill Caruso hadn't always been a knockout. She was, at best, cute through grade school but kind of tall, gawky and awkward in high school. Had the boys taken the time to notice her striking cheekbones and the dark, sexually inviting orbit of her eyes, more of her male classmates could have claimed to have taken a spin with someone who'd become a New York fashion model.

One boy can claim to have taken special notice of Belinda in high school and his name was John Vesque. Johnny formed a band with some of his friends and crowned himself the lead singer. By high school standards, they'd done pretty well for themselves. They'd actually cut a demo which was financed by their parents. The demo had even received a limited amount of local airplay. Of course, this was when a local band could actually get a local radio station to play their music without representation. While the band never toured, they wailed away at local VFW halls and friends parties. Belinda was immediately hooked, not necessarily on the lead singer Johnny, but on musicians and their lifestyle. One night, the group had played a battle of the bands in a neighboring town and after their performance; the local girls stormed the bands dressing room. The town police were brought in to escort the boys safely out of the building and out of town. The police never once questioned the bands about their use of drugs and booze, which was littered throughout the under age group's dressing room. The attention and excitement, not to mention the intoxicants, were definitely for her.

Belinda graduated high school without distinction and without the singer. She'd enrolled in a small Junior college in Southern California just south of LA that specialized in Liberal Arts. As her looks began to mature and her figure blossomed she delved into the nightlife of L.A. and became a regular groupie on the music scene around the time Guns and Roses and other rock bands were earning their bones. Disco was finally dying and rock music was on its way back. Belinda found herself right in the middle of this scene and couldn't have been happier.

The idea that rock stars had predetermined signals with roadies to bring attractive women from the crowd backstage was no urban myth. Belinda was a regular backstage at most rock shows and at most LA "rocker" parties. She was a groupie in every definition of the word except for the fact that she didn't sleep around. Unfortunately, this qualification was a must on the list of most rock stars, whether they were self-imagined rock stars, budding artists, or bona fide stars. Belinda's sex appeal and pleasant personality combined, kept her a regular on the scene, but didn't get her a boyfriend who was willing to support her. Tired of working as a record store clerk or a coat check girl, which didn't pay much in a climate like LA, Belinda began thinking about a more satisfying means of supporting herself.

After a G'N'F' and R; Guns and Fucking Roses as they would later become known by their hardcore fans, show at The Whiskey, Belinda met a small time agent backstage. While he was clearly hitting on her, he mentioned that his college roommate worked in a modeling agency in New York and he said he'd be willing to get in touch with him and if she gave him her number, she'd get a call. Belinda had been mistaken for a model before by small time strip club operators, which she saw for what it was and had no interest. This guy's offer hadn't been contingent on sleeping with him, so she figured what the hell and gave the guy her number. Much to her surprise, she received a call a few days later asking for headshots and a bio. Two weeks later, she was in New York signing a contract with a small modeling agency. As far as she was concerned, the only thing that mattered was that the agency was legitimate. She'd determined this by the fact that the agency had paid for her first class ticket and moving expenses to New York City. Her basis for her more recent decision's wasn't as thorough as it had been in the past.

Modeling suited her perfectly as it indulged her insatiable need for adulation. It also paid well and musicians' penchant for models was almost as strong as it was for chemicals. She made a decent living by New York City standards; a fortune by any other. The hours were long but they afforded her plenty of time to pursue her two favorite hobbies: music and musicians. There was a saying by virtually everyone involved in the music business. Whether you were a member of the Rolling Stones, an entertainment attorney who never had a hit act, a groupie or a fan, if music was in your blood, you chased the high forever. Belinda was no different.

She was smart enough to realize that given her age, her agency, and her late start in the modeling business, her career wasn't going to last forever. As she grew tired of the parties and her way of life she began to acknowledge that a change in her lifestyle needed to take place if she was to acquire any sort of security. The reality of her type of lifestyle was that anyone inclined to living it usually grows tired of enduring it. The body simply can't recover as age sets in and the physical and mental fatigue becomes too far advanced before it is actually realized. Belinda had no intention of letting her lifestyle ruin her life.

As her modeling career advanced Belinda began to meet a higher caliber of people. The restaurants and parties she started to attend were with the jet set. She was finally being introduced to men who were the *real players* in the music industry. Even though she loved where her career was taking her, she could still could not escape the allure and charisma of the artists themselves. That was how she met Billy McCarthy. He had come through town as a guitar player on a promo tour with a recently signed band whose lead singer was a female rocker chick that went by the name Heroine. She remembered thinking he wasn't that striking, not a GQ kind of guy, but he was cute, funny and sincere; and sincerity wasn't something that she found could easily be faked. As she chatted with him she recalled thinking that acting was never going to be in his future. Unfortunately, after seeing the band's performance, she wasn't sure that guitar playing was in his future, either. This created a problem for by now she'd grown accustomed to a certain lifestyle. She was ready to fall in love with someone but she wanted to fall within the right tax bracket. Given the amount of money the label had spent on the party, however, it appeared that this act just may be a hit; a hit despite the guitar player's musical shortcomings. Anyone who was anyone in the music or fashion business was at the party including a few actors and actresses. The dramatic branch of performing artists usually felt musicians were beneath them. Although actresses, like every other female, often fell under the spell of a musician's charms-in the short term, anyway. She may have had a hard time remembering the name of his band, but she had no trouble remembering the fact that she had taken him home. The result, for her at the time, was an unusual one-night stand that she was surprised to find memorable long after. Billy claimed the same, though not very convincingly, as he was leaving the next morning. She wasn't sure if the lasting memory of the evening was due to Billy being an attentive, experienced lover, or if it had just been so long both before and after since she'd had a lover she was actually still interested in the next morning.

Billy proved fairly faithful in their budding relationship for a guitar player in a rock and roll band. He called regularly and spent every tour break with Belinda when he was in New York. She wasn't, however, naïve as to what transpired on the road with touring musicians and the groupies they encountered after each show. After all, she had been a groupie herself. In light of the fact that the sex they'd shared the first night had proved to be more than just beginner's luck, it was clear that he really liked her. Ultimately, his band was dropped after the millions of their label's marketing dollars were spent. The band attempted to continue without a record deal but everything was changing as rumors of infighting amongst the band members and cancelled tour dates escalated. Normally carefree and laid back, Billy started to change as he became overly stressed and withdrawn. As he began to change, their relationship took the brunt of it as he became more and more distant and distracted while he licked the wounds inflicted by the corporate reality of the music business. She knew these wounds would result in permanent scars and a daily reminder of a dream realized, but unfulfilled. His failure left her dream unfulfilled in the financial sense. Billy drifted back to his home North of Boston and eventually stopped calling. She hated herself for making the mistake she'd in the past tried so hard to avoid-she fell for a musician without a trust fund. Then and there, she swore off the music maker and set her sights on the money maker…of the music business. She had the ability to have her cake and eat it too, it was time to stop just licking the frosting.

Chapter 11

Billy had every intention of speaking with his father after the interview with WXKL but he fell back asleep instead. From his perspective, it wasn't unreasonable, given that he'd only had twenty hours of sleep since Monday and it was now Friday. The irrationality of it all was the fact that it was his decision not to sleep as he chose to party for four days, and that was how his father would view it. Like all the familiar obstacles in most father/son relationships, his lifestyle and his father's disapproval of it, had been the constant deal breaker. All things considered, by the time he awoke Friday to the afternoon sun, his father was in no mood to talk and his mannerisms made that perfectly clear. In turn, this set Billy off, who was still feeling the effects of the week, not to mention the previous night's festivities. He decided to spend the afternoon looking for painkillers; not the hair of the dog that bit you as liquor had little effect on the tolerance of those who partied like a rock star. He needed opiates; percocet, oxycontin, H, "Dancing with Mr. D."

Unfortunately, his mission turned out to be a success and he found what he was looking for. He scored a few twenty-milligram of oxys at a local bar. Without delay he went to the men's bathroom where he swallowed two, then crushed and snorted the third on the bathroom sink. Immediately he began to feel better, at least physically, as the mental hangover would take more than a narcotic. The oxy he'd snorted instantly began distributing a warm, numbing feeling, as gravity pulled the drug from his brain down through his bloodstream. Later, the time-release pills he swallowed would catch up, providing him with a first-rate high for a number of hours.

He subsequently went to another local tavern, *The Haven*, where few people knew him and those who did could care less that he was a wanna-be rock star. It was a place where only a very few would think of finding him. After his appearance at the *One-Two* last night word had probably spread through the small town that he was back. Those that were close to him would know that if he was at *The Haven*, he wasn't in the mood to socialize. Being at *The Haven* eliminated having to deal with any so-called friends who would be hunting him down for a job on the upcoming tour, or tickets. They didn't want tickets to Drown, but tickets to the Stones, the Who or U2-all who were rumored to be heading out this summer. This was one of the downsides of hanging out in local bars in your home town. You drank too much and bragged about being a success and some people actually took you seriously. At *The Haven* the patrons had their own problems and dreams of a fun night out were something they stopped having a long time ago.

Billy began feeling that his trip home had been a mistake. He hadn't even thought about Nacy—not because he had a change of heart but rather because he had been so wasted he couldn't even feel his heart. Once again he'd managed to piss off his father just by showing up and that always created tension in his family and he knew it hurt his mother which was something he just didn't want to dwell on. Finally, he was using hard drugs again, and this wasn't the way he wanted to kick off the tour-strung out. Also, Wednesday night in New York with Belinda had been a disaster, and that was putting it mildly. He knocked back a few more pints as the pills began their slow, much awaited time release and his troubles began to melt away at least temporarily.

The Haven was your stereotypical dive bar and even though it was dimly lit the aura just felt grimy. The once majestic but now worn and chipped mahogany bar was long and narrow, approximately fifty feet long by tenty feet wide. Located behind the bar, the mahogany liquor shelves sat against a mirrored backdrop which ran from the height of the bar to the ceiling. Even though the shelves were dusted regularly, their well-worn sheen gave them a permanently dusty look. The other three walls were once painted white but were now yellowed with the combination of age and stale cigarette smoke. The asphalt floor was the Haven's unique attraction; the result of some town workers who had spent an afternoon drinking and taking a practical joke too far. This was a bar for people who could hold their booze. The stools were all old and uneven. As a result, if you couldn't maintain your center of gravity as your buzz progressed, you were likely to take a serious header, literally, onto the asphalt.

Billy left *The Haven* early and headed back for the guest room at his parents. His mood wasn't any better but he felt grateful that at least he wasn't feeling anything at all. At this point that was about all he could ask for.

Once again, he woke up to semi familiar surroundings. He immediately realized where he was for the first time in two years and this included his previous night's stay. Unfortunately, he had become used to feeling disoriented. It was 9:00 am according to the clock on the nightstand next to his bed as the sun glared through the window, its path having found its way through the partially opened shade.

He had a lot to do today as the tour was starting tomorrow night at the Paradise and he had to pick up his band for rehearsal later tonight at a rented soundstage located in the Fenway. Before that he had to meet the tour bus and tour manager at the hotel in Boston where they all would be staying. These responsibilities provided him with some peace of mind and a sense of purpose and he was grateful knowing that he'd be staying somewhere else tonight. Deep down he couldn't deny that his relationship with his father constantly weighed on him and the fact that they didn't see eye to eye was something he took for granted. After a couple of days, the tension was taking its toll on his mother who had the unenviable position of being stuck in the middle between two men cut from the same cloth; two men who never could see the forest through the trees. This was the simple result of focusing their anger on each other rather than taking a glimpse within. It was a fact his mother had given up pointing out a long time ago.

In addition, Billy was actually looking forward to seeing his tour manager, Dick Poole, who had been the road manager for his last tour and he felt they really had a connection. Dick rarely mentioned it, but he'd also been Led Zeppelin's road manager and this fact impressed Billy for two reasons. Zeppelin was one of the greatest musical groups at one of the historic peaks of rock music, but also because Dick was a consummate professional, which you'd have to be to be hired by such a well known band. If he could handle those lunatics-and by most accounts Led Zep was well behaved by 60's standards—he could certainly handle Drown on this 50-city tour.

Billy stripped the covers from the bed while slowly and deliberately placing his feet on the floor. He'd begun doing this since he turned the age of 33. He never remembered feeling the after effects of drugs prior to that age. He knew it was due in part to age but also to the increased strength and the amount of drugs he was taking. You didn't have to be a genius to figure this out. Nonetheless, for a smart guy up until now, it hadn't made him stop, which was the obvious solution to many, if not all of his problems. *I should just stop inflicting this pain upon myself.*

Other than feeling a little "jiggy" from the detox of the oxys, he felt pretty good. Despite the fact that pharmaceutical opiates provide for a very light sleep, it was more rest than he'd had had in two years. He cursed himself, just as he did every time he took pills, for not saving an oxy for the next morning. This would have eliminated the "snakes" he could feel that were lightly crawling up and down his skin. The good news was that he had a busy day and wouldn't have a lot of time to focus on the physical after effects of his two-day alcohol and narcotic binge. Likewise, since he'd been relatively free of drugs prior to Wednesday, he knew the prickly way he was feeling would last only one day. This was good for a number of reasons, not the least of which was that Dick Poole had been clean for twenty years and had agreed to do this tour at a reduced rate, as long as Billy was going to make a serious effort. He would overlook a lot: broads, drug use, even tardiness-though not for performances, but never sub par performances or problems as the result of dope sickness. Billy had hired him because he knew how lucky he was in landing this record deal and he had no intentions of blowing it and with the help of Dick keeping things together, it should be a done deal.

As someone once told him in regards to yet another relationship which he'd fucked up, "a few of us get second chances, Billy, but ain't nobody gets a third chance."

He dragged his ass into the shower and as the warm water cascaded down over his skin, he started to feel better. He wasn't aware of any material items that could soothe the soul. Leaning against the shower wall he began reminiscing about how he'd arrived at this point in his life. He would've been better served thinking about the busy day ahead, but somehow he couldn't shake the mood. Procrastination, along with the ability to go long periods of time without speaking to his father, were two characteristics that had been handed down to him through the generations on his paternal side of the family.

After the crash and burn of his first band, Heroine, and attaining a first hand view of the ugly side of the music business, he'd returned home. He considered going to law school as he began working for his father. But within the short span of a month, they weren't speaking and he basically wasn't working. Around this time he began dating Nacy. They fell in love with almost immediately. His parents, however, didn't approve of her but this was nothing new as his parents didn't really approve of anybody he dated. This was a common trait with parents of his generation. No one was ever a good enough mate for their offspring. The irony was that most of his parents' generation were self-made and came from humble beginnings, a fact they overlooked when judging one's latest flame. Another thing, if marrying money was so easy, why hadn't his parents or any of their friends done it? Furthermore, money always married money, did his parents really think that anyone in power wanted to empower the lower classes?

The closest he got to flirting with money was when he briefly dated the Secretary of State's daughter, almost certainly while she was going through her rebel phase. The relationship was over and done with when he asked if Air Force 3-or whatever plane the Secretary of State flew-could fly them to a Grateful Dead Concert. To say the Secretary herself disregarded him would be a nice way of characterizing their relationship. On his first and last introduction to the Secretary, in the Presidential Suite at the Waldorf in New York, the Secretary inquired whether he aspired to be Mayor of Boston, Senator of Massachusetts, or President. When he came back with rock star, he was abruptly dismissed. After getting the Secretary's daughter totally sloshed in Greenwich Village and then sleeping with her on the hotel floor of the Astoria, his political career, if he desired one, was over before it could begin. Needless to say, this was much to his parent's chagrin because they were even willing to overlook the fact that she was Protestant.

Initially, like most woman who became enmeshed with him, Nacy was attracted to him because of his music. Her interest diminished, as she wanted a more stable life. She came to know what everyone else knew; Billy was smart and he could do anything, but a half ass effort at his age in the music business was a million to one shot. A half ass effort at anything at his age was a million to one shot. Whether it was due to the drugs, some type of mental condition or the fact that he honestly believed that he'd peaked at 18, he couldn't find a way to apply himself to anything for very long. Nacy began losing her patience and any understanding she had left. He really cared about her but music was his real mistress and therefore would always be his forbidden and irresistible true love. She figured out she was doomed and so they split. Billy was allowed back home solely upon the insistence of his mother who always had a weak spot for him and believed his excuses. His father was tough and inflexible but he knew that his old man respected his wife and her decisions. She rarely stood up to her husband because to do so would be a waste energy but there were exceptions, however, when it came to her son. She always stood up for Billy and in this she always prevailed.

The water slowly washed him back to reality and his first thought was, *Man I feel like shit!* He opened the shower door a crack and reached for a fresh laundered towel that was left courtesy of his mother. Once he grabbed the towel he slammed the shower door closed before the warm moisture in the stall could give way to the cool, spring air seeping in through the bathroom window. Despite the lethargy of his body, his mind began to focus. He had to pick up the band, all of whom had stayed in New York after the show.

His band was pretty good considering this was a low paying tour. He was fair when it came to his band by giving out points in the record, a fair share of the song writing/publishing and an equal share of tour revenues.

For a new or developing "solo" artist like Billy, this was more than fair as most solo artists relied on studio musicians and paid union scale whether it be in the studio or on the road. No solo artists gave up song writing/ publishing as songwriters often hired publishers and the publishers enforced the songwriter's rights and collected royalties in exchange for a percentage of the proceeds. This made sense for most artists, as the time and costs in connection with these duties were significant—most publishers would be willing to pay the artist a cash advance for the publisher's rights and proceeds. Given the artist's need for cash, along with the extreme risk in that the publishing could ultimately be worthless if the artist stiffed, most artists entered into a publishing agreement.

A few artists like Neil Diamond, realizing the ultimate worth of publishing, decided to retain all rights, thereby turning down publishing deals early in their careers. Songwriting/Publishing is arguably the most lucrative aspect of the music business. and one of the few revenue streams paid directly to the artist/songwriter. This meant that the record company, as well as managers and agents who may have acquired an interest in the recording, along with a pound of the artist's flesh, had no rights to the publishing income which could be significant.

Songwriting/Publishing income included all the so-called public performance income, meaning royalties in exchange for songs being publicly played on television, radio, jukeboxes, arenas, department stores and supermarkets. Each of these entities paid blanket licenses to so-called public performance royalty collection agencies of which there were two: Associated Society for Collection of Artist Payments (ASCAP) and Business Music International (BMI). Anyone who's read the liner notes or the back of a CD jacket has seen these initials. In addition to public performance payments the songwriter receives a certain number of cents per song, per record sold. This amount, set by statute, presently stood around seven cents per song. More importantly, failure to pay these royalties was a violation of Federal Copyright Law and carried significant punitive damages. Finally, the songwriter/publisher also received compensation for any use in movie, television, or advertising, an amount which could easily reach seven figures, if used as the basis for a major marketing campaign—for example, The Verve's "Bitter Sweet Symphony" by Nike.

Initially, most rock and roll artists refused to license their music for commercials. This refusal was based on the decision that their art wasn't created for the purpose of selling anything other than albums. In the early 80's a rock band called the Del Fuegos, a couple of whom attended the same boarding school as Billy, licensed the rights of one of their songs to Budweiser. There was a universal outcry form the music community—a cutting edge band selling out, went against everything artists worked for and stood up against.

The hypocrisy of the Del Fuegos' contemporaries and critics was twofold. First, at the time the band actually needed the money. Second, as the alimony, palimony and expensive habits added up, most artists couldn't resist the six and seven figure offers from corporate America whose target demographics had grown up on the artists' music. This resulted in the licensing deals of Eric Clapton's, "After Midnight" for Michelob and The Beatles', "Come Together" for a technology company. The cardinal sin, in Billy's opinion, was that The Stones, "Start Me Up" was sold to Ford fucking Motors, of all people.

There were many infamous stories concerning song writing/publishing royalties and the saddest involved the outright theft of these rights and royalties from the artists. The most well-known was by record executives overseeing the artists in the 50's and 60's. This was particularly true in the case of black artists. These artists were either never informed of these royalties, or forced to sign them away. In other cases, executives listed themselves and/or relatives as the songwriter and registered the songs in their names with the US Copyright office. Allegedly, during the 80's, a representative from a royalty collection agency attempted to collect these royalties from one executive. The executive and his associates opened the window of their office several floors above Manhattan, held the representative upside down by his ankles and screamed, "If you want royalties, go to London." That was the last time anyone attempted to collect publishing royalties on behalf of these artists.

Unfortunately, this remains the case to this day. This left many artists destitute and uncompensated after generating millions in sales for record companies. These arrangements were not limited to less informed artists. Even the Rolling Stones and Beatles entered into agreements which at one time limited their share of publishing royalties.

The Rolling Stones had their publishing royalties stolen from them by one of their manager/producers, Andrew Lloyd Oldham. Though The Stones later successfully sued, Oldham avoided the multi-million dollar judgment by filing bankruptcy. Although British, the Stones developed Irish Alzheimer's over the years, which is to say that they failed to remember anything but their grudges. This was probably due in part to their history of substance abuse that, according to Keith, was "an occupational hazard." In the case of the Stones, they were able to exact some measure of revenge when Oldham produced the above referenced "Bitter Sweet Symphony" for the Verve. Unbeknownst to the Verve, the record company or The Rolling Stones, Oldham used an unauthorized sample from a Rolling Stones song; a previous recording used in a new song. Very common in rap music, the use of samples required both permission and compensation. Since Oldham saw no need to pay the Stones what was rightfully theirs in the 60's, he probably figured why start paying royalties thirty years later? Once again, the Stones found out, sued successfully and obtained a judgment. Not only were the Stones entitled to all of the royalties to "Bitter Sweet Symphony", they also obtained the right to license the song which they did, to Nike. For a band like the Verve, licensing their material for commercial use was against what they represented. Licensing to a symbol of corporate American greed, like Nike, which allegedly used child labor to maximize profits, would normally be unthinkable. Payback is a bitch-just ask Mick and Keith.

Chapter 12

Sleeker and shinier than any Greyhound motor coach, the tour bus idled at the curb in front of Boston's Four Seasons glass and brick façade, directly across from Boston's public gardens.

As Dickie slowly unfolded his long, gaunt frame out from one of the berths he ran his fingers through his thinning salt and pepper hair. His body was too big to have spent his life living on a bus, but like most things in his life, he'd come to this realization too late. His lean frame was a result of keeping physically fit, not a result of being strung out. His smooth, wrinkle-free skin and his clear, chrome colored eyes further enhanced his overall manifestation of superior health. Considering the life he led, he was still in his prime, regardless of his age.

Dressed in Gabardine slacks and a gray, hand tailored silk shirt, he looked every bit the English country gentleman. This was not the case, however, he'd spent his early years on the road with Led Zeppelin and having barely survived that experience he'd decided to retire to Venice, figuring the rest of the loose nuts had already rolled to California, so why not him?

In spite of all the aggravation and irritating minor duties involved, he enjoyed being a road manager. The road manager was the ringleader, and every rock and roll tour, regardless of how professional, was nothing more than a traveling circus. The bands that didn't use drugs or alcohol tended to be worse than the bands that did. He knew first hand that all the "clean" bands wanted were broads, broads and more broads. Forgoing drugs and alcohol you had to have something to do between shows. In Dickie's humble opinion he knew that the broads were often more trouble than the booze and the drugs combined.

The road manager's duties entailed total responsibility for the band, as the band was totally incapable of taking responsibility for themselves. These responsibilities included, but not limited to: Getting the band to the bus and on time, getting them to the show on time, in reasonable condition and competent to perform, keeping track of the band members and their whereabouts before, during and after the show, keeping track of who was hanging around the band and for exactly what purpose they were hanging around. Was it money, drugs, sex, to buy or to sell or all six possibilities? Road managers were also known to obtain women and drugs for the band members. His age, experience and reputation made it clear to all his clients that this was no longer part of his job description if in fact it ever was, he didn't procur drugs and women—he was a professional not a pimp.

He began to walking down the aisle of the tour bus. On the road, the tour bus became the band's home, the only refuge from the madness that surrounded every rock tour. He had certain rules regarding his bands and their home away from home. The golden rule being nobody but the band members could travel on the bus. It was okay for people to hang out after a show and the guys could screw broads on the bus, but no one else was allowed to travel when the wheels were rolling. This rule applied to the wives and significant others of the band members as well as the strangers they encountered on the road. They could protest as vehemently as they wanted but he saw this rule as essential to keeping the peace in the bus and between the band members.

Many of the wives were not fond of this rule and conjured up all kinds of excuses why it should be broken for them but Dickie and his rule prevailed, this point was non-negotiable. The smartest of the wives who wanted to stay married didn't want to know about what went on in the bus because they were aware of the real reason for the rule and resigned themselves to the reality of life with a musician prior to involving themselves with a rock star. He knew of many rock stars who loved and even missed their wife and kids on the road, but as of yet, he hadn't met one who'd remained completely faithful, which was another occupational hazard of their careers. Some guys could resist temptation better than others, but when a couple of strippers dragged you into the showers in the Bulls Locker room at the United Center in Chicago, what was a guy to do?

Dickie continued moving toward the front of the bus while behind him, at the very rear of the bus, was the "lounge" which consisted of a round, three-quarter black table surrounded by black leather couches. Mahogany cabinets and shelves framed the space between the couches and the roof of the bus and located in the center of the shelves was a 64" flatscreen, and beneath the TV sat a DVD player and the box which controlled the satellite dish on top of the bus. Moving forward toward the front of the bus on the left side of the aisle was a mahogany door that led to the toilet and shower stall. On the right side were six single mahogany bunks, two rows of three. On each bunk was a top of the line mattress, which in turn was covered in Egyptian cotton sheets and a down filled duvet. Two tapestry-like shades hung from the inner tops of each berth, one on the window side and one on the aisle side so they could be pulled down like a window shade to provide privacy. Further up the left side of the aisle was a small kitchenette. Black, leather couches surrounded the mahogany dining table.

Above the center and to the right of the kitchen area were tinted windows and to the left against the back of the shower stall wall were more mahogany shelves that held a microwave and toaster oven. Across from the kitchenette and just in front of the sleeping berths were two captain's chairs. Diagonally opposite the Captain's chairs in front of and below the kitchenette was the driver's seat. The driver's personal mementos hung from the visor; plastic laminated backstage passes with neck strings that allowed the holder access to all the given events on a tour as well as keepsakes which included but were not limited to; stuffed animals, bottle openers and pictures appreciatively given by artists in return for safe passage. In addition, this particular driver, Charlie Daniels, a retired Tennessee truck driver and veteran tour bus operator had a picture of his dearly departed wife, Isabel, front and center just above the dashboard.

Tour buses were fashioned like a traveling dorm room, some being the equivalent of a dorm room at a Backwater University and others, like the tour bus Drown was presently using, were the comparable to a suite at Harvard. Total cost to the record company and ultimately the artist was at four thousand dollars a week. There were many and assorted comforts designed to ease the thousands of miles traveled by the five or six men in such a confining space. By the end of a tour it was not unusual for members to be barely speaking to one another and occupying separate corners of the bus. "fifteen hundred miles, three thousand more in two days, You ask me why another road song, funny but I bet you never left home," that's how Chris and Rich Robinson of the Black Crowes sang it.

As Dickie neared the front of the bus he turned to his left and pulled up the shades covering the bunks. As he did, he noticed the pedestrians as they passed by on the sidewalk between the bus and the carport of the Four Seasons. Most of the younger kids hesitated or walked slowly past staring at the gray ghost, hoping it carried someone of a musical note and maybe they'd get a glimpse. The older crowd continued on by without notice, either unaware or indifferent to the bus' occupants. All those who approached the bus from the left, however, stopped upon reading the buses destination sign which read… *All those who wander are not lost*.

As he continued to stare out the window above the kitchenette he could see clear across Boylston Street, relatively busy on this early Saturday evening. Across from Boylston was the Public Garden. The flowerbeds in the Garden had been cleaned in anticipation of their summer guests' arrival. Likewise, the Frog Pond was completely melted and it wouldn't be long before the famous Swan boats were dropped into the water. Beyond the pond at the far northeast corner of the park were the bronze statues commemorating McKlusky's, "Make Way for Ducklings." A favorite past time of the local hooligans was to steal one of the duckling statues which guaranteed its mention in the local news and thus, in turn, was then anonymously returned.

Through the black, five foot high wrought iron gate surrounding the Public Garden and the tall oaks guarding the air space above the gates, he could just make out Billy Sunday as he came within view of the bus. His first notion that it was Billy was by the way he was dressed; the ripped blue jeans, a white thermal shirt covered by a baggy, navy blue well-worn sweater. He was glad to see that he had dressed for the occasion. *At least he's on time.* He had taken this gig because he genuinely liked Billy and he believed that he respected Dickie enough to keep himself together for a successful tour.

As Billy drew nearer to the bus he wasn't able to notice Dickie watching him through the tinted windows.

Dickie watched him as he come closer and noticed he looked tired and that the color of his skin was a ghostly pale, with a tinge of gray and black circles under his eyes indicating to him that he'd been doing some partying. It took a junkie to know a junkie and he knew that Billy's schedule, like most musicians, had been grueling. He also knew that the showcase in New York in front of the industry had put a lot of pressure on him. This show had to go well, not only because it was his last chance, but because he had been around long enough to know that without respect for the business he'd be lost. Dickie disagreed with Billy's idea to return to Boston immediately after the showcase, particularly since he knew his real reason for returning was he was in search of the one thing he was never going to find. What he was looking for was somewhere within himself and did not come in the shape of a woman, the stealth of a syringe or the bottom of a glass. Dickie had spent a large part of his own life looking everywhere else for the answer to all of his problems and he knew all he found was more problems. The temporary relief a gorgeous actress or flawless model provided was only a bandage and was no cure for soul sickness that caused the wound. He knew Billy would eventually have to find out that his only mistress right now was the road and he wasn't ready to leave her quite yet. Once he found peace within himself he might then be able to bring peace and stability to a relationship with someone else. Most people went through their whole life without finding that special someone because they never looked within before looking out.

Dickie felt he should have said something to Billy about keeping the band in New York and then have everyone drive up to Boston together to hook up with Charlie and the bus but it really wasn't his call to make. They'd been through wars together and alone, so Dickie tended to treat Billy as an equal and for the most part, he let him make his own decisions.

Looking at him now, he knew he'd made a mistake. If Billy started using again now, to quell his emotions, he wouldn't survive this tour and that would turn out to be a problem for everyone.

The bus door retreated just as Billy raised his hand to knock and the opening made that swooshing sound known to every commuter worldwide. As he boarded the bus they entered into a strong, firm embrace. "Aye, Mate, you look like Shite," Dickie said in a pronounced British accent.

He knew that was coming and replied, "Good to see you, too, asshole."

"I'm not going to start on you, but I will if I have to," said Dickie, sternly enough so Billy wouldn't take him lightly.

"Medicinal reasons only," assured Billy, unable to look Dickie in the eye. It was an instant sign to Dickie that he was using and he was headed for trouble but he decided to save the lecture for the rest of the band, as well. "So, how's it been being back home here in Boston?" he asked.

"You know, Dickie…same circus, different clowns."

"What time are we picking up the band?" inquired Dickie.

"The first of them should be flying in around now," Billy replied as he glanced around his new surroundings, he was pleased.

Seeing Billy's reaction, Dickie said, "It's the Scorpions bus. They owed me a favor."

"Yeah, but how did you get Phil Caruso to pay for it?"

"Easy, I told him I'd get you to amend your contract so that you were responsible for 100 % of tour support."

"Why the fuck not?" was his response, "We're never going to sell enough records to recoup and pay for it anyway."

"Spoken like a true tortured artist," said Dickie with a smile.

"You're kidding, right?" questioned Billy, with no sense of amusement in his voice. Dickie just continued to smile. *Fuck it, what difference did it make?* thought Billy.

"How are we getting to Logan?" asked Dickie. "I have a rent-a-car."

"Fuck that. Call Charlie and lets ride in style, it's the last time I'll ever roll like a rock star." said Billy, still conveying the tortured persona.

Almost on cue, dressed in crisp new blue jeans, a red and black

L.L.Bean, lumberjack shirt and new black, ostrich cowboy boots, Charlie appeared in the doorway to the bus which had been left open. Charlie, in his late 60's, carried almost two-hundred and eighty pounds on his 5'9 frame. Despite his age and girth Charlie bounded up the bus steps two at a time. "Billy, it's my pleasure."

"No, Charlie, it's my honor," he assured him.

Though they had never ridden together, like Dickie, Charlie was a legend and Billy knew he was traveling with the best.

"Enough of this fucking mutual dick holding," shouted Dickie, "Let's roll."

"I can see that his professional asshole side has kicked in," stated Charlie, as he eased into the driver's seat.

"What's the name of this band?" asked Dickie, feigning the inability to recall the band's name.

"Oh yeah, Clusterfuck, that's right," said Dickie, answering his own question.

"Billy Benoit on keys, Johnny Chez on drums, Bobby Brothers on bass, and Jimmy The White Russian or Russian, for short, on lead guitar. The tightest group of badass motherfuckers you've ever seen. And the name, for your information, is D-R-O-W-N," Billy proudly asserted.

"Yeah, like I said, Clusterfuck," was Dickies comeback.

Billy ignored the razzing. "C'mon Charlie, the sooner we go, the sooner we're home."

With that, Charlie gently eased the big bus from the curb and moved into traffic as gracefully as a swan boat leaving the shore of the frog pond in the Public Garden.

Chapter 13

Jimmy Gerard hated working Saturdays and it wasn't because he was lazy. He was single and with no one around to pester him with a honey-do list he morphed into your typical workaholic. But every Saturday for the past twenty years he'd been hungover and the only thing that differed from one Saturday to the next was the degree of the hangover he had to contend with. Today, dressed in khaki slacks, a white, button down Polo shirt and a blue, Brooks Brother's blazer with wooden buttons, he made his way into midtown's 18th Precinct. His outfit was his idea of casual as he always tried to appear what he felt he was, a consummate professional, regardless of his hangover.

He entered the precinct and he headed toward the elevators. Normally, he'd have taken the stairs to the third floor homicide office, but given his degree of hangover, even the elevator was going to pose a challenge. He'd spent last night drinking Jameson's Blackbush with black and tan chasers, what he considered a real tribute to the homeland. Actually, it was a real tribute to Margie Markowitz, the city's premiere gossip columnist of Page 6 in the New York Post. As far as today's degree of hangover, it was off the charts.

After a long Friday of interviews about a celebrity murder and arguing with DA McBride, the power hungry bitch, all he really wanted to do was take up his regular seat at McGinty's and watch the Yankees while nursing the only known cure for his ailment: displeasure for the state of the world caused primarily by those who presently inhabited his universe.

DROWN

Last night, before his intuition told him he shouldn't go home first, *Go right to McGinty's,* he decided to change clothes and almost as soon as he entered his apartment, the phone rang. Again, his intuition spoke up and told him not to answer but given the day's earlier discovery, he figured it could be the captain wanting an update. So for the second time in less than five minutes, his intuition had been right, he shouldn't have gone home and he most certainly shouldn't have picked up the phone. After twenty years as a cop you'd think that he'd have learned to trust his intuition.

"Jimmy, glad I caught you," came Margie Markowitz's seductive voice from the other end of the phone line. The cheerful tone told him that she wanted something and he had a feeling he knew what it was she wanted. She was looking for anything and everything on Belinda Caruso and her untimely demise but before Jimmy could answer, Margie continued. "Heard you found New York's lead rock and roll groupie dead in a quite compromising position, so to speak?"

"No comment," said Jimmy.

"Also heard you already have a suspect," Margie continued.

"How the fuck do you come up with these things?" queried Jimmy.

"For one, I'm good-like you," Margie replied in a patently obvious attempt at flattery.

"Do you think you're the only one who can speak to witnesses? Unlike the Police Department, which relies on a sense of civic obligation, I can be a little more persuasive."

"You bribe them," stated Jimmy.

"We prefer to call it compensating them for their services," finished Margie. She always remained vague because she would never allow him to identify her sources.

"It's way too early in the investigation for me to have anything concrete to give you. Belinda was found dead in an apartment on the Upper East Side early this morning. Technically, we have a number of people who were apparently seen with her at some point just prior to her death. Again, it's the Department's position that its way too early to name anyone as a suspect."

As if she didn't hear a word he said, she couldn't resist adding, "I hear it's some washed up, wanna be rock star who goes by the name Billy Sunday?"

"That's simply not true." He said, trying to figure out how someone could be washed up and a wannabe at the same time. She could really irritate him.

"All right, I'll just run something generic for now, but I'm telling you this is the murder of the year, maybe even since OJ, given the players involved. This is going to stretch far and wide and I'm going to be all over this investigation. Thanks Jimmy. Ciao!" Margie made some kissing sounds as she hung up the phone.

"Murder of the fucking decade," Jimmy deadpanned into the receiver. "What a way to make a living." *No*, he thought to himself, *Having to solve the murder of the decade in a week, now that's no way to make a fucking living.*" When did celebrity culture become news in this society never mind the lead fucking story? His Grandmother was right the world is going to H-E—double hockey sticks in a hand basket.

Jimmy had always felt obligated to Margie. She started out as a celebrity groupie and hung out down in the village in the early days where he'd met her at a party twenty years ago when one thing had led to another. True to form, he'd never called her back after that night, and she never mentioned it or seemed to care.

Margie was able to parlay her hobby into becoming one the biggest gossip columnist in New York City's where gossip now took center stage. Now, because of some Catholic guilt bullshit he still felt he owed her something. *What is that saying-the Irish feel guilty about nothing except sex and the Jewish feel guilty about everything but sex, or something along those lines?* He really should have taken up the Department's offer for therapy when it was recommended. She was a hell of a lay, as that night still brought a smile to his face twenty years later, and she was a professional, in that she wouldn't ever write anything that would jeopardize him or his sources. Like Zen, with the good also comes the bad and his conversations with Margie always made him drink heavily.

The motion of the elevator jerking up made his stomach queasy as the taste of Jameson's slowly rose back up his esophagus and into his mouth. As the elevator stopped at the third floor he stepped out directly across from a door marked, *DETECTIVES, HOMICIDE DIVISION.* Like everything else on the floor, the door was painted battleship gray and the cracked linoleum floor, while polished to a shine, was yellowed with specks of faded gray. The fluorescent lights overhead beamed off the floor and seared his eyeballs.

His head was pounding as he entered the squad room. To his right and left were two equally spaced metal desks and located at the far end of the room was a big white marker board where Kelly stood with her shapely back to him. Like Jimmy, she was always dressed for the job but today, being Saturday, she allowed herself the casual look of black slacks with a sleeveless, tight fitting, black, mock turtleneck top. In front of her, stuck to the white board, were three pictures and one blank spot. The first picture was of Phil Caruso and looked like a photo from the latest Artiste annual report. Next to the picture of Caruso was one of Billy Sunday. *Kind of an average looking guy for a rock star* thought Jimmy. He had shaggy, brown hair, bright blue eyes and a tightly cropped goatee. *He didn't look like a murderer, but who did these days?* The third picture was that of Billy Brill. His face was thin and drawn. He had a thick chain with a padlock around his neck and dragon tattoos on both sides of his neck. He also had four or five hoop earrings in each ear and a nose ring. His young face was pitted with a few acne scars and out of his head grew a shock of bright orange hair. *Now, he looks like a murderer,* thought Jimmy. The fourth space was the same size as the previously three, but blank and underneath this space were the words, *Record Executive.* Underneath each picture was a column that listed the following words: motive, opportunity, and means. The bottom half of the board was blank under the words: *Notes/Misc.* To the right of Kelly was a smaller, white drawing board and centered at the top was the name *BELINDA CARUSO.* Beneath it was her headshot which looked like it had been taken from a newspaper article.

Man, was she good looking. I should have been a rock star, Jimmy thought he might have said out loud, as he looked at her photo appraisingly.

Beneath the glamour shot were the photos of the grim crime scene; different angle shots of Belinda on the bed. A close up of her head and neck that give you an idea about the severity of the bruise. And beneath these photos were the following outlines: *Time of Death, Cause of Death,*

Coroner's Report. Like the bigger board, all of these headings were followed by blanks.

"Spent last night with Margie, I take it," said Kelly, without turning.

"How did you guess?" asked Jimmy as he walked toward her.

"I can smell her perfume escaping from your every pore, every time. Jameson's Black-nothing but the best for Margie."

"That bad?" asked Jimmy skeptically

"No. Actually, somehow she got my pager number and like an asshole I called her back," she informed him. "But I figured if she got to me, she got to you and then you got to the Jameson's."

"*You* ought to be a fucking detective," replied Jimmy. "What did she tell you?"

"She's got a source who likes our cutie boy, Billy Sunday."

"I don't find him that cute, but she basically told me the same thing. I didn't get a chance to grab a paper this morning. How did it read?"

"Generic, just like she promised," assured Kelly. "It's on my desk."

He picked up the paper and read through the Page 6 story. "Body of a young, record executive's wife found dead on the Upper East Side. Husband grieving and the police aren't saying much. A couple of suspects rumored, ya da ya da ya da."

"Well what do we have, exactly?" asked Jimmy, removing his sport coat and throwing it over the metal chair at his desk.

"We have some preliminary forensics," Kelly relayed, as she caught him up to date. She began writing on the board while she continued to fill him in. "Time of death is estimated somewhere around early Thursday morning between midnight and 2:00 am. Cause of death is strangulation with some type of ligature yet to be determined. Right now, we're thinking maybe one of her stockings. One seems to be more stretched than the other. You can see it in the photos, if you look close enough. Preliminary toxicology report reveals alcohol, cocaine, heroin and oxycontin. Belinda may have been a walking pharmacy but she hadn't ingested enough to kill herself, apparently. There were some other unidentified toxins but none known to be fatal."

"Could make for a good defense," suggested Jimmy as he couldn't resist adding, "She was going to OD anyway." Kelly didn't see the humor in that and let him know it without having to vocalize her feelings. *If looks could kill.* He thought as he continued. "So the killer strangled her and then reattached her stocking to her garter belt? I don't buy that. Any fingerprints?"

"Lots of partials," she continued. "Obviously the victim's prints were present throughout the apartment. Mr. Sunday's and Mr. Brill's were also present. I have two other sets that we haven't been able to identify, one male and one female. I'm guessing the male set belongs to our mysterious record executive and the other is probably a female friend."

"So Kelly, are we thinking murder, crime of passion, sex crime or accidental strangulation?" asked Jimmy.

"Homicide, definitely. A crime of passion is still a homicide. She doesn't appear to have been raped but we're still waiting for those tests to come back. How often is strangulation accidental? After a brief discussion with Joe Briggs in sex crimes, people who are into bondage or S&M aren't usually bound as tightly as Belinda was. This way, the person tied up can release themselves, if things get too sticky. In role playing, the partners usually have a safe word indicating that one partner is getting uncomfortable and the other should stop."

"There weren't any signs of a struggle on her arms or legs, no other bruising that would indicate she was tied up against her will," Jimmy pointed out. "Not that I need to start learning about S&M at my age. I can't even get laid in the missionary position, for Christ sakes."

Kelly's laughter was cut short by the ringing of the phone.

"Let me guess, the bitchstrict attorney?" Jimmy was willing to place a bet.

"I'll get it," Kelly replied. "Agis," she answered as she picked up the phone. "Hi, Beth. Yes, Beth, we have some very preliminary forensic reports and I have some junior detectives running backgrounds on the possible perps. Yes, they were identified from both witnesses and the prints lifted at the scene. No, I wouldn't say we had a real suspect at this point. The next step is for Detective Gerard and myself to track Mrs. Caruso's movements on the day of her death. I'm not going to bring anyone in for questioning until I have all of the background. A press conference? 6:00 o'clock tonight? I think that would be very premature,

Beth. All right, I'll get back to you by five o'clock with what we have at that point. Yes, I'm sure the captain knows to make it a top priority."

"Fucking A," started Jimmy, as Kelly hung up the phone.

"Save it, Jimmy. We don't have the time. Let's go see the grieving husband again," Kelly said, with more than a touch of sarcasm.

Chapter 14

Even on Saturdays, Johnny Vell's phone rang constantly. He was the type of person who wanted to let other people know that he was important, even on weekends. It was mid-afternoon on an unusually warm Saturday and Boston's Newbury Street was bustling with its international cast of inhabitants as people continuously poured out of the classic Back Bay brick brownstones. Vell was fully clad in Armani, all black, including his loafers and sunglasses and was just crossing Dartmouth Street when his phone rang. It was Luke from Artiste. Vell had to give the kid credit. He may have had a lousy record with The Dead Boys, but he sure had the makings of a great promotion man. His perseverance was an asset that could one day overcome his lack of talent. "Vell here."

"Hey, Johnny," Luke said in his downtrodden voice. "Johnny, this ain't about The Dead Boys."

"What's up?"

"Belinda Caruso is dead."

He stopped right where he was, in the middle of Dartmouth Street, as a yuppie in a silver Range Rover slammed on his brakes and came to a screeching stop mere inches in front of him.

"Asshole," the typical Boston driver yelled out his window while flipping his middle finger.

As Johnny regained his senses and stumbled to the curb in front of the restaurant Fridays, he asked, "Dead how? Was she murdered?"

"They think murder," replied Luke. "I just thought," Luke continued, "I mean, it's none of my business, but you know people talk and..."

Vell interrupted, "Listen Luke, I really appreciate the heads up. I'll make sure The Dead Boys is a go next week on WXKL."

"That's not why I called."

"I know," said Vell, "do you know anything else? Like any details?"

"There are not a lot of details. They say she was found Friday morning in the Rocket Science Records office slash apartment. Supposedly, the cops have a couple of suspects."

"Thanks, Luke. Keep me posted, would you?"

"Okay, thanks for The Dead Boys."

Vell was stunned. Phil Caruso was never going to pay him when he found out Vell was banging his wife. He should have never gone back to her apartment and he knew it was a mistake as soon as he left. Lunch was enough, yet Belinda had a way of leading men around by their dicks. Fuck, his fingerprints were all over the apartment, not to mention her. He stared at his cell phone in disbelief. *All of the so-called important numbers and not one criminal defense lawyer*, was Vell's only thought as he began dialing four-one-one, still totally oblivious to the heavy Newbury Street traffic all around him.

Chapter 15

Two miles away from the street corner where Vell was standing, the Drown tour bus was pulling up to the Delta Shuttle terminal at Boston's Logan International Airport. Standing in front of the terminal were four individuals who had no problem being identified as musicians. Billy Benoit was a good looking guy, noticeably thin with a silver hoop hanging from his left earlobe, he was encased in black from his close-cropped black hair down to his shit kicking scuffed boots and propped up next to him was a tall black case with the word *YAMAHA* printed on the outside. Alongside Billy was Bobby Brothers who was rocking back and forth on his red, high top Converse Chuck Taylors. Dressed in jeans and a green flannel button down shirt, he looked inconspicuous. Next to Bobby was Jimmy Belanda, A.K.A., the White Russian. Dragging on the cigarette hanging from the side of his mouth, his long golden locks framing his well-defined facial features, he had the looks and swagger of a rock star. Wearing a buttoned down yellow and blue paisley silk shirt neatly tucked into his black leather pants he was the whole package. His nickname didn't come from his heritage but from his favorite libation and he was already a few white Russians into the afternoon. Six guitar cases stood situated amongst the group, the cases held vintage instruments now worth thousands of dollars each. Behind all of this was Johnny Chez, timekeeper extraordinaire. Decked out in black Chuck Taylors, black jeans and a red These United States t-shirt, he was the first to see the bus pull up as he tossed his non-filter camel into the gutter and began gathering up his drum kit cases.

Normally, the driver and road manager would load the gear, but because of Dickie and Charlie's reputation the guys had no problem with loading their own gear into the cargo hold under the bus.

Each band member then strutted up the stairs of the bus like they'd done it a million times before as Billy stood at the top and greeted each member with a mischievous smile and a hug.

"Great job the other night, guys. C'mon, get settled. No need to introduce Charlie and Dickie," welcomed Billy and with that the doors closed and the Drown tour was officially underway.

The bus exited Logan airport and headed through the Callahan Tunnel back toward downtown Boston. Leaving the tunnel, Charlie eased the bus onto the Central Artery for one exit and then commenced to weave through city traffic headed for Kenmore Square. In the back of the bus the guys began making drinks, rolling joints, cutting up lines and checking provisions. Dickie had made sure the bus was well stocked with nothing but the best: Kettle One Vodka, cases of Heineken, bottled water, carbonated and non-carbonated, pomegranate juice and Gatorade, original flavor. Billy sat in front with Dickie, comfortable being back on the road with the only responsibility being having to entertain a few thousand strangers a couple of hours a night.

As the pavement rushed by below, Billy's mind began to wander to the tours he'd performed in the past where he believed he was running toward something or sometimes running from something. The reality, he now realized, was that he was simply running. The thoughts of running to or from something brought him back to thoughts of Nacy. He'd gone home with the intention of seeing her and telling her how he really felt and that after this one last hurrah he'd settle down with her for good. "Gonna give up the booze and the one night stands, then he'll settle down, find a piece of land in a quiet little town and forget about everything," or whatever Gerry Rafferty had sung. The certainty was that Nacy probably wanted nothing to do with him and why would she since he really wanted nothing to do with himself. His mood quickly changed from one of happiness to dread so he excused himself from Dickie's company and made his way to the bathroom. Once inside, he reached into his pocket and pulled out two small glassine bags that he'd picked up, just in case. One baggie was filled with coke and the other was a heat-sealed packet printed with an image of a red devil and the words *Red Hot* which contained heroin. He carefully opened each package, dumping the contents on the sink and with a razor blade began chopping each pile into a fine powder then mixing the two together. The end result looked like two matchsticks the color of beach sand when chopped and aligned. He rolled a dollar bill and with a quick sniff inhaled the concoction. *Not great for the heart,* he thought, *but great for the head.* His eyeballs rolled slightly back in his head, as a warm effortless feeling began to spread from his brain through the rest of his body. Once the sensation encompassed his whole being, he slowly and methodically cleaned up the residue left on the sink as a small wave of guilt passed over him. The guilt lifted as he told himself these chemicals were for medicinal reasons only. He was reminded of Keith Richards singing, "Booze and pills and powders you can choose your medicine…"

Coming out of the bathroom he went straight to the back of the bus because he didn't feel like facing Dickie-not that Dickie didn't know what he was doing. The lines were spread across the lounge table and everyone was excited about the start of the tour. They were all feeling good and ready to terrorize the women in every city they played. The myth was that drug use was down, even in the music business, but that was a total fallacy. Because of the political incorrectness now associated with illicit drugs, their use had only returned to the closet while the drugs being used today were harder, stronger and more addictive, both physically and mentally.

As he drew near the table the laughter stopped and the band turned their attention to him. Each band was like a sports team and each player had a designated role. Billy was ten years older than the other guys and had paid his dues and earned their respect. More importantly, he agreed to pay them an equal share of the tour receipts over and above whatever Artiste had agreed to pay them. Since he wrote, recorded and produced all of the songs, he took a larger portion of the receipts.

Billy felt it was important that this tour be done as a band and not promoted as a solo act. He was already broke so what difference would splitting the proceeds make to him? He figured splitting the money would keep up moral which would be important on a long tour such as this one.

As he took a seat in the back the Russian stopped strumming the acoustic guitar he was playing and moved his free hand in an offering gesture to what was laid out on the table. *What the fuck?* Billy thought. The chemicals in the bathroom had only given him a taste for more. That was the problem with narcotics. One was too many and a thousand was never enough. Tolerance and taste developed quickly. He leaned over and snorted a line of coke and a line of dope.

He allowed a few seconds for the chemicals to infiltrate his bloodstream before addressing the band.

"All right, guys, rehearsal tonight, as long as it takes, we have another big show Tuesday night in New York. The label reps will be there tomorrow and they've promised a big radio push for the single. So, let's make a good impression, all right?"

Just as he was finishing his little pep talk, Charlie was pulling the bus into Kenmore Square. He drove past the Boston University dorms and frat houses and made a left at Pizzeria Uno. He then made another quick left at The Cask & Flagon onto Lansdowne Street and passed behind Fenway Park's Green Monster. Now totally jammed, the Russian, a native New Yorker, yelled, "Hey Billy, tell the guys how the Sox ruined your life!"

"Which time?" Billy asked the Russian.

"The first time. You never get over your first broken heart, man."

"You would know Whitey. Yours gets broken in every city," Johnny Chez chimed in.

"That's cruel, man," the White Russian responded.

The guys then gave Billy their undivided attention.

"1986, Game Six. My parents were on vacation for a month and I was house-sitting. I was lying on the floor with this gorgeous model I was dating, and I do mean fucking gorgeous. I'm lying there and I'm thinking this is going to be the best fucking night of my life. I have this amazing broad in my arms that's dying to screw me and the Red Sox are going to win the goddamn World Series. I would have absolutely nothing to live for after this night. My dreams were going to come true."

By now, everyone, including Dickie and Charlie, were listening to his tale as he was a good storyteller, a trait that came through in his music, as well.

Billy continued, "Okay, so, I go down to my father's wine cellar and get the absolute best bottle of Champagne I can find. I mean, the old man isn't going to care because the Sox are going to win the fucking World Series, for Christ sakes. I go back upstairs and my girl is half-naked on the Oriental rug so I pop the Champagne and pour two glasses and the scoreboard was flashing Bruce Hurst, the Red Sox pitcher, as MVP. I mean, God chose this day to smile on me, right? I mean, they're going to write songs about this. Next fucking thing I know, Stanley throws a wild pitch, which everyone forgets. Stanley blew the fucking game! Anyway, I start drinking the Champagne a little faster as the ball goes through Billy fucking Buckner's legs and now I'm guzzling the Champagne out of the bottle. The next thing I remember, I wake up and the TV is nothing but snow since we didn't have cable. The girl is gone and I never fucking saw her again and the five-thousand dollar bottle of champagne is spilled all over the thirty-thousand dollar Oriental rug." He looked down, deflated from the memory. "And I've been pretty much been fucked over ever since." After a mournful pause, they all burst into laughter.

"Now I'm thirty-five, I don't have a single possession and I'm stuck with you jamokes on another pointless journey. No wonder I'm snorting junk again." Everyone continued laughing.

Dickie turned around, still smiling and looked directly at Charlie. "What do you think, Charlie?"

"We'll be all right, Dickie. Ya know, these guys have all been around. They know the score. They're just excited, getting a chance to do what they love to do-just like us, I guess. Tomorrow night is a home game for Billy, so that adds to the excitement."

"Yeah, I guess your right," Dickie replied.

Still, something about Billy was making Dickie feel uneasy. At this point, he was willing to write it off as nervous energy about the upcoming tour on both their parts.

Chapter 16

Attorney Clarence Weatherby was screaming at Phil in his office. "I told you that broad was nothing but trouble!"

The filtered sunlight shimmered off of the chrome furnishings and recently polished mahogany woodwork. "Listen, I don't need the I told you so lecture right now," Phil replied, frankly, "I need some serious fucking legal representation."

"I hope to fuck you didn't kill this broad." Weatherby continued.

"I told you, I was in the office all day working The Dead Boys record and then I was at home working the record from there."

"The only fucking dead boy being worked is going to be you when NYPD gets here. And I'm not talking about the TV show you were thinking about when you decided to speak with them yesterday, without my representation. You are lucky I'm blaming myself. I never should have let you go through with marriage to that groupie."

Weatherby noticed the sting his last remark had caused by the grimace on Phil's face. Even for a lawyer, that was over the top when all Weatherby was trying to get across was just how much trouble Phil could potentially be in. Murdering his wife, which Clarence didn't think was possible, was one thing, but Phil was going to be in trouble with Artiste's Board of Director's who would not tolerate a scandal of this sort. This was definitely going to cost him his career. The fucking incompetent, no talent midget was finally getting what was coming to him. Even though he had represented him for a number of years, he never grew to like him socially, like he had with many of his other clients.

Trying to regain his composure, Phil began, "I have an alibi."

"You were by yourself. You don't have an alibi. Don't get smart with me, either. You're lucky I know Detective Gerard from the old neighborhood. Right now, all he would tell me was that, at the moment, you're being considered as a suspect until you can be irrefutably ruled out. That means they have a good reason to think you did it, or at the very least, were somehow involved. You're lucky he was considerate enough to interview you here at your office, and not the police station where the DA would have paraded you around in front of the media. I don't think I need to tell you that that would have been a complete circus, particularly with Margie Markowitz printing every aspect of this investigation she can weedle out of anyone she can get her hands on. Considering all of the above, I expect you to be sincere, considerate and contrite and not your usual asshole, smug self. Are we clear?"

Phil was too angry at being talked down to and refused to respond orally. As a result, he returned Clarence's verbal undressing with a curt nod.

"I don't know how we're going to explain that you knew nothing about the apartment where her body was found especially since Artiste has been paying five grand a month for the mortgage," Clarence said skeptically.

Phil, continuing to take offense, managed, "I told you that the condo was leased to Rocket Science Records. They're an independent imprint I established for Belinda to run and they have been funding her budget so quite frankly, I never really had to look at how the money was spent." Clarence began rolling his eyes. Phil continued, "Apparently…"

"Not fucking apparently, absolutely!" Weatherby interrupted. Now, Phil was steaming.

He probably made three times as much as this asshole attorney, therefore, he figured he was smarter. It was a common misperception among most high-level record executives who measured their intelligence by their salaries; salaries that were usually the equivalent of seven figures time's their IQ.

"If RSR is funded by Artiste and the rent is ultimately paid by Artiste how is it possible you know absolutely nothing about it?" inquired Clarence.

"It's obvious Artiste is a big entity and I can't possibly know everything that goes on," Phil bemoaned.

Clarence jumped out of his seat, grabbed the chair and tossed it the length of Phil's office. Chair throwing is a favorite past time for attorneys with short tempers. "Have you ever heard of Enron or Health South? You are the fucking C-E-O. You sign the financials which indicates that you read the financials and understand the financials, which also means you know where the money goes and finally that the financials are an accurate description of how the money is both made and spent. Thank god there are no laws against stupidity or you'd be doing life. From the looks of things, you may end up doing that anyway," Clarence concluded.

Phil was now visibly seething and Clarence knew it wasn't wise to work his client into a fury immediately prior to a police interrogation. But Phil was so arrogant and incompetent that it was simply impossible to stop his rampage whose only effect was to further infuriate Phil. He decided to spend a few minutes rehabilitating his witness, so to speak. "I don't mean to offend you or aggravate you, Phil, it's just that these are very serious charges and after this interview, I want to be certain that you're no longer a suspect. Your conduct and your answers are going to be very important."

As Phil's face began to relax he no longer looked like he was ready to boil over or fire Clarence the minute the Police left.

"If you weren't at the apartment, which I believe you when you say you weren't since you didn't even know it existed until I told you, then there should be no physical evidence to tie you there. The police are probably going to try and connect you with either the killer or killers. Since at the moment they don't know who murdered Belinda, they can't tie you to the murderer. I don't think they've yet made the connection with the rent and Artiste, but they will. Given what's before us, I think we'll be just fine," assured Clarence.

Phil had a look like, "Now that's the type of representation I'm looking for from you, Clarence." However, Phil noticed that at no point in their conversation did Clarence make any serious inquiry as to whether or not he was actually involved in his wife's murder. These thoughts were abruptly interrupted by a firm knock on his office door.

Clarence walked quickly across the room and righted the chair he threw and then walked up to Phil and straightened his tie then gave him a reassuring pat on the back. After checking his own appearance in the reflection of the plate glass window, he turned 180 degrees and opened the door with a confident smile. "Detective Agis, Jimmy, please come in. Let me begin by thanking you for the courtesy of allowing my client to meet with you here. As you can imagine, he hasn't had a chance to begin processing his grief and" Jimmy cut him off. "Clarence, we go back, so let's cut the bullshit. Okay? I'll be as fair as always and you be as straight with me, as always, and everything will be copasetic."

Clarence smiled. Jimmy would have made a damn good lawyer. "Please then, Detectives, sit down."

Kelly and Jimmy sat on the leather couch that was situated in the middle of the office while Phil and Clarence sat opposite on the two chairs that were turned around in front of Phil's desk.

After their initial encounter with Phil earlier, neither Kelly nor Jimmy were inclined to give him any courtesy or cut him any slack and as a result skipped all pleasantries. At this point, Jimmy believed that he was somehow involved.

Jimmy began the interrogation. "Mr. Caruso, because of both the personal relationship and professional respect I have for your counsel, I'm going to be direct. In turn, I expect you to be the same and that way we should be able to save each other a lot of time. Understand?"

"Understood," answered Phil, as he sat motionless, staring at the Detectives.

Jimmy nodded and continued. "At this time, we have no physical evidence linking you to the crime scene."

"Then why are we here, detectives?" Clarence interjected.

"We're here because your client didn't seem all that broken up yesterday, for starters," Jimmy continued.

"Detective, come on, my client was obviously in shock."

"I thought we were going to be straight, Clarence?" Jimmy asked.

"I'm sorry. What are you getting at?"

"We know that Mrs. Caruso hasn't exactly been faithful during your marriage and we also know your finances indicate you may benefit financially by her death." Jimmy knew Clarence would see right through this circumstantial sweeping statement, however, thanks to the bitchstrict attorney and her insistence on an early evening press conference today, they had no time to properly prepare for this interview. They spent some time on the Internet before leaving the station but that left them only a couple of possible motives. Clarence was right, what was the point of this interview? "We do know Artiste stock has been headed south since you took over and I suspect that means your stock options might not be enough to support your, or more importantly your wife's, lifestyle. We do know that your wife was adequately insured. As you may be aware, the husband is usually guilty in about seventy percent of murder cases." His experience in dealing with guys who were soft, was to try and break them right away.

Weatherby, however, had been around the block a couple of times, as well and as Phil started to answer, he raised his outstretched hand with his palm in the air, indicating that he should stop.

"Detective," Clarence's formal tone toward Jimmy indicated that the battle had begun. "Except for your last statistic, all you have at this point is what you've been able to cull from the newspapers and innuendo. If you have any further specific questions, based on actual evidence we are willing to answer them to assist in your investigation. We, also, want my client's wife's killer brought to justice. So, if you have nothing further to ask, I'd say we are finished here." He'd made the intuitive conclusion that Jimmy was going to be more than Phil could handle. Suave, his client was not. Since during the interview he hadn't disclosed that Artiste was paying the mortgage where Belinda was found, he didn't have much and for now Phil might not be further implicated, at least for today. He knew, however, that the Detectives would have this information by the end of the weekend.

"Well then, I guess we're finished here," said Jimmy as he motioned for Kelly to rise from the couch.

"Good enough. Let me show you out," offered Clarence.

As Kelly walked to the door, she glanced at Phil as he stared blankly out the window at Times Square. *He looks like a drowning man,* she thought. As they rode down the elevator, Jimmy asked, "What do you think?"

"Certainly acted like he had something to hide," replied Kelly.

"Yeah, might as well go back to the office and see if the backgrounds on our suspects are back."

Neither one said another thing but both were feeling McBride's pressure to conduct a 6:00 o'clock news conference.

Chapter 17

Jonathan Vell walked into the entrance of One Beacon Street, a tall skyscraper that accomodated many of Boston's largest and most successful law firms. As Vell strode through the gray and white, marble lobby it was all but deserted on this late Saturday afternoon. His stride was no longer as confident as it had been prior to Luke's phone call.

He rode the elevator to the fifteenth floor, exited to the right and followed the maroon colored carpet to the law office of Attorney Barry McGregor. The office, from where he stood, appeared deserted, but the door was open and inside was a small reception area with a floor lamp, a coffee table and a white, micro-suede covered love seat. Looking further he saw an empty receptionist's station and beyond the receptionist station was a hallway leading off to the right. He walked around the station and turned right down the hallway along a green carpet toward the office that was situated at the end of the hallway that was painted with ivory-white and were lined with antique picture frames encasing photographs of judges and courtroom scenes. The office door was partially opened and he paused before knocking

"Come on in, Johnny," Barry McGregor welcomed, even before he could push open the door and get a visual. Upon entering he encountered McGregor situated behind an imposing, antique mahogany desk whose desk drawers faced both in and out with brass handles on both sides. The legs tapered down to brass lion's paws. The floor of the office was covered with a vivid, blue and red Oriental rug. Two antique chairs that matched the desk in design were turned to face the desk. Beyond the desk was a large window overlooking the impressive view of Boston Harbor. The far wall also had a floor to ceiling window which overlooked the Common and further out toward Quincy. On a clear day like today, the view almost reached Cape Cod. Barry, seated behind his desk, was dressed casually in beige slacks and a white button down shirt, no tie. His hair was covered in gray and his face bore a resemblance to that of Harrison Ford.

"Thanks for seeing me on a Saturday and on such short notice," Vell said.

"No problem. Any friend of Will McCarthy Sr. is a friend of mine." Vell's world was getting smaller and he had a feeling that the shrinking was going to continue. "What's so urgent?" Barry asked.

"Well, I don't know if it made the news here in Boston, but apparently Phil Caruso's wife was found murdered in New York City yesterday."

"Okay, whoever the fuck Phil Caruso or his wife is," Barry replied.

"Phil Caruso is the President of Artiste Records."

"One of your clients, I take it, Johnny?"

"Yes, and his wife was an, ah, I'm not sure how to put this?"

"Why don't I say it for you," interjected Barry. "You were screwing his wife and you were screwing her in relative proximity to the time and place her body was discovered."

"Basically."

"You fucking guys in the music biz get yourselves into more jackpots. All right, take me through what the fuck happened." Barry's directness made Vell somewhat uncomfortable, although he figured this was a quality he'd want in his attorney. At three-hundred dollars an hour he needed McGregor to get to the point.

As Vell began relaying the events of his most recent trip to New York City, the color slowly began to drain from his face. "I was in New York on business Wednesday morning. I've known Belinda for a while."

"Intimately?" Barry interjected.

"To know Belinda is to know her intimately, if you know what I mean. Anyway..." Vell continued, "Belinda runs a small independent imprint distributed through Artiste. We had tentative plans for lunch."

"You mean, Mr. Caruso is funding a label run by his wife? That's not too fucking bright," said McGregor. "What's the name of the label?"

"Rocket Science Records, RSR," answered Vell.

"All right, I'm sorry. Get on with your story."

"We had lunch at a place in the village where I know the chef. Then, after lunch, I had a couple of hours to kill so she suggested we go to her place to discuss the new releases I'd be working on, so to speak."

Both Vell and McGregor laughed. "Did you have sex with her?" asked Barry with a look of interest.

"Actually, I didn't," answered Vell.

"Let me back up," said Barry, "When you say you went to her place, are you saying the home where she lived with her husband?"

"No," he answered. "She has or I guess had, a small place on the Upper East Side where she runs RSR. But it's more of a bungalow than an office type of place."

"And that's where the body was found?" inquired Barry.

"I guess," answered Vell.

"I'm not sure which is worse," McGregor said, almost to himself.

"So, were you planning to have sex with her?" he continued his questioning.

"I was hoping to," answered Vell, partially laughing.

"So, what happened? Why didn't you?"

"Once we got there she said she wasn't feeling well and then one of her artist's stopped by," said Vell.

"And who was this artist?"

"A guy named Billy Brill."

"And he is?"

"The lead singer of a band called The Dead Boys."

"So then what happened?"

"The kid and I spoke about his record and then I left."

"Was this Brill still there when you left?"

"Yes."

"Was Mrs. Caruso still alive when you left?" Barry asked with a smile.

"Yes, absolutely!"

"Then what are you worried about? Aside from the fact that when this comes out Artiste isn't going to pay you what it owes you?" said Barry.

"I'm worried about the kid putting me at the scene and/or my fingerprints being found at the scene. I mean, what if the kid did it and says I did it?" Vell was starting to sweat. "Not to mention the whole industry finding out that I was having an affair with Belinda."

Barry paused, leaned over his desk and formed a triangle with his fingertips. "First of all, you shouldn't have been fucking her if you were worried about people finding out. And that's going to happen, so prepare yourself. Secondly, you seem to have an awfully guilty conscience for something you didn't do. If in fact the police place you at the scene through a witness or forensic evidence or both, they are going to want to question you. The question now is whether you do it voluntarily or wait and see if they contact you. I'm sure the tabloids down in New York are going to be all over this. My inclination is to wait and see what the police do. Why bring yourself into it sooner than necessary, if at all? Call me if and when you hear from NYPD. My guess is that it will be soon."

"Okay," Vell said, as he rose from his chair.

"Out of curiosity, did Bill McCarthy Sr.'s son know this Belinda?" asked Barry.

"Know her?" Vell countered, "He was just signed to her label."

"One last thing," inquired Barry. "You and Billy, Jr. ever patch things up?"

"No," he answered without explanation.

Vell and Billy had known each other through the music business and never really liked each other. It had something to do with Billy's old band, Heroine. There were rumors that Vell had refused to work on Heroine's first single which was ultimately a bomb. The fact that both of them had been sleeping with Belinda had become the latest skirmish in an ongoing war.

Chapter 18

Billy was oblivious to the fact that he was a central figure in the eye of a brewing storm. In fact, from the moment the investigation into Belinda's death began, he was just about oblivious to everything. The tour bus was parked on Lansdowne Street in front of a small club called Axis and just in front of the bus was a mid-size Ryder Truck that carried the band's gear along with the road crew. After the band unloaded their personal gear from the luggage compartment they all filed into the club.

Axis is a small music club that is found situated among many other nightclubs along Lansdowne Street, which runs parallel to the Fenway's Green Monster. As you pass through the door into the club you come upon a ticket booth to your right and a coat check to your left. The first thing your senses perceive is that everything in the nightclub; the floor, the ceiling and the walls, are all black. Once Billy and the band passed through the narrow hallway they entered a room that was no bigger than forty by eighty feet wide. At one end of this room was a stage and at the opposite end was the sound and light board. On each side of the club was a bar and there was a small set of stairs that led down to the floor of the club. "Techie," the band's only sound and light guy, was behind the sound and light board doing his best to curse with a small flashlight clenched between his teeth. Each member of the band greeted him in their own way as they passed by him as they made their way to the stage.

"Listen you fuckers, you're late as usual. We've only five hours till they open the club." Looking at them all with skepticism he couldn't resist adding, "From the looks of you fuck-ups, someone better start sharing or you won't hear a fucking note during rehearsal!"

"Good to see you too, Techie," cajoled Billy. "Hey, somebody hook up Techie here, and fast."

"Back of the bus," one of the band members yelled. "Help yourself."

"Yeah, but don't be a glutton," said another voice in the dark. It was probably the Russian. Billy may have been the bandleader, but the Russian was definitely the conductor.

The band stood facing the stage trying to determine how to set up for the rest of the tour. Tour rehearsal was making small decisions that had big ramifications which were multiplied by each stop on the tour. Techie captured the sounds which gave him a general feel for the players and how they liked to play; how loud, etc. Individual sound checks would have to be repeated at every venue on the tour. Once he was satisfied with the sounds being produced the band would then be able to formulate and rehearse the set list for their Sunday night show at the Paradise.

Once everybody became focused on the task at hand, Billy took charge. "Let's start with what we know works. We'll put the drummer in the back center. I'll be front and center which leaves three spots to fill."

"I'll take stage right, your left, Billy," said the Russian.

"All right, we'll put keys and bass to left then," finished Billy.

With that settled they began setting up their personal gear. The Russian was touring with a 1963 sunburst, a red and yellow Les Paul guitar that had a clean sound and was used by the majority of lead guitar players such as Joe Perry, of Aerosmith and Ace Frehley, of Kiss.

Billy played the rhythm guitar and for acoustic he used a hand made, high-end acoustic guitar called a Takimini. For electric, he played a 1973 Blond Fender Telecaster; the type of guitar preferred by rock and roll poster boy, the man, the myth, and the legend of rock, Keith Richards. Bruce Springsteen also preferred the Telecaster. It provided that electric, country twang. On bass, Bobby played a Fender Music Man that was standard issue for most rock bands and Johnny Chez banged away on a set of custom Pearl drums with Zildjian cymbals. This band was a professional rock band, both on and off the playing field. Once they were done setting up Techie spent an additional hour going through the individual sound checks.

Once all the preliminary set up matters had been addressed Billy once again took over and announced, "Okay, let's run through the set. I wanna open with Betrayed and I want it to fucking rock. Count it down, Johnny."

Johnny clicked his sticks three times at equal intervals,—*click, click, click*. On the fourth click, a cacophony of sound erupted into the empty room. Dickie, who was standing behind the soundboard, felt somewhat relieved when the band kicked in. They sounded pretty good, even though they were three-quarters into the proverbial wrapper. He managed to convince himself that that at tomorrow night's show they'd have their game face on which meant they wouldn't be this fucked up.

Chapter 19

Immediately upon returning to the station house, Kelly picked up her phone. "Beth McBride, please," Jimmy heard her say. "Detective Kelly Agis, I'll hold." After a few minutes pause, he heard her continue. "Beth, Kelly, hi. It's going fine. Listen, there is no way you can hold a press conference today. It's just too premature. Yes, I understand the political pressure you're under and the feeding frenzy Markowitz is creating. I know it's good PR for the department..." she turned toward Jimmy and rolled her eyes, as she said, "But if we give out any information that turns out later to be incorrect you'll more than regret it. We just have too many loose ends right now. No, it's far from clear at this point that Sunday is our primary suspect. We know from his prints and a couple of eyewitnesses that he was in the apartment, but we haven't been able to prove if he was there on that particular night. And we don't even know where he is right now. All right, I agree, that's the right thing to do. Yes, we will try and put something together by 6:00 o'clock tomorrow." With that, she hung up the phone.

"Thanks," Jimmy said, truly gracious. "Why is it everybody likes this Billy Sunday?"

"I don't know," replied Kelly, "But let's try and find out."

There were three dossiers on Jimmy's desk. "Let's start with the not so charming Phil Caruso," said Jimmy, picking up the folders.

"Good a place as any," agreed Kelly.

"Philip Antonio Caruso, was born on June 6, 1946. A career record man, promoted up through the ranks and married the lovely and recently departed, Belinda Carlisle on the Fourth of July, two years ago. It's clear her marriage vows didn't alter or curb her enthusiasm for the wilder side of life. It looks like Artiste Records stock has been dropping like a rock since Phil took over." This was partly due to market conditions and illegal Internet downloading, but mostly due to the death knell of every record company a—lack—of—hits. "No way to tell, but obviously poor performance negatively effected Mr. Caruso's compensation." Rumor around town was that he was on notice from the Board of Directors about the company's performance. "Belinda signed a pre-nuptial agreement which expired this past December. Another tidbit of info, life insurance on Belinda was initially a cool $2,000,000. That, Kelly, is the oldest motive in the world…m-o-n-e-y. Divorce for Mr. Caruso would have been very expensive. Murder, on the other hand, would be highly profitable."

"Actually, two of the oldest motives around," reflected Kelly, "Money and adultery."

"Very good, Detective, the old kill two birds with one stone, so to speak."

"Or one strangle, depending on how you look at it," said Kelly, joining in the sarcasm.

"Opportunity?" asked Jimmy.

"Doesn't look like it," she replied. "We'd have to establish his whereabouts on the day and the night of the murder."

"I spoke with Clarence yesterday when I was setting up the interview. Off the record, he assures me that Caruso has an airtight alibi. I honestly don't think he even knew the apartment existed, let alone its location." He began flipping through the pages of Caruso's folder. "Let's see, yup, just as I thought," continued Jimmy. "RSR was paid by Artiste and on their payroll was Belinda's apartment. That explains why Clarence was so defensive this morning."

"Either that or his client's involved and/or guilty," suggested Kelly.

"Always the possibility," replied Jimmy.

Kelly wrote the word *no* next to Opportunity under Phil's name. "Means?" she inquired.

"Definitely," said Jimmy. "He had the money and could easily have hired someone."

"Okay, the alibi we still have to verify. Next possible?" she asked, moving right along.

"Everybody's favorite so far, Mr. Billy Sunday," said Jimmy, as if he were introducing a Vegas act.

"According to his rap sheet," Jimmy continued.

Kelly interrupted. "Let me guess…possession?"

"How did you know?"

"Billy Sunday, A.K.A. William McCarthy, he was born twenty miles north of Boston in 1968. Graduated Phillips Academy and then Holy Cross in 1986. He was arrested in 1992 on an O.U.I, with a possession charge of cocaine, along with a litany of other motor vehicle violations.

"I know he was in a band but I can't remember the name, they weren't very big, but I remember he was driving a Porsche 911 and there were rumors that he had a passenger but that was never disclosed. Some political connection, maybe a congressman's daughter, I think. The only reason it rings a bell with me. Something the tabloid's grabbed onto but nothing very newsworthy at that time anyway.

"Apparently someone sent lawyers, guns and money. The OUI was continued without a finding and everything else got dismissed," Jimmy paraphrased from the material he was reading. "Then nothing until two years ago, possession of heroin, charges later dropped."

"Long way from possession to murder," stated Kelly, matter of factly.

"A pharmacy of drugs found at the scene, though," Jimmy said, by way of explanation. "An array of opiates, oxys and heroin were found. Maybe they got a little too high and something went bad? Do we know where Mr. Sunday is today?"

"He's promoting a tour with his band and they call themselves Drown. They've been around a couple of years but they just signed a record deal." said Kelly.

"Too bad the band wasn't called The Strangled or The Stranglers," mused Jimmy, taking the joke too far.

"Oh, check this out…" remembered Kelly, now ignoring Jimmy. She continued before he could answer. "According to his Website, Drown will be playing in New York next Tuesday at the Acme Lounge in the Village. How much you wanna bet we can get a warrant? We know we can at least nab him on a drug charge."

"I don't think it will go over big in the music industry here in New York if we start shaking down visiting musicians for doing drugs," replied Jimmy.

"Then again, who knows, maybe we'll have enough evidence for a murder warrant by Tuesday," said Kelly, optimistically.

"Maybe, but something tells me it's not going to be Mr. Sunday we end up charging," said Jimmy.

"He is kind of cute, in a way. Nice eyes," said Kelly, while staring at his photo.

"Listen, I've been telling you that you need a boyfriend," said Jimmy, "but not a fucking rock star, for Christ sakes. A rock star would be bad enough but a rock star suspected of homicide? That'll really solve all of your problems. All right, enough fucking around, don't forget we have the bitschstrict attorney's press conference to set up," said Jimmy.

"I hate it when you call her that," said Kelly. "C'mon, let's finish with Sunday: motive, question mark; opportunity, yes, he clearly had access; alibi, question mark." She rattled this information off like she was filling out a questionnaire in a Cosmopolitan magazine. Despite her short career she had accumulated quite a bit of experience.

"And our next great American is John Quartermain, A.K.A. Billy Brill, lead singer of The Dead Boys," Jimmy read the information out of the third and final folder. "What is it with musicians and aliases?"

"You have to sound cool, capture your audience's imagination, you know? If you were a singer, would you rather be called Jimmy Gerard or Mick Jagger?"

Jimmy rolled his eyes. "Date of birth 1978. He's just a baby. Looks like he has some juvenile violations but that's all been sealed. He's acquired some minor incidents since then; possession of marijuana, resisting arrest, a couple A& B's on photographers. I'd say a typical rap sheet for a rock star."

"Yeah, but the A & B's show a tendency for violence," Kelly pointed out.

"If I was famous, I'd take a whack at those fucking paparazzi, too," said Jimmy.

"Yeah, you're probably right."

"Let's see," continued Jimmy, "His present address is down in Greenwich Village somewhere."

"Looks like he's in the same category as Mr. Sunday, as far as this investigation is concerned," replied Kelly. "Motive is a question mark; opportunity, yes, means, yes, alibi? I guess we'll find out when we go see him."

"What about our mystery record executive?"

"No ID yet." answered Kelly.

"What about the other two sets of prints?"

"Nothings come back yet. So what's next?"

"We still need to track Belinda's actions on the day of her unlikely demise."

"And where do you propose we start?"

"Well, let's see, since she's dead, asking her is pretty much ruled out."

"Wise ass," said Kelly.

"Mr. Sunday is presently in the wind. Phil Caruso has lawyered up so that leaves us Billy Brill of The Dead Boys fame." Jimmy looked at his watch. "Four o'clock. We can probably catch him just waking up. If not, there's a bar down in the village that I always liked."

"You really should stop talking to Markowitz, especially on weekends," said Kelly.

Jimmy grabbed his blazer and Kelly followed him out the door and into the elevator.

Jimmy was partial to Greenwich Village because his fondest memories happened when he hung out there in the 60's and early 70's; getting laid, smoking grass, and listening as Dylan emerged onto the scene. He was there and was a part of it and consequently it was now a part of him. He didn't follow the modern day rock groups but that didn't matter. Dylan was not only the greatest musical artist of the Twentieth Century but he was also the most influential artist—period.

As they walked down Bleecker Street, Jimmy absorbed every aspect of the scene that unfolded before him. The Saturday afternoon traffic crawled along the cracked asphalt as the sun that filtered through the clouds lit up the village like it was a Broadway marquee. He couldn't stop smiling while listening to the sound of the taxi's horns and the overall din of the city's pedestrian traffic in its hippest borough. He watched as the varied characters in front of him cavorted in and out of the leather shops, dive bars, gay bars, vintage shops and bodegas. Kelly couldn't help but notice the added bounce in his step as they made their way to 112 Bleecker.

112 Bleecker turned out to be a three-story walk-up that had seen better days. They rang the buzzer for Apartment 3, the top floor and there was no answer. Jimmy looked at the old double door with its chipped emerald green paint and its cracked smoked glass windows and just as he was about to put his shoulder to the door, a young, nasally voice came through the intercom. "Yeah?"

"NYPD."

After a moment of hesitation, another anonymous voice came through the intercom system. "Yo, what up?"

"NYPD. We just want to ask you a few questions," answered Jimmy. "About what?"

"We'd rather discuss this in person," said Jimmy. Through the intercom they could hear muffled voices and bottles clanking.

Jimmy, deciding he'd save everyone some time, "Listen, we're here to ask a few questions about Billy Brill. We don't really care who or what is up there, we just need to speak with Mr. Brill in regards to an ongoing investigation."

Another pause, then, "Am I in some kind of trouble?"

"Only if you don't open the door in the next ten fucking seconds," said Jimmy, starting to lose his patience. Kelly had a hard time holding back her laughter.

After another slight pause, the door buzzed and the intercom spit out, "Top Floor."

"No shit. We're detectives remember?" Jimmy said, shaking his head. By now Kelly was laughing so hard she was bent over. "C'mon, it's not that fucking funny."

The hallway and rickety stairs were the same washed out emerald green as the door and blue flecks of paint showed that the wall's original blue color was interspersed amongst the green. As they trudged slowly up the stairs they could hear a door on the third floor landing being unlocked and opened. Upon arriving at the landing, Jimmy pushed open the door and allowed Kelly to pass through first, always the gentleman.

Immediately upon entering the apartment to the right of the door was a second hand, well-worn gray couch. In front of the couch was a white Formica topped coffee table that was littered with empty wine bottles, beer bottles and overflowing ashtrays. Jimmy's eyes immediately focused on a glass stem resting in one of the ashtrays. The stem could be used for only one thing-smoking crack. On the far right wall were two windows that overlooked Bleecker Street. The walls were yellowed with age, water damage and smoke. To the left of the doorway was a small kitchen area with a refrigerator, stove, and sink. In the middle of the far wall across from the door was another door that was closed and presumably led to a bedroom. In the right hand corner of the living room, across the scratched and washed out wood floor, stood Billy Brill. He looked like he'd just woken up with his red hair plastered on top of his head. He wore a wrinkled, black Eric Lindell T-shirt which appeared slept in along with baggy plaid pajama bottoms. Looking directly into Brill's eyes Jimmy became aware of the fact that he'd made time for a morning fix. His eyelids were at half-mast and his pupils were constricted.

Jimmy could tell just by looking at him that he was a punk. Furthermore, Jimmy's hangover had descended from the painful headache stage to the weary and fatigued physical stage. He was in no mood to put up with any shit from this kid and demanded, "You Billy Brill?"

"Who wants to know?"

They flashed their badges simultaneously.

"What the fuck do you want then, coppers?" snarled Billy. Before he could move, Jimmy crouched down and quickly pulled a needle from under Billy's chair. Holding up the needle, he responded with no amount of affection, "What I really want to do right now is bust a punk like you for dope and crack. But since I gave you my word, I won't, for the moment anyway. But my word is contingent upon your cooperation, understand? Belinda Caruso was found dead yesterday in an apartment you were seen leaving, capiche?" Jimmy twirled the syringe in his fingertips.

Brill's persona did a one-eighty. Gone was the snarling punk and in his place sat a humble servant.

"Listen, Belinda is my aunt. She got me signed to Artiste. Why would I possibly kill her? If that's what you're implying." He answered with no real emotion.

"Why don't you take us through your last visit with your aunt," ordered Jimmy.

"My band, The Dead Boys, we were signed to Artiste just before the holidays. We've been in New York a few months, waiting for the record to be released and rehearsing for a tour. Wednesday afternoon before rehearsal I went to see my aunt because the single had been released and I wanted to discuss radio play. I was hoping she would talk to her husband and make us a priority. I was actually glad I stopped by, as it turned out."

"Why is that, whiz kid?" asked Jimmy.

"Because she was there with a friend of hers who is an independent record promoter," said Brill. Jimmy and Kelly looked at each other, *Bingo* they both thought. "What's his name?" asked Kelly.

"Johnny Vell. He's the biggest alternative record promoter in the country."

"Who does he work for?" inquired Kelly.

"Himself, I think, out of Boston," answered Brill.

"All right, what happened on Wednesday when you met Vell in your aunt's apartment?" Kelly asked, re-starting the interview.

"Nothing, I talked to Vell about getting more airplay and then I left."

"Was Vell still there when you left?"

"Yes. Yeah, he was still there."

"How did Vell and your aunt seem to be getting along? What were they talking about?"

"You know, the music business…general shit. That the "Drown" record was coming out on Rocket Science Records next week. Vell didn't seem real thrilled about that, exactly."

Jimmy and Kelly tried not to show any emotion.

"Anything else you think we should know?" Kelly asked, wrapping things up.

"Yeah, maybe," said Brill, clearly hesitating. "It seemed like my aunt and Vell, you know, wanted me to leave. Seemed like they were more than just business associates."

Chapter 20

Back in the unmarked cruiser and sitting in the passenger seat, Jimmy came upon an idea and turning to Kelly said, "Let's go back to the station house for a minute."

"Where else were we going to go?" she asked. As she made her way through traffic, she commented, "The music industry is one incestuous, fucked up business."

"And we haven't even scratched the surface yet," said Jimmy. "Let's talk about what we have so far."

Kelly started, "We have a not so upset, not so jealous, soon to be not so broke husband. Apparently, we have a nephew who became famous the old fashioned way, nepotism. We've identified our mystery record executive, but don't know much about him and have little chance of reaching him considering it's a weekend."

"Let me worry about that," Jimmy interrupted.

"Finally, we have our favorite suspect, Billy Sunday, who is still in the wind, so to speak. Oh, and we still have two unidentified prints. I have to say that even though Phil's a total asshole, I don't think he's our guy," said Kelly.

"Why?" asked Jimmy.

"Well, we don't have any forensic evidence linking him to the scene. It's unlikely the three people we can place at the murder scene would have conspired with Phil."

Again, Jimmy asked, "Why?" "Looks like Billy Sunday's band was on

RSR which was owned by Artiste. Maybe Phil tells Billy do me a favor off my wife make it look like an OD and I'll see to it you finally get the fame and fortune you so richly deserve."

"Artists are notorious for hating their record executives, particularly a swell guy like Phil. Likewise, independent record promoters hate label execs and vice versa. It's purely a marriage of convenience and not attraction when it comes to Indies and execs."

"And you, Ms. Kelly, know all of this, how?"

"An ex-boyfriend of mine was in a band. Not a very good band, but he knew the business," she answered.

"I tend to agree with you, although you know what happens when you make assumptions…" said Jimmy.

"I know, I know," exclaimed Kelly. They spent the rest of the drive back to the station house in silence, each going over the case in their respective minds. After ten minutes, she eased the car back into the station house motor pool.

"All right, our priorities are to get in touch with Vell and Sunday," said Jimmy, as they rode the elevator up to the squad room. "I'll track down Vell," he said, "We know Sunday will be in New York on Tuesday, but why don't you go online and figure out where he might be now."

"Fine," said Kelly. She exited the elevator on the third floor as Jimmy continued on to four. Upon entering the squad room, she noticed that there were new medical reports on one of the metal desks. She grabbed the reports, sat down at her desk and began to look through them. The documents provided the evidence that Belinda had both intercourse and anal sex shortly prior to her death. *No big surprise there*, she thought to herself. Traces of semen were found in both Belinda's stomach and colon but not in her vagina. The samples were being sent out for DNA testing along with other physical traces. In addition, the report noted that the sex was considered to have been consensual as there were no signs of bruising or tears that would imply forced entry, indicating rape.

Waiting for Jimmy to join her on the third floor, she put the report back on her desk, sat down in her chair and placed her head in her hands. She was starting to acquire a bad feeling about this investigation that went along with the wide-ranging bad feelings she'd been having about the rest of her life. She knew now wasn't the time to ponder these feelings but she couldn't stop her mind from racing to that place which no part of her physical or spiritual being wanted to go.

She was in her early thirties and her life consisted of nothing but her job. Lately, as the work became less and less fulfilling, she wondered what her true purpose was. Now, this so-called high profile murder investigation comes along. Solving murders and putting away dangerous people was why she entered the field and believed it would be gratifying, but in a case like this other people's motivation and not justice seemed the true motivation behind convicting somebody, anybody. This wasn't about finding the guilty party or convicting the right person, it was about getting a conviction, any conviction, if it would stick in time for the fall primary elections. She'd been successful in her career to date but had not advanced toward any of her personal goals. Her success placed her in the position of pursuing someone else's agenda and oftentimes those agendas conflicted with the oath she took to preserve justice. It became a balancing act-did she follow what she believed or bend the rules to further both her and someone else's career? She was smart enough to realize that that person would only take her along until it was her who became the most expedient to blame.

Her professional life on the outside seemed perfect as the trajectory of her career was moving along without any obstacles impeding her progress, regardless of her age and sex, which were known past impediments. Her personal life, however, left her no sense of satisfaction. Kelly hadn't had a date with a man in over a year and the dates she had been on before this dry spell had been pointless. She'd had a few brief interludes in the past with other women but realized that wasn't what she was looking for. The sex had been great, as woman instinctively knew what another woman wanted. This switch to the other side of the street, so to speak, had only served to further confuse her and ultimately made her feel guilty. She loved men, enjoyed the way they could make her feel and those affairs with other women had at least made her realize what it was that she truly wanted. She was beginning to think it would be impossible to find the right guy. She wasn't looking for her soul mate because she figured that was an urban myth. She just wanted someone who was kind, compassionate and who could perform in bed half as good as he thought he could. This combination of her ebbing interest and conflicts in her job and her non-existent personal life had become a distraction that was only getting worse. To top it off, she couldn't help thinking that these were supposed to be her best years-a career, a family, and a future—not simply marking time at the opportunistic age of 32. All she really wanted was the hope that she had a future but she wasn't feeling a lot of hope at this point, either. Luckily, the closing of the door behind Jimmy as he entered the squad room brought her mind back to the issues at hand.

As it stood right now, each of the four suspects had a 25 % chance of being arrested and a slightly less chance of being convicted. Neither of them liked arresting someone based on these odds but they both knew that with District Attorney McBride's track record, she was willing to arrest anyone at anytime and then work towards a conviction later if it would increase her popularity in the polls.

While Kelly had been pondering the meaning of her life, Jimmy had been upstairs in the evidence room retrieving Belinda's purse. As he entered the squad room with the purse his cell phone began to ring and with his free hand he retrieved the phone. As he answered, he appreciated that his hangover was finally starting to somewhat abate.

"Hello?"

"Jimmy," Margie's voice reverberated so loud he had to move the phone away from his ear. *So much for the disappearing hangover*, he thought.

"Hear we have a sex crime? Also hear we've identified our record executive?" Margie stated matter of factly.

"Yeah, tell me what else you hear," he asked frankly.

"Belinda was tied up spread eagle and was raped. I also hear the record exec in question is Johnny Vell, a music guy and a guy only he himself could love," she prattled on.

"I'm not going to confirm or deny anything but I will tell you that you're dead wrong about the rape," assured Jimmy.

"But not the tied up part, right?" asked Margie.

"Cannot confirm or deny."

"Listen, Jimmy…" As she started to bargain, he walked into the squad room with Kelly staring at him, holding the purse in one hand and the cell phone in the other.

"Markowitz," he mouthed to Kelly as he continued walking toward her. She immediately rolled her eyes.

Margie continued, "The news of this murder is spreading across the city and you know I can't fall behind. I'm running a story tomorrow morning, naming the four suspects."

"Who are?" he asked without rancor.

"Phil Caruso, Billy Brill, Vell, and Billy Sunday," Margie rattled the names so quickly one would think she'd known them forever.

Jimmy couldn't believe it and was dumbfounded. Markowitz knew as much or more than they did.

"I don't need to tell you that Caruso and Vell have the money to sue if you're wrong about them. As far as the two kids you named are concerned, all you're going to do for them is help them sell their records."

"As long as I'm technically right in that they're being considered as suspects, so be it. Thanks Jimmy, you're a doll."

"Listen, Margie, while we're being flattering, there's no need to bother Detective Agis. Deal with me on this thing."

"But I like to get a woman's perspective, a woman's point of view, particularly in connection with a crime like this one." She said teasingly.

"I'm telling you, Margie. I ain't fucking asking!"

"All right, All right, Jimmy. You're still a doll in my book."

Kelly thanked him as he closed his cell phone.

Addressing Kelly, he said, "We better get moving. She's running a story tomorrow morning, naming the suspects. Once the press gets this thing, everyone's going to lawyer up and then we'll be spending all our time trying to avoid the press and dodging lawyers. The media's going to have a real field day with this one. I swear to god, this is my last case. I'm way too old for this shit." He walked over to the board marked Belinda Caruso and with a black marker he formed a new column on the right hand side of the board marked, *Leaks*. He turned back toward Kelly. "Right now, she has a very good source and obviously someone with intimate knowledge. I mean, she has as much information as we do, for

Christ sakes. We need to shut it down. We need to speak with both Vell and Sunday, pronto."

"I'll hit the Internet and Google Sunday," Kelly replied.

Jimmy sat down, put Belinda Caruso's purse in his lap and reached inside. He pulled out her cell phone, turned it on and after pushing a few buttons he motioned to Kelly, "Viola, Johnny Vell...office, home and cell."

"Anything on Sunday?" she inquired.

After hitting a few more buttons, "Nada."

"McCarthy?"

"No, I checked that, too. I also checked Drown. Nothing."

"All right, lets try Vell's cell," she responded hopefully.

Chapter 21

As Billy and the band were finishing their rehearsal set he noticed the local promotion guy from Artiste, Luke, talking to Dickie. From his perspective, still standing on the stage, he noted the conversation appeared serious.

Fuck, was his first thought. He knew going to see Belinda had been a mistake, but it was unavoidable, wasn't it? *I mean, she ran the label. Her husband had found out about what happened about him and Belinda. But he had to go see her what choice did he have really?* He knew the music industry was full of bands that had been dropped from their record companies for political or other non-music related reasons. He just couldn't take that chance given this was his last chance.

The band had finished their set and the drummer Johnny Chez leaned over to Billy and asked, "What Dead song, man?" Somewhere, in every Drown set, Billy played a Grateful Dead song as a tribute to both the deceased Jerry Garcia and to the years he'd spent following the band. Looking briefly back on his life he believed those Dead shows held the happiest and most intense times of his life; times when he knew he was right where he belonged.

If Jerry singing, "I'm standing on the moon with a beautiful view of heaven, but I'd rather be with you," didn't bring a tear to your eye, you were fucking already dead and just didn't know it yet. Of course, his overall opinion was that most people were living their life according to someone else's expectations and were thereby already dead. Deadheads may not have had much of a life in material assets, but at least it was their own. "Live for the moments, not for the days," was the Deadhead's rallying cry. The only problem with that philosophy was there were a lot of days in between the moments-particularly of late, for Billy at least.

"There Comes a Time," was Billy's answer to Johnny. This was one of the bands favorite tunes. He picked up his acoustic guitar and began softly strumming. He sang with his eyes closed and a pained expression on his face, "There comes a time when a blind man takes your hand and says, don't you see."

Techie, Dickie and Luke stopped what they were doing and turned their attention to the stage. The band was delivering a powerful rendition of a powerful song. When Billy finished singing he opened his eyes he noted Luke was gone and Dickie was motioning for Billy to join him. Dickie looked sullen as Billy climbed down from the stage while the rest of the band milled about onstage talking, smoking and drinking.

"Let's go out to the bus," said Dickie, motioning for Billy to follow him. Billy knew the feeling that was quickly coming over him the feeling you get when you are about to get that soft spoken lecture from someone you respected but whom you'd recently disappointed. He was going to get the disappointment speech, not the five-minute ballistic rant and rave emotional undressing. Maybe Artiste had heard about the band's drug use and in particularly Billy's return to using? Billy wasn't a big enough talent to invest $1,000,000 of promotion dollars with persistent drug use going on. Billy's drug use had always ultimately cost him as much as everyone said it would; everything

As they took seats across from each other in the bus' kitchenette Billy comprehended the fact that he had never seen Dickie look so grave and serious. "You saw me talking to Luke. I've got bad news. Belinda Caruso is dead and it appears that you are a suspect."

Billy sat stunned feeling the narcotic buzz and the adrenaline of rehearsal swiftly ebb away. "This is some type of joke, right? You guys are pretty fucking sick," was all he could say.

"It's no joke, Billy. It's none of my fucking business but I know you and Belinda go way back. Far enough back for there to have been good times and bad times. I also know you saw her in New York."

"Yeah, we've always been pretty close," he answered as he began slipping into a total daze. "As far as me seeing her in New York, I mean, she runs the label, Dickie. You know that."

"Billy, I saw you arguing with her."

"What, Dickie? You think I'm capable of murdering her?" Billy replied with anger and hurt.

"No, I don't think that. But I know you're using pretty heavy and I also know you've been putting a lot of pressure on yourself to make it this time. Maybe things with Belinda somehow got out of control?"

Shit, Billy thought. From the picture Dickie formulated he made it sound like he was there. Then again, when it came to Belinda, everyone knew things always got out of control. "Look, Dickie, I may be a junkie and I may be tilting at windmills with this band, but I'm no fucking murderer."

"No, Billy," Dickie said softly, "You're no murderer."

Chapter 22

"Vell here."

"Hello, Mr. Vell. Kelly Agis, NYPD." Kelly and Jimmy had figured that Vell would be more comfortable speaking to a woman so Jimmy was now surfing the Web for any info on Billy Sunday while Kelly pursued the conversation with Vell.

By now, she was used to the uncomfortable pause created on the other end of the line after introduced herself for the first time, particularly when she was addressing a guilty person.

"What can I do for you, Miss Agis?"

"My partner and I would like to speak with you regarding a murder investigation we are conducting."

"Am I a suspect?" Vell asked, point blank.

"Not at the moment," was her answer.

"Not at this time, indicates to me, that I may become a suspect at a later date, in which case, I think it best you call my attorney." And with that Vell rattled off the phone number. "Thank you and have a nice day." He promptly hung up.

"Conceited prick," said Kelly, slamming down the office phone.

"What's up?" asked Jimmy, who was still typing away on the Internet.

"Vell has lawyered up, all right, and up in Boston. No surprise there," she concluded.

"I'm on this Goggles.com and I can't find anything on Sunday or DROWN," said Jimmy.

Kelly couldn't suppress her laugh. "Move." She sat down at the keyboard and began typing away like a stenographer. In just a few seconds she was able to pull up what they were looking for; *billysundayanddrown.com*. After a couple more seconds the homepage appeared and the computer screen filled with a photo of the band in a typical rock star pose; Billy Sunday, lead singer, in jeans and a black T-shirt standing sideways and in front of the other band members. Kelly found the link marked *Live* and clicked on it and the page re-loaded with a list of cities and dates that was superimposed over the faded home page photo.

"Bingo," said Kelly, "Pack your bags, we're headed for Boston. Drown's homecoming is at the Paradise Rock Club this Sunday night and is sponsored by WXKL. We can kill two birds with one stone by interviewing both Vell and Sunday in Boston."

"Only two problems," replied Jimmy, "Vell's lawyered up and there's no guarantee Sunday will speak with us, either."

"I'll leave a message with Vell's lawyer. If he agrees to a meeting, we'll go," said Kelly. "As far as Sunday is concerned," Kelly said, flashing a seductive smile, "Leave that to me. I know what musicians like."

Kelly called DA McBride and updated her on the latest developments in their investigation. McBride willingly moved the press conference to Monday. With that, they wrapped up the investigation for Saturday.

No one involved in the investigation or those under investigation, in connection with the murder of Belinda Caruso, could have predicted what was going to happen on Sunday morning.

The Sunday headline of the New York Post read *Sex, Drugs, Rock-N-Roll and MURDER*. Beneath the caption was presented a crude photo of Belinda Caruso's upper body showing it tied to the headboard. Beneath that centered photo were the pictures of the four suspects; Phil Caruso, Billy Brill, Johnny Vell and Billy Sunday. The by-line was *Margie Markowitz*.

Beth McBride was bullshit. She rang up Kelly at 5:00 on Sunday morning ranting at her and accusing Gerard of being the source of this leak. Kelly listened and offered up defenses for him for over half an hour, relaying over and over that she'd personally heard the conversation Jimmy had with Markowitz and could vouch it was not him who leaked the story or the photos. She quickly pointed out that the photo printed wasn't one that the department had taken, which meant somebody other than NYPD was responsible for giving Markowitz the photo. McBride wasn't so much bullshit that the story had run because she wanted the press on this case, she was bullshit that the story's spin was that the Post's investigation was ahead of both the police department's and the DA's office. McBride instructed Kelly and Gerard to get up to Boston, "ASAP! Speak to Vell, speak to Sunday and figure out who was with Belinda last on Wednesday night and come back with a definitive suspect before the scheduled press conference on Monday."

The circus in New York was well underway and the big top was just going up in Boston when Kelly and Jimmy landed at Logan International at 10:00 am. Kelly was conservatively dressed in a light grey, wool skirt and jacket to match. Her black tights and tight fitting black blouse accented her desirable figure. Jimmy was dressed in tan slacks, a white shirt, beige blazer and a yellow and blue striped tie. He'd stayed at home the night before and watched the Yankee game. He was feeling a whole lot better then the previous morning and despite their age difference, they actually made a good looking couple.

Kelly complimented Jimmy on the way he looked, jokingly mentioning to him, "You know, if I was 20 years older, just maybe…"

This drew a smile from Jimmy who'd also started his day on the phone with DA McBride.

"Compliment in there somewhere?" was his only reply.

They disembarked from the shuttle and stopped in the terminal to retrieve their weapons. They stepped outside the terminal door into the cool air that represented springtime in New England. *There's something about spring mornings*, thought Jimmy, *you can almost smell the cleanliness in the air.* Being mid morning on Sunday the airport traffic was light as they stepped to the front of the taxi line and grabbed the first cab that was waiting.

"One Beacon Street," instructed Jimmy, and off they went. Without much traffic, the ride from the airport through the tunnel and into the city took less than ten minutes.

Downtown in Barry McGregor's office, Vell and McGregor were

awaiting the detectives' arrival. "We have the same story this morning as yesterday?" McGregor asked Vell.

"I swear to you, Barry, that's how it went down."

"You see today's New York Post?" McGregor asked.

"Not yet, but I figured something was up when The Boston Globe called me at 7:45 this morning and The Boston Herald called at 8:00."

Barry began pulling up the Post on-line as Vell gazed out the window. The sun was bright and crawling above Boston Harbor, illuminating the Back Bay and beyond. It seemed the sun shone all the way to New York City where Vell's mind was presently residing. He'd always wanted to be famous and within the industry he was, but his ego wanted more than that. He felt he needed to show everyone he was better than they were. He'd hoped to become famous by making others infamous but now it looked like that plan had backfired.

McGregor said, "Come here," as he motioned Vell over to the computer monitor and as he looking at the screen his face went blank.

"All right," Barry said, "We're in a real fucking jackpot here. I think the best approach is to be honest and straightforward. I don't think there here to arrest you at this point."

"You don't *think* there here to arrest me?' asked Vell in total disbelief.

"Why, you didn't bring your toothbrush?" deadpanned Barry, now having some fun with Vell.

Vell started to get up and leave.

"Sit back down," said Barry, "I'm just kidding. Detective Gerard is supposed to be a real straight shooter and he would have warned me if they wanted to arrest you. They would have wanted me to surrender you in New York, save themselves the plane fare. The broad, on the other hand, is supposed to be a real looker and tough, as well. So just remember what put you in that seat." Taking all of this in, Vell was subdued, to say the least.

They heard a faint knock at the door.

"All right, show time, as you entertainment types are so fond of saying," said Barry. At least one of them was relaxed. "Pause after each question is asked and give me an opportunity to answer first. If I don't say anything, you can answer. Okay? Lighten up, you'll be fine."

Barry briefly considered blasting the Detectives about The Post story but he'd had been around long enough to know that they were probably as bullshit as he was about the article. He also knew Beth McBride by reputation and in his opinion she was incompetent. This, to him, meant his client might just be high profile enough for McBride to charge him with murder, regardless of the evidence.

Barry walked down the hall and opened the door. "Good Morning Officers," He said in a cordial tone but businesslike.

"Detective Jimmy Gerard," Jimmy said offering his hand, "and this is Detective Kelly Agis."

"Good morning, detectives," Barry replied.

"Not exactly," said Jimmy.

"None of us should be working on a Sunday," said Barry.

"That's true, but not what I was referring to, exactly," implied Jimmy.

"Oh? What were you referring to?" asked Barry.

"That fucking New York Post story, excuse my language," replied Jimmy. He figured he'd be on the offensive as far as the issue of The Post story. He knew that no attorney would be happy to be caught by surprise with a story like the Post's.

"I'm not exactly thrilled about the story, either," said Barry. "But I figure it wasn't any of your doing. Markowitz has quite a source. At this point, she seems to know more about the murder than anyone. I'm sensing that can only hurt your investigation. McBride must be bullshit her picture wasn't included on the front page."

Kelly laughed. "Already heard about it at 5:00 this morning?"

"I guess Boston isn't that provincial, after all," added Jimmy, as they entered Barry's office.

Vell was shifting nervously in one of the antique chairs as he waited in the office. When they entered he rose to his feet as Barry offered introductions. "Johnny Vell—Detectives Gerard and Agis."

Handshakes were exchanged and in spite of McGregor's forewarning, Vell couldn't help but notice how attractive he found Kelly Agis. He tried not to be obvious as his eyes began wandering up and down her body. Barry become aware of Vells appraisal of Detective Agis and knew it was best to get things started and this interview over as quickly as possible, with as little information as possible.

"So, where are we at, Detectives? According to The New York Post story my client here is a suspect."

"Not at this time, as far as we're concerned," replied Jimmy. As Barry had done with Gerard, he, in turn, had also spoken to The Boston Police Department about McGregor. He found out that McGregor was old school and a straight shooter. BPD told him if you were straight with McGregor, he'd be straight with you and if you weren't straight with him, you'd pay. Barry was known for defending a couple of Boston cops on corruption charges that ended with mixed results. Still, BPD had a very favorable opinion of Barry McGregor.

"As we notified you on the phone," said Kelly, "We have a couple of witnesses who place your client at the apartment with the victim on the day of the murder."

"But not around the time of death," McGregor interjected.

Kelly failed to acknowledge McGregor's point.

"Right now, we're interested in tracking Mrs. Caruso's movements on the day of her death," stated Jimmy. Barry noticed they had yet to mention any forensic evidence concerning his client which meant one of two things: Either they didn't have any, or they had nothing to match with which to match said evidence. Either way, it was a good sign for his client.

"All right, off the record, no notes or recordings," informed Barry. "I'd ask for immunity, but I get the feeling neither of you want to deal with McBride right now. However, I can tell you immunity will be a condition, should you require my client to testify. Are we clear, Detectives?"

"Crystal," they answered in unison.

"Kindly give me a minute to confer with my client and we can begin," asked Barry.

Kelly and Jimmy rose, walked out the door and closed it behind them.

Once Barry was sure they were out of hearing range, he addressed Johnny. "Okay, here's the deal. You heard what I said. Now, while they're willing to go along, it doesn't mean they won't use what you tell them against you, understand? It appears they have no forensic evidence concerning you right now, so I think talking to them is a relatively safe strategy at this point. The way the press has a hold on this thing the sooner you're ruled out as a suspect the better, agreed?"

"Whatever you think is best, Barry."

"Okay, let's bring them back in then," said Barry.

Once they were back in and all seated Barry began, "All right, Detectives, are we in agreement on the ground rules?" He looked at Kelly, as he asked his question.

"Agreed," she concluded.

The four of them formed a square in the middle of Barry's office with Barry and Johnny sitting with their backs to the window overlooking the harbor as Jimmy and Kelly sat facing them.

Jimmy began his line of questions, "Mr. Vell, you were in New York City last Wednesday, is that correct?"

Johnny paused while looking at Barry, who nodded. "Yes," he managed.

"Can you take us through your day in the city, paying particular attention to the time you spent with Belinda Caruso?" asked Jimmy.

"I got on the 8:30 shuttle. I was heading to New York on business. At about 10:00 in the morning I arrived at Universal Music where I met with clients at, Polygram, Interscope and London Records till about noon. I had a scheduled appointment in the village for lunch with Belinda to discuss RSR's new releases."

Out of habit, Kelly grabbed her purse to reach for her notebook. Leaning over, she caught Barry's stare and remembered the agreement while discretely returning the notebook to her bag.

Vell continued. "Rocket Science Records, as you may know by now, is an independent label distributed by Artiste. We met at a sushi place in the village where one of the chef's is a friend of mine."

"Name?" Kelly asked formally.

Vell paused, looking directly at his attorney. Again, Barry nodded and he answered, "Red Tails on 11th and Bleecker." He didn't offer the chef's name, and they didn't ask.

Jimmy figured there was no way Barry was going to allow him to give it up voluntarily. *It didn't really matter*, he thought. With a little extra legwork, they would come up with the name.

"We were at the restaurant for a couple of hours," he began again, "Then, Belinda asked me to come to her, ah, office, to listen to a couple of new releases. So we grabbed a cab to the Upper East Side."

"To the so called office?" interrupted Kelly as she eyed him surreptitiously, waiting for his answer. This drew a glare from Barry, but she couldn't resist sticking it to Vell, just a little. He was gaining confidence and she wanted to knock him down a peg.

"Yes, to the office," he answered. "I was only there a couple of minutes when Billy Brill arrived. We talked briefly about his record and then I left. Kelly shot a quick glance at Jimmy. Barry picked it up not knowing what it meant, but he made a mental note to review its significance later.

Vell went on, "Belinda said she wasn't feeling well."

"So you left and Brill was still there?" Kelly interjected.

There it is, thought Barry. Brills alibi is that he left before Vell.

Barry spoke up, "That's been asked and answered."

Jimmy wanted to push the issue but Kelly had been a little too anxious in trying to set a trap for Vell and it looked like McGregor was onto Kelly's plan.

"I saw Belinda again at about 8:00 o'clock," Vell suddenly offered without even looking at Barry. Barry immediately turned toward him and gave him a look of utter dismay. It was a lawyer's worst nightmare when a client provided information the attorney was never even aware existed.

"I saw her at CBGB's. Drown was showcasing their new album and I talked with Belinda briefly backstage when she saw Billy McCarthy, I mean Sunday, or whatever he calls himself. That, was the last time I saw Belinda. She and Billy got into a pretty heated discussion so I left them alone."

"Did you stay long enough to witness the discussion?" asked Jimmy.

"I saw part of it but I couldn't hear it," he said. "She seemed pretty upset when she saw him and that was the last I saw of her. I stayed and watched the band do a couple of songs and then left."

"That's it?" asked Kelly without any belief in what he was saying.

"That's pretty much it," was Vell's answer.

"Okay, Mr. Vell, Mr. McGregor, you've been very helpful," said Jimmy, as Kelly stood up to leave. "Oh, one more thing, if you don't mind?" Jimmy directed his question to Barry.

"That depends on what it is?"

"Mr. Vell, how do you and Mr. Sunday get along?"

"Actually, we're done here," Barry ended the questioning before Vell could answer. It was clear to everyone in the room that McGregor was pissed.

As they entered the elevator, Kelly realized it was one of the few times she'd seen Jimmy speechless.

"You mean to tell me Vell and Sunday…"

Jimmy answered, "Yes," before she could finish asking a complete question.

"Oh, what motherfucking tangled webs we weave, right?" asked Jimmy.

"It's 11:30. We have three hours until Billy's sound check," informed Kelly.

"Soundcheck? What the hell is a soundcheck? And how do you know all of this shit?" asked Jimmy, shaking his head.

"I keep trying to tell you that I'm a groupie at heart. Let's get something to eat and compare notes," she said.

Chapter 23

Dickie could see Billy was hurting both physically and mentally. He knew Billy and Belinda had a stormy relationship over the years and that her death would have a serious effect.

Billy was in the back of the tour bus with a guitar, pen, and paper and drinking jasmine tea while working on a new song. The Cowboy Junkies song *500 miles,* played softly in the background.

To anyone else it looked as if Billy hadn't slept in quite a long time but Dickie knew he was pale and drawn because he was dopesick. When using opiates like heroin, even for a short period of time, the physical withdrawal is often referred to as being dope sick. It is extremely unpleasant, highly uncomfortable and produces high anxiety, dry heaves, vomiting (blood and bile mostly), sweats, and insomnia. Feeling strung out creates the necessity to use again to alleviate the physical symptoms that happen when the drug leaves your body. This feeling is what leads to the mental and physical dependency that never seems to end.

"What's up?" Billy asked, eyeing Dickie as he approached.

"Not much. You look like shit, though" he replied in all earnestness.

"Thanks. Got any dope?" He said, trying to make light of the situation.

Dickie slid in next to Billy and wrapped his arm tightly around his shoulder and as he did he could feel Billy's body tense up, as he was trying to hold back his tears.

"Maybe everybody was right, Dickie?" Billy mumbled with his head down.

"You mean the constant searching and the never finding?" questioned Dickie.

Billy didn't respond. He just lifted his gaze toward the front of the bus like he was in a trance.

"Maybe I'm too old for this shit? Maybe it's a younger man's game?"

"Tell me about it," said Dickie with a sigh.

"The drugs come back so quick. All the same problems right after," said Billy.

"But you already knew that," presented Dickie.

Billy reached into his pocket and pulled out a pillbox. He slipped a mustard colored 40-mg oxycontin into his mouth, bit the pill in half and washed it down with Jasmine tea. "Sorry," he said to Dickie, looking like a kid who just got caught with his hand in the cookie jar.

"You know that isn't going to solve anything," said Dickie, trying to use a sympathetic tone.

"I know. I'm not that sick. It's just a little something to take the edge off, you know-get right."

"Whatever you say Billy, but you're in for a world of shit with this Belinda thing. You need your head on straight and to be thinking clearly."

"Yeah," he whispered. He was strumming a slow chord progression on his guitar.

"New song?" inquired Dickie.

"Yeah, want to hear it?" Billy asked, rhetorically. He began to play before he got an answer.

> "My lady friend laid down with the devil, like so many times before
> Tonight, however Lucifer was going to take just a little more
> With pills and powders he convinced her he was on the level
> And then he stole her soul and now she belonged to the devil

(Chorus)
> "Did you ever stop to think
> That today (today) could be your last day (last day)
> Probably never gave it a moments thought
> More worried about the bills you had to pay

But for someone else it ended up that way
So what would you do different
If you knew it was your last day (last day)

"The prince's plane left late that early summer day
Too inexperienced to know the tricks New England
weather could play
The wind and fog came up, and the plane went down
All his ancestry and riches couldn't turn that plane around.

(Chorus)   "Did you ever stop to think
That today (today) could be your last day (last day)
Probably never gave it a moments thought
More worried about the bills you had to pay
But for someone else it ended up that way
So what would you do different
If you knew it was your last day (last day)

"Just nineteen and didn't know much about conflict
much less war
Join the army going to see some places he had never been
before
But in that Middle Eastern desert he ran into that snipers
bullet's way
Spilt blood for us spilt blood for oil on his last day, (last day)

(Chorus Out) "Did you ever stop to think
That today (today) could be your last day (last day)
Probably never gave it a moments thought
More worried about the bills you had to pay
But for someone else it ended up that way
So what would you do different
If you knew it was your last day (last day)

"Pretty," responded Dickie. "Playing it tonight?" He could see Billy's eyes were slowly beginning to constrict and his color was beginning to return, as the narcotic began to release in his bloodstream.

"Yeah, we can work it up in sound check." Sound check was the best time for the guys and the only time they had on tour to rehearse new material.

"We need to go over tonight, Billy."

"Okay, let's do it."

"I just woke the guys up and they're all fucked up, as I'm sure you can imagine. They have an hour to get straightened out and then everyone should be there for soundcheck. I've been up to The Paradise and it's already a fucking zoo," Dickie exclaimed. "Not only are all of the local Boston stations there, but all the fucking New York stations. CNN, HNN, I mean, it's a real fucking circus, Billy. I also spoke with a friend of mine at the Boston Police Department and they tell me there were two New York detectives in town this morning and they interviewed Johnny Vell at a friend of your father's office. No word on what exactly it was about. Have you talked to your father?"

"No," he answered curtly, clearly not wanting to discuss this.

"My guess is these detectives are going to want to speak with you at some point tonight," said Dickie. "So, here's what we're going to do. We can drop you off two blocks down from The Paradise. You throw on a Red Sox cap and walk up to the McDonald's, turn right and then take your first left into the alley where Techie will be loading up."

"Dickie, I'm from Boston, remember? I must have played The Paradise about a hundred times. I think I know where the load-in is located." As soon as he said it, he apologized, "Sorry, Dickie, I'm just a little stressed out right now."

"No problem, kid. This too, shall pass,"

The bus door opened and the band began staggering up the steps of the bus. They were showered and had on clean clothes, but were still looking a little worse for wear.

"You boys finally learn your lesson last night?" asked Dickie.

A collective, "Yes" escaped from their lips as they stumbled in and sank into various areas of the bus. The Russian made it to the first bunk and crawled right in.

"Two strippers at once. It killed him, again," said Johnny Chez, looking at Billy but nodding toward the Russian.

"I need a little pick me up," the Russian moaned. "Throw me a CD, somebody."

A Drown promotional CD was tossed into the bunk.

"At least these CD's are good for something-this and coasters." Billy and the rest of the band laughed.

The Russian reached into his pocket and produced a glassine baggie. He dumped its contents of cocaine and heroin; a speedball, into a pile on the CD. Someone else threw a straw onto the bunk. The White Russian inhaled deeply, throwing his head back once and the pile was gone.

There was an uneasiness in the air as the band lounged around the bus and both Billy and Dickie could feel it. Feeling better now, the Russian swung his legs out of the bunk and placed his black Beatle boots firmly onto the floor as he pulled a crumpled slip of paper out of his pocket. Billy and Dickie were still seated at the back of the bus watching him. "Good time last night, Russian?" asked Billy.

"I'll tell ya, Billy, Boston girls are all right," the Russian replied.

"You say that in every city," said Billy.

"Not Memphis." The Russian's ex-wife had been from Memphis. He'd made the mistake of falling for that Southern Belle act in his early years and now steered clear of southern charm.

"Billy, throw me my address book. It's in my jacket back there somewhere." He found the Russian's address book and tossed it to him. He caught it and opened the book and began transcribing numbers from the crumpled piece of paper. Johnny Chez walked over to see what he was writing.

"The girls names are Merlot and Cheyenne?" asked Chez, bending awkwardly at the neck trying to read what he was writing.

"I think that's what it says," he replied. He moved the scrap of paper back and forth in front of eyes, while he spoke. He squinted and then opened his eyes simultaneously with the movement of the paper. This had everyone on the bus smiling.

"But you're listing the names under B?" Chez asked while looking at him queerly.

The Russian looked at Chez like he had three heads. "Ya and...?" He rolled his free hand waiting for him to get to his point.

"Shouldn't the names be under M and C?" Chez asked.

"M and C?" asked the Russian, looking puzzled. "No. We're still in Boston, right? B is for Boston." He looked down and continued writing. Everyone on the bus laughed.

"Fucking Russian," said Billy.

The Russian finished writing closed the book and slid it into his back pocket. "Listen, Billy, I think I speak for everybody here when I say we're truly sorry about Belinda. We know you had nothing to do with it. So, let's go play a kick ass show."

With that, the tension on the bus started to dissipate. Band brawls were legendary: Lennon-McCartney, Jagger-Richards, and the two Robinson brothers of The Black Crowes. When push came to shove, the good bands banded together, closed ranks, and stuck together. Billy knew he had a great band.

Charlie was the last to board. "We ready to roll, Dickie?"

"Full steam ahead, Captain."

"Aye, aye, Sir."

The tour bus pulled out from The Four Seasons, made a left on Charles, passed between the Public Gardens and the Boston Common, made a left onto Beacon Street and cruised up past the brownstones. Billy made his way up to the front of the bus as Charlie had pulled up behind a hearse.

"Is this some type of omen?" Billy asked, looking at Dickie.

"Let's hope not," he answered.

"You know what I don't understand?" Billy continued before Dickie could answer. "When you die, they let you run every red light on your way to the cemetery. I mean, what's the hurry? Seriously, at that point what's the fucking rush?"

"I never looked at it that way, but you're right," said Dickie, laughing.

"Plus, at this rate, I'll be there sooner then you will, Dickie," Billy said, gesturing toward the hearse.

"You're probably right," Dickie replied, "but how exactly do you figure?"

"I'm aging twice as fast as you are," he answered, dead serious. "When I was twenty you were forty, right?"

"That's right."

"So I was half as old as you were. But when you're sixty, I'll be forty, right?"

"Right, your point being?"

"At that point, I'll be two thirds as old as you are. Forty is two thirds of sixty. So even though I'm younger, I'm actually aging twice as fast as you are, you see?"

Totally perplexed, he looked at Billy. "You're being serious, aren't you?"

"As a heart attack," said Billy. "I mean, its simple math, and math doesn't lie. I'm aging twice as fast as you are."

"You sure have a strange way of looking at things," said Dickie, as he slid a little further away from Billy.

"I do. I'm so fucked," Billy sighed. "It's like if you're having a good time and time goes by fast. Is your life actually shorter than if you were bored all the time and time just crept by?"

At this point in the conversation, Dickie decided it was best to get up and stretch. He moved away quickly as if Billy's point of view might be contagious. He was more concerned given the fact that Billy was obviously completely serious. Worse yet, after giving it some thought, he was beginning to see his logic. *It's way too early in the tour to start agreeing with the artists*, Dickie thought, as he stretched his hands over his head in the aisle of the bus.

Charlie easily maneuvered the bus through the un-congested Sunday afternoon traffic. In Kenmore Square, Charlie bore right onto Commonwealth Ave where Beacon Street and Commonwealth Ave split. A couple of blocks after the split, he eased the bus to the curb in front of a large unassuming Boston University building. Dickie threw Billy an Olde Towne team cap which he donned, as he hopped off the bus, completely unnoticed. The bus resumed moving up Commonwealth Ave and pulled to a stop directly in front of The Paradise Rock Club as the

Boston police had reserved a spot for the bus in advance. In addition, the police had cordoned off the sidewalk from the bus to the entrance, so the band could walk right off the bus and into the club without being accosted.

As a long time road manager, Dickie was familiar with the cops in every city. Some cops he knew for good reasons: tickets, well paying security details, and backstage passes for the cops' kids. Other cops he knew for bad reasons: band member arrests and drug raids. Fortunately, Boston was a city where he knew the police for good reasons. As such, it was too late before Kelly and Jimmy realized where the BPD had positioned them. It appeared they had a great vantage point situated right next to the bus door, however, once the bus door was open their view was actually blocked. It didn't really matter as they only saw the backs of four members of the band as they disembarked and entered The Paradise for soundcheck and Billy was not among them.

Along with the rest of the media horde they moved toward the Paradise's black doors as they quickly closed. Meanwhile, as the news cameras and press photographers jockeyed for position in front of the club, less then twenty feet away Billy made his right in front of the McDonald's on the corner and walked twenty yards to the small alley, completely unnoticed.

Once inside the doors to the club, Dickie said to nobody in particular, "A few more Indians than we originally planned on, Mr. Custer."

The Paradise bouncers and Boston Police stood in front of the door preventing anyone from the press on entering. Flashing their badges, Jimmy and Kelly worked their way swiftly to the front of the crowd.

"Sorry guys, strict orders. No warrant, no admission until show time," said one of the cops.

"So much for professional courtesy," muttered Jimmy. The fact that the Boston cop had asked for a warrant meant someone had tipped the BPD off to their arrival in Boston. He had figured this would be the case knowing Billy was from Boston and his father had represented the BPD officers in court with McGregor. He didn't bother putting up much of an argument with Boston's finest. Little did he know, it was actually Dickie who was pulling the strings.

Jimmy and Kelly worked their way around the crowd. "Maybe he's still on the bus?" asked Kelly as she looked around her for signs of Billy.

"No, he went in the back. I think I saw him on the corner as the other guys went in. I should have thought of that," responded Jimmy. "Now that we know that, we'll catch him on the way out. I'll take the front. You take the back."

"Fuck," uttered Kelly in exasperation. "He's twenty feet away and we can't get near him. Looks like we will have to stay here tonight. These bands don't go on stage until 10:00 or 11:00 o'clock.

"That won't make the bitchstrict…"

"All right," Kelly interrupted, before he could finish. "I'm the one who has to deal with her."

"Even if we stay and do catch up with him, there's nothing that says he'll agree to speak with us," admitted Jimmy.

"Maybe he has an alibi?" suggested Kelly.

"If he did, he would have been on the bus and not have avoided us." said Jimmy.

The band began its sound check inside the club. The Paradise had a top-notch in-house sound system that Techie was familiar with having worked here a number of times before. The band worked up "Last Day" during most of the hour and a half of allotted time. After sound check, Billy hung out in the dressing room and with the oxycontin time releasing its soothing narcotic, he simply spent the rest of the afternoon talking to the guys and nursing a couple of Heineken's.

At 7:00 pm sharp, The Paradise doors opened. By now, Commonwealth Avenue near The Paradise was complete and utter chaos. In this day and age of 24-hour cable news and tabloid TV, a story like this was a dream for every network. There were television crews everywhere. Like most stories that quickly became sensationalized, up until now it had been a total non-story with little to actually report. Even the Post story was a non-story. The Post had basically reported that the body of a pseudo-celebrity had been found dead and the suspected cause of death had been murder. There had been no real new news or facts to report since The Post story. The so-called journalists outside The Paradise were working the story into whatever fed the frenzy, they didn't need facts. In addition to the media, Drown fans were milling about who had actually come for the musical aspect of the show. Boston's rock and roll royalty was also well represented as members of Aerosmith, the Cars, The Real Kids, J. Geils, and the Del Fuegos were all present. By now, the members of various *Stop Violence Against Women* type of groups had begun protesting and setting up camp. Apparently, nobody knew that Billy had recently done a number of concerts benefiting women's rights and advocacy groups, including a group called Deana's Fund.

Deana's Fund was a charity formed by two of Billy's closest friends who'd lost a daughter to domestic violence. This charity specialized in education in an attempt to educate young people to the epidemic that domestic violence had become in the United States. Inherently lazy, the media had no desire to discover this or if they did, they had no intention of reporting anything positive about Billy or any worthwhile cause for that matter. They were after dirt.

Dickie and Charlie glanced through the front window of the bus. "No business like show business, hey, Charlie?" observed Dickie.

"That poor kid can't even mourn his friend's death and they already have him convicted," was Charlie's reply. "That boy couldn't hurt no one."

"Well, let's head back in," said Dickie.

As they walked through the doors of The Paradise, to their immediate left was a small ticket window. A few steps further in was the bathroom and beyond that a coat check closet and a merchandise booth. They entered a short tunnel-like hallway with dim lighting and a low ceiling. The walls were painted in psychedelic colors and at the end of the tunnel was an opening that faced the stage. The stage was all black and elevated four feet off the ground. The center of the stage had the appearance of being framed by two, four-foot wide columns reaching from the floor to the ceiling. In reality, the two pillars were located halfway between the stage and the tunnel's entrance. The interior of the low-lit club was all black. To the left and right of the stage at the edges of the floor were small booths and tables, they were staggered from the floor to just below the club ceiling in bleacher-like fashion. Immediately opposite the stage and above the entranceway was a catwalk that connected the two booth sections. Centered in the middle of the catwalk was the sound and light board booth which was empty. The stage was also dark and empty. Songs from The Rolling Stone's, "Exile on Main Street" and The Beatles, "White Album" alternated softly over the house sound system. These were the two greatest rock and roll albums ever recorded-not only in Billy's opinion, but many other's as well. Billy and the band were in the dressing room located to the left of the backstage area.

On the outside of the dressing room door was a piece of paper with the words *Band Only*, *NO EXCEPTIONS* written in black marker. Normally, Billy would have been welcoming well-wishers like models, strippers and other potential paramours. Outside the door was Brad, a Paradise bouncer, who stood watch along with a uniformed Boston Police officer. Brad had a band called Big Block 454 and knew Billy from the Boston music scene. He was a good looking guy, stocky, with dark smooth skin and closely cropped black hair. He was dressed in black jeans and a black T-shirt with the Paradise logo on the front and *STAFF* written in bold white letters on the back. Brad wasn't anybody somebody was going to fuck with in an attempt to get to Billy. A few journalists, mostly attractive women, tried to persuade him with their wiles but having been in a band and around the music scene for most of his life, he'd heard every story in the book and nobody was going to make it past him. Billy was appreciative as the lack of distractions allowed him to concentrate solely on the show. He promised Brad's new band a few opening slots on the present Drown tour.

The inside of the dressing room was a long narrow rectangular hall out-fitted two black, faded leather couches. In front of one of the couches was a coffee table that was littered with partially full Heineken bottles, overflowing ashtrays and lines of various chemicals layed out. Since it was right before the start of the show, the band members were going slow and not using much. A *good sign* thought Dickie, as he took in and surveyed the room. Billy was on the back couch strumming his acoustic guitar with Johnny Chez next to him, quietly tapping his drumsticks on the table looking lost in thought. The other guys were pacing about, trying to burn off the nervous energy that gathers before a performance.

Dickie spoke up, "Half hour, Gentlemen. 8-3-0 sharp, set time, Okay?"

Each band member nodded in answer.

Billy spoke up, addressing the band for the first time. "I appreciate your support." He paused to gather himself and his thoughts. "I think we've made a great record and this is going to be the beginning of a long journey that will result in the breaking out of this record and this band."

The group formed a circle and put their hands in the center, one on top of another.

Billy said, "One, two, three." They made a downward motion with their outstretched hands and then raised them simultaneously. They broke the circle. The White Russian began bouncing on his toes. A couple of guys went to finish what was left of their beer or dope. Billy handed his guitar to Dickie and in turn, he handed it out the dressing room door to a roadie. Billy stretched his hands skyward and pivoted on his toes back toward the back of the dressing room.

"Hey, Russian, fix me a little something for my head." Everyone in the room noticed it was the first time during the day Billy had cracked a smile.

The Russian responded, "Full beverage, dude," and smiled back. "Yes sir, Mr. Boss man, sir. The usual, Monsieur?"

"Oui," Billy responded, "Tiny, tiny, tiny, though."

The Russian put out about a half-inch line of coke and a matching tan line of smack. Using a credit card, he repeatedly swiped his hand left back and forth until there remained only a perfect, thin sand colored line.

"Voila, Monsieur," said the Russian. Billy leaned toward the coffee table and Benoit handed him a rolled dollar bill as he passed. He reached the table and in one motion bent over and sniffed the line. As the chemicals hit the membrane in his nostril he straightened and tilted his head back. The mixture of the adrenaline rush before a show with the added benefit of the narcotics was like no other high in the world for the performer.

Just outside the dressing room on the stage the roadies were making last minute checks of the band's gear. A couple of beats of the drums, a pluck of the guitar, each sound brought a louder response from the crowd as the anticipation grew. The room was filled to capacity with was a set of eyes in every conceivable nook and cranny of the Paradise.

After the instruments were checked one of the roadies began lighting the white candles that sat atop the amplifiers and the drum riser. Set lists; what the band intended to play and in what order, were taped to the floor in front of each microphone. Techie seemingly appeared out of nowhere in the sound and light booth. The activity in and around the stage was a sure sign to any concert veteran that the band would be taking the stage any moment now. As the crowd murmur continued to build the house sound system went silent. The flames from the candles swiveled on their wicks and their reflections danced on the walls and ceilings.

Billy confidently stepped onstage, dressed in an olive Strangefolk T-shirt, faded blue jeans and brown suede, English walking boots. In his left hand, he carried a red plastic beer cup and in his right hand he held his acoustic guitar by the neck. He strode over to his amplifier, put down his beer, then turned and sat down with his guitar in his lap.

As the crowd cheered, hooted and hollered he received a warm, hometown welcome. After a couple of minutes, the crowds noise began to die down and the nervous energy could still be heard in the scraping of moving feet and the rustle of bodies rubbing up against one another.

Billy was normally stoic on-stage, however, tonight he felt the need to say something. "Hi, thank you, thanks for coming," he said in an awe shucks manner. "Tonight's a home game!" he shouted with more depth.

The crowd once again roared its approval and as the applause died down, a female voice rose above the din and screamed, "We love you, Billy." Simultaneously, a group of red roses seemingly fell from the sky down to Billy's feet.

He shifted his weight and began to play a sequence of single notes in a particular key. It wasn't any particular song, arrangement or melody, rather, he was noodling. Slowly, Techie bathed him in a halo of soft purple light and as he continued to play, the crowd barely noticed as the other band members slipped into their respective spots on stage.

Slowly Billy's noodling morphed into an actual melody and his playing became a more recognizable sequence. The anticipation and applause all at once built with the recognition of each familiar note. Slowly he rose from the amplifier and stood in front of the center stage microphone. The stage lights went white as the whole band kicked into "Betrayed." Billy closed his eyes, leaned into the microphone and sang the first notes and everything else drained from his mind. Billy always found it ironic that artists, the most insecure souls on the planet were most secure baring their sick thoughts, souls and demons to hundreds of strangers every night.

Thankfully, the tour was officially underway.

Jimmy and Kelly found themselves jammed against the back of bar on the left-hand side of the room. With the size of the crowd it was all Jimmy could do to pivot and order a couple of Budweisers. They slowly pulled on the bar bottles, as Billy and the band ran through the new album. When they went into a cover of Dylan's "Just Like Tom Thumb's Blues." Jimmy couldn't help but sing along. "Started out on Burgundy, but soon hit the harder stuff," Billy sang, "Everyone said they'd stand behind me when the going got rough, but when I turned around there was nobody there, nobody even to call my bluff, I'm going back to New York City, I do believe I've had enough." The irony of Dylan's lyrics wasn't lost on Jimmy or Billy. They completed the set with the Dead's, "There Comes A Time." At the end of the song, Billy and the band walked off stage without saying a word. The crowd roared. It was a great performance and Billy smiled at Dickie as he came off stage with his T-shirt soaked in sweat from the heat of the stage lights. "Sometimes the lights all shining on me," said Billy, to no one in particular, "Other times, I can barely see." After a few minutes-enough time to swig down a Heineken and blow a couple of quick lines-the band bounded back on stage for the encore.

Billy pulled the mic back toward him and lowered the stand as he sat down on his amplifier so he could sit and sing. The crowd quieted. Almost in a mumble, he said, "This is a new song for an old friend who recently passed away." With that, the band went into a stirring and emotional rendition of his newly penned, "Last Day." Given the fact that the audience knew exactly what he was referring to, there wasn't a dry eye left in the house.

At the end of the song, in a soft tone the Russian said, "Thank you and Good Night."

Even Jimmy and Kelly had enjoyed the show and were moved by the set's last song.

After a couple of minutes, Jimmy said to Kelly, "Let's get to work." As the crowd began to thin, he swore he saw Margie Markowitz stage right, with a note pad in hand.

Chapter 24

Jimmy and Kelly milled about as the people in the Paradise serpentined their way out the central door. They'd given the backstage area a try and were unsuccessful which didn't surprise them. The roadies were in the process of breaking down the gear and hauling it out through the club's open, double back door. As Techie was rolling up the cables between his palm and elbow, he noticed a fan running on stage and grabbing something. He yelled at the fan to get off the stage, but he really wasn't upset since it was usual for fans to try and grab set lists or picks that were left behind by the band. As long as it wasn't anything of value, he really didn't give a shit. It was around 10:00 pm when the club had completely emptied. Jimmy was now at the front door and Kelly was at the back. She'd been asked to leave several times by both Techie and the roadies. Not looking for problems with their New York brethren the Boston Police intervened and allowed her to stay. Notwithstanding, Techie and the boys inconvenienced her as much as possible as they tried to run her over with amplifiers, hit her with guitar cases and just gave her overall dirty looks.

After a half an hour Jimmy called her on his Nextel, "What's up?"

"Nothing yet," she relayed.

"It's 10:30. Maybe we missed him? I think we should try and make the last shuttle."

"I agree," as she glanced around her. "Tuesday night in New York will be a home game for us. It'll be a totally different story."

"I hope so."

Meanwhile, Billy was already on the bus and elated that the show had gone well, but even happier that he wasn't in NYPD custody. Immediately after the show was over, he'd ducked into the dressing room, changed his T-shirt and donned his Red Sox cap. He trailed Brad and came out through the backstage door and instead of going on stage, they went directly to the Paradise floor and blending into the exiting crowd, they walked right by Jimmy and Kelly. At least Billy assumed they were the two New York cops. He didn't recognize them. He'd signed autographs for most of the Boston cops working the detail and they didn't look like typical Drown fans. He could have sworn he saw a gun under Jimmy's jacket as they passed. Getting past them had been Billy's first obstacle. Getting from the door of the club to the door of the bus had been his second. The Boston Police had cordoned off an alley and he only had ten yards to cover. Since the crowd was spilling out at the same time nobody noticed the bus door opening in the commotion with Billy quietly slipping inside.

Chapter 25

BILLY SUNDAY DROWNS HIS SORROWS—By-Line, Margie Markowitz *Boston, MA. Billy Sunday, a suspect in the murder of Belinda Caruso, opened his U.S. tour last night here in Boston at The Paradise Rock Club. Billy Sunday, looking slightly intoxicated, played a moving new song, "Last Day" as an apparent eulogy to his deceased friend.*

Jimmy scanned further down the article. *In other aspects of the investigation, Independent record promoter Johnny Vell also spoke to police and appears to have been cleared of any wrongdoing.* Strangely, District Attorney McBride's office had no comment. The bitchstrict attorney would be out for blood, namely his and Agis'. Jimmy rubbed his eyes, he was still tired from yesterday's trip to Boston and besides, he really hadn't slept. To him, it still wasn't clear whether any of the four known suspects was the killer. The song and performance of "Last Day" was a moving artistic tribute and to pull that off, Sunday was either a stone cold killer or he was innocent. He didn't know Billy at all, but he didn't have the persona of a guy who could commit a murder and then weep at the funeral. He appeared genuine. It was only 6:00 am. Rubbing his eyes again, the phone rang. "Hi Kelly," he spoke into the phone before she could speak.

"Been up all night?"

"Pretty much."

"I just got off the phone with McBride," she said. "As you can imagine, I did most of the listening. You're not going to like this but..."

"But what?"

"She wants us to start building a case against Billy Sunday."

"Has she ever heard of building a case against the guilty party?"

"It gets worse."

"You have to be kidding me, right?"

"She wants us to pick him up at the concert tomorrow night. She's going to be there with the press, I can only imagine."

"Are you fucking kidding me?" Jimmy screamed.

Kelly would laugh at his use of profanity but this wasn't funny to either of them. Jimmy was literally hopping mad.

"That's it! I'm handing in my badge and gun. She's gone from incompetent to in-fucking-sane, you understand that, don't you?" Kelly continued to let him rant. "And guess who's going to hang when it turns out this is another McBride, McMotherfuckin W-F-G-C."

"A what?" She couldn't resist asking, stifling her laugh.

"A wild fucking goose chase, you never heard that before? You and me-that's who will hang. I ain't gonna do it. I'm telling you, Kelly, I ain't fucking doing it." He'd finally talked himself out.

"Look, can you meet me at the office at 8:00 am? I have something that'll help make the case against Sunday," she managed before he started ranting again.

The brisk morning air was retreating against the warm spring breeze and heat from the sun. It was going to be another beautiful spring day. Jimmy was dressed in off-white, pleated Banana Republic chinos, a white dress shirt and a tan, light wool blazer. He headed off the elevator into the squad room where he met Kelly who was also dressed for spring in sheer stockings, a mauve lycra skirt, and a pink, gauze sleeveless top. She was standing beside her gray gunmetal desk with a red beer cup sitting on top.

"What's that?" pointed Jimmy, still clearly seething and in no mood for pleasantries.

"The cup Billy Sunday was drinking out of onstage," said Kelly.

"What's in it?"

"A Billy Sunday of course," she admonished, as if he should have already known.

Jimmy gave her a quizzical look.

Kelly continued, "The residue of Kettle One Vodka, pomegranate juice and Gatorade. Billy prefers the lemon/lime." She'd begun talking about rock stars like most other fans did, as if they knew them personally.

Jimmy laughed nervously at first. His exhaustion fueled the release of endorphins and he immediately began laughing hysterically.

"What's so funny?" grinned Kelly.

"This day, this case, Kettle One and Gatorade. Take your pick. Every aspect of the suspects. The so-called evidence. The DA. They're all fucking cuckoo," pointing his right finger against his right temple he made a circling motion.

"Anyway, it's not what's in the cup that's important. It what's left on the cup," she said, holding the cup aloft.

"DNA," replied Jimmy. "Billy's DNA. What about the seizure of the cup?"

"Hey, he left it in public in plain sight where he should have had a reasonable expectation that it would be seized," she explained.

"Not exactly what the case law says, but I'll leave that argument to defense counsel. Anyway, we'll never get a DNA match with the sperm samples by Tuesday."

"No," she realized, "but with eyewitness testimony and the forensic evidence we have already, it should be enough to pick him up and question him."

"Well, I'm not sure we have enough right now." He surmised.

"No, I tend to agree," said Kelly. "Although, I thought we should check out Vell's story first and see if he can be concretely ruled out, as a suspect."

"As Good a place to start as any," agreed Jimmy. "Kelly, you know that working the case this way-from the suspect on back, things are bound to get fucked up. I mean, working under these conditions goes against everything we were taught."

"Yeah, I know."

"And it'll be our asses on the line. McBride will sell us down the river in a heartbeat. No looking back."

"I would like to think not, Jimmy, but deep down I know you're right. I'm starting to think I'm not cut out for this line of work."

"No, you're definitely cut out for this line of work. You're just not cut out for the political bullshit that goes along with it. Nobody is cut out for it except for the politicians. Ever since OJ and the advent of Court TV, criminal trials have become nothing more than entertainment for the masses. The politicians are the producers, the media are the scriptwriters, and the cops, suspects and victims are merely stage actors. Justice is no longer relevant. That's because the just result doesn't always garner the best ratings. As a result, we now race to convict innocent people which is exactly what we're likely to do in this case. In the alternative, like OJ, through judicial incompetence, we let the killer go free because it makes for a better ending. Shakespeare would have loved us. First, we kill all the lawyers…wasn't that him? He was onto something."

"The two prosecutors, Darden and what's her name, were ridiculously incompetent. That's what happened in OJ. I don't think it was any grand conspiracy," responded Kelly.

"Probably right," said Jimmy. "But they, too, got caught up in the drama and lost sight of their true purpose which was first and foremost to bring justice for both the victims and the system. Their purpose wasn't to advance their careers or promote their book deals, but that is ultimately what they ended up doing. Although, looking back, hopefully that trial will be used in law schools as the perfect example of how not to prosecute a case."

"Back to this case, you really think Billy Sunday is innocent?" she asked, wondering what she really believed.

"I don't know if he's guilty at this point, but I won't doubt if he's found not guilty because we're being forced to prosecute him rather than pursuing the person to whom good, solid detective work leads us. We're not being given the opportunity to investigate and follow through."

"All right, Detective," said Kelly, "I think its time we began doing some solid detective work."

"You're right. It's just that McBride has us going about this in completely the wrong way. Making the evidence fit the suspect is totally ass backwards."

"C'mon," said Kelly, "Let's get down to Red Tails and see what Vell and Belinda had for lunch. Then we can go over to CBGB's and see if anyone witnessed an argument between Billy and Belinda."

"Sounds good. I'm getting hungry anyway," he agreed.

It took them a while to make it from mid-town Manhattan to the Village given the Monday morning commuter traffic so by the time they entered Red Tails, the restaurant employees were in the middle of setting up for lunch. They flashed their badges toward one of the Japanese waiters and asked to see the chef and watched as the waiter disappeared into the kitchen. Standing close enough by the door to the kitchen they could just make out two voices conversing in Japanese then the waiter came back out through the kitchen door and motioned with his hand for them to approach. They walked among the glass topped covered tables and red cushioned chairs and had to walk behind the sushi bar as the kitchen door was centered right behind it.

A large Japanese man in a white chef's hat and apron asked in perfect English, "How can I help NYPD's finest?" It sounded as if he'd rehearsed his question beforehand.

"We need to know if you remember a couple of customers," said Kelly, flashing the 8 x10 photos they procured of Vell and Belinda.

"Not familiar customers. Her, I would have remembered," was the chef's reply. "When did they come in?"

"Wednesday for lunch," answered Kelly.

"I didn't work Wednesday. Charlie work Wednesday. Yeah, Charlie work Wednesday, but I don't see him since."

"You haven't seen him since when?" questioned Jimmy.

"He hasn't been in since work on Wednesday."

"I don't suppose you have any employment records on Charlie?" Jimmy inquired.

"No, he's how you say, an independent contractor?"

Jimmy wasn't surprised and figured as much. Immigration issues, tax issues, employment issues, take your pick, in the ethnic restaurant business in New York, the less employers knew about their employees, the better off the employers were. If the employee showed up and worked hard, he was paid cash for the day. If he showed up the next day, fine. If he didn't there were always others eager for work.

"Do you mind if we speak with some of your employees and see if they remember them?" asked Kelly.

"Fine." The chef motioned out the kitchen door. "Be my guest."

Jimmy and Kelly got lucky with the first waiter they met.

"Yes, he came in last week with the very pretty girl," said the waiter, while looking at the photos. The short thin Japanese waiter was dressed in the universal wait staff uniform, white dress shirt, black pants and black sneakers.

"He know Charlie. Charlie make him something special not on menu."

"Do you happen to know what it was?" asked Jimmy.

"No, you have to ask Charlie."

"Do you know Charlie or where we can find him?" Kelly chimed in.

"No, I not know Charlie except from here," the waiter replied, looking at his shoes.

The waiter's body language said to Jimmy that he did in fact know Charlie but was lying about it. What the fuck could he do about it? It's not like he could beat it out of him but for a split second, he thought about it thinking that beating a witness until he talked might actually make him feel better. But what had the waiter ever done to him? Beth McBride's actions concerning this case were going to ruin a few careers as it was and he didn't plan on letting his career be one of them. McBride had swore to him after the last fiasco involving one of her cases that she would be out for his blood if he didn't go along with her. He always considered the possibility that she would end up backstabbing him and it would be her incompetence that was going to do them all in. Her ineptitude is what had him considering beating up an innocent illegal alien. *What was he thinking?* He asked himself as he walked away-right out the front door. Kelly finished the interview for them.

"How were they getting along? Friendly? Angry? Did you notice anything about the way they interacted?"

"They get along fine-laugh, joke, drink sake, speak to Charlie. They leave together, hand in hand."

"Hand in hand, huh?" Kelly had hoped this interview was going to simplify matters. Like everything else in this case, the interview only further complicated things; only further clouded the issues.

"That was fucking helpful," remarked Jimmy as Kelly entered the unmarked cruiser. "I'm at the point where I don't know what to think."

"Me too," she agreed. "Almost everyone suspected has a motive but nothing compelling enough to actually commit murder. They all seem to have had the opportunity, but not the window of opportunity that rules out the others.

"And everyone seems to have had the means." Jimmy finished the thought for her. "Let's see if we can find out what the argument at the club was all about."

Jimmy eased the cruiser to the curb directly in front of CBGB's. Being mid-afternoon on a Monday there was little activity in or around the club and they were hoping they'd get lucky and find someone who was working. Fortunately for them Monday was delivery day and the manager, Sam, was in. As they walked through the unlocked front door they were confronted with the noxious odor of ammonia and once inside the door the ammonia, stale beer and sweat mixed all together and the cleaning agent they used only amplified, rather than masked, the unpleasant odors. Like most empty nightclubs, CBGB was dusky and dingy, which was part of the allure of the place. CBGB's was most famous for breaking early alternative acts like the Talking Heads, returning the favor; The Talking Heads had immortalized the club in their song, "Life During War Time."

Dressed in the standard club uniform, Sam was wearing dark jeans and a black T-shirt with the CBGB logo, standing behind the bar holding a clipboard in front of a stack of beer cases and checking off the liquor delivery.

"Hello." Jimmy said by way of introduction as he and Kelly reached for their badges, although there really was no need.

Through his peripheral vision, Sam saw them and immediately knew they were cops figuring who else would be here in the middle of the afternoon dressed like C.S.I detectives? They certainly weren't tourists asking for directions.

"We'd like to ask you about a concert here last Wednesday night," informed Jimmy.

"A showcase, an industry showcase," added Kelly.

Jimmy gave her a strange look. *She actually is a fucking groupie.*

"Figured someone like you'd be coming around, just surprised it took you this long," said Sam, keeping his eyes focused on his clipboard. "Billy Sunday and Drown. Yeah, they played Wednesday and drew a nice crowd. Pretty good show, too. Billy's one of the good guys. Belinda Caruso was here, too, looking as sweet as ever. She was alive when she came in and alive when she left, if that's what you want to know. Does that about cover it?"

Neither could tell if Sam was being an asshole, was just busy or both.

"Did you happen to see who Belinda left with?" asked Kelly.

"She left with Johnny Vell, Mr.Extraordinaire, just ask him," intoned Sam, "He's an all-around narcissistic, world class asshole. Just ask anyone besides him. The fact that they left together was kind of strange though."

"Why do you say it was strange?" inquired Kelly.

"Because her husband was here and he wasn't too happy when she left with Vell."

Jimmy took over the interview, "Let me venture a guess. Was Billy Brill of The Dead Boys here, too?"

"Yup."

"We heard Billy Sunday and Belinda had an argument backstage at some point?" alluded Jimmy.

"Don't know anything about that since I was pretty much working the front of the room. Little Stevie was working the backstage area. Maybe he can help you."

Jimmy automatically figured that Little Stevie was going to turn out to be another Charlie being that the employee benefit plan was the same in the nightclub business as it was in the small restaurant business. Jimmy assumed Stevie was going to be about as available as Charlie and they were both surprised when Sam said, "Stevie is downstairs. If you wait a minute, I'll go and get him for you." Sam continued making a few more check marks before putting down the clipboard. He turned, opened a trap door and leisurely disappeared down the stairs to return a few minutes later followed by a thin, young boy.

Little Stevie's head was topped off by a flat top hair cut and his face was covered in acne. An aquamarine T-shirt emblazoned with the Drown logo hung off his shoulders while his black jeans hung even lower on his hips. Red Chuck Taylor's completed his attire and he looked 18, at best.

Sam said by way of introduction, "Stevie here is our new bar back and was working the backstage area the night your interested in."

Stevie piped up, "Hey, I don't want to get anyone in trouble. I mean, Mr. Sunday was a really nice guy."

"He give you that nice T-shirt?" Jimmy asked sarcastically.

"Yeah, I mean yes," said Stevie, not quite catching on. "All I did was bring the guys beer, just the usual."

Jimmy could see Stevie's nostrils were red, raw and glistening, "You sell them any drugs? Like maybe a little blow or crystal meth?"

"No, nothing like that," he responded, looking everywhere but at Jimmy.

"So, you wouldn't mind if we searched you? Right?" added Kelly.

"All right, all right, I'll cooperate, but you gotta keep my name out of it," was Stevie's response. "I'm not going to testify, though. I mean, I'm just getting started in this business. I mean, if these bands think I'm a snitch, I'll be out before I'm in."

Jimmy decided he'd deal with the legalities later but he wasn't making any promises. "Just tell us what you know."

"Everything was normal before the show, I guess. A few label execs came backstage and did the industry press photo thing. Then the band played. When they came off stage, this attractive woman, I mean, a real piece of eye candy, approached Billy."

"Was this her?" flashing a picture of Belinda, Kelly was smiling at the eye candy comment.

"Yeah, that's her. Anyway, they went to a corner out back. I kind of followed. I was curious. Plus, that broad was real easy on the eyes."

"Yeah, we get the picture on the broad," said Jimmy, "Just continue."

"She had Billy over in the corner and she was facing him so neither one could see me. I was making myself look busy, moving cases of beer back and forth."

"Did you get the gist of their conversation?" asked Kelly.

"You want the gist of the conversation?" he repeated, "Or the actual conversation? I mean I was pretty much close enough to hear everything."

In unison they gave Stevie a look like, *Why don't you think about what we're looking for, genius?* Stevie finally caught their drift.

Another rocket scientist for a witness in this case, thought Jimmy, *God fucking help us.*

"There was this really good looking blond woman…" After Jimmy's prior warning, Stevie mad an effort to tone down on the hyperbole. "She had on a tight white halter top and tight and I mean tight, hot pink, leather pants. Well, she was all over Billy as soon as he came off stage. I'd say they were pretty close. She was touching Billy's arm whenever she talked to him and Billy had his arm wrapped around her waist as he was introducing her to the guys. I couldn't help but notice his hand rubbing her ass on account of her ass was so fucking hot." With his eyes, Jimmy warned Stevie again. "I mean, I just couldn't stop looking staring," he finished, with his head down.

"Enough with the editorial comments," said Kelly, her patience being tried.

"Huh?" responded Stevie. "Anyway, when the other woman came backstage, you know, the one in the picture, well, she went right up to Billy and pulled his arm away from the blond chick. That's when they moved to the corner to talk in private. Apparently, the picture chick, what's her name again?"

"Belinda," Kelly responded.

Stevie obviously didn't get up early enough to catch The Post's early edition, Jimmy thought. *For that matter, maybe this kid is totally brain dead since the whole city is talking about this murder and lil, ol' Stevie here doesn't seem to have the foggiest idea why they were even having this conversation.*

"So Belinda, apparently, she has something to do with Billy's record company. Which is why I was listening in the first place, because my band has a killer demo tape and I was trying to figure out to whom I should give copies.

"Why don't we stick to the story here, Stevie," managed Kelly through clenched teeth. *This is going nowhere.* All Jimmy could do was roll his eyes.

"Okay, she's accusing Billy of having a threesome with the blond who was here and some stripper the night before the gig." Kelly and Jimmy braced themselves for Stevie's next insight. "Man, I can't wait to be a rock star," he sighed. Kelly gave him an un-approving look as he continued on, undeterred.

"Billy was denying it, but even I could tell he was lying. He's not a good liar. This Belinda was saying that as long as he was signed to her label, he was expected to stay faithful to her. She was going on that if he wanted a three-some, that was fine, as long as she was part of the equation."

Kelly believed he remembered the quote verbatim as the pun was totally lost on him.

"She went on saying that this included tonight, you know, last Wednesday night, that she expected to see him after he was finished here."

"Did she mention where that was going to be?" asked Kelly.

"If she did, I didn't hear it."

"Did you get Billy's reaction?" she continued grilling him.

"Something about her being married and what they had was over and she should accept it."

"Did she have a reaction to that?"

"She just whipped around and walked away on those thigh high, black heeled boots of hers. I did catch her saying, "No later than midnight and don't bring the tramp. I'll find somebody suitable for us."

"And what did Billy do after she walked away?"

"He kind of shook his head for a minute and walked back into the backstage crowd like nothing had happened."

"You didn't happen to catch the name of the blond girl by any chance?"

"No, but if you have a picture of her, I'd like to keep it." This brought a laugh from Billy and Kelly. If they couldn't laugh they'd both be crying at this point. "One more question, Stevie," said Kelly, "Did you see Billy leave?"

"Yeah, he was the last to leave, Him and his road manager. He thanked me, signed a couple of CDs, tipped me $100 and asked if I could call him a taxi."

"Do you remember which taxi company you called?"

"Yeah, the numbers up front, I'll get it."

Chapter 26

At the same time that Jimmy and Kelly were finishing their interviews in the village, Billy and the boys were boarding the bus in front of the Four Seasons. Once the band woke up, at Dickie's prodding, they found a change in their tour books. Tour books were just that; small, leather bound books containing information on the individual dates of the tour, in particular, their daily events and schedules which included radio show appearances, record store appearances and, of course, their concert performances. The information included their arrival times, check-in times, load—in times, set times and load-out times. Musicians were inherently lazy and always late and Dickie had to maintain constant vigilance. Drown was originally scheduled to drive down to New York on Tuesday afternoon. Dickie figured that by then the media circus would be laying in wait so he decided to change the departure time, arrival time and hotel accommodations and so far his plan was working flawlessly. There was nobody to see Drown off as the bus once again circled the Public Garden and made a left on Arlington Street, passing Commonwealth Ave., the Old Ritz Hotel, and Newbury Street. After crossing Boylston Street they took a right and merged onto the Mass Pike heading for New York.

Billy positioned himself in one of the front seats with Dickie beside him. "You don't look too worse for wear," noticed Dickie.

"I'm feeling all right," he answered.

"The old self detox."

"Yeah."

"Listen, we were able to work some magic up in Boston in part because it's your home town, but my contacts in New York tell me it's soon going to be a different story when we get down there. Detective Gerard is a good guy, old school. Don't know too much about the broad."

"We know she's pretty," Billy commented.

"Only you would think of getting involved with a broad whose job it is to send you to the death chamber," replied Dickie rather dramatically. "Who do think you are? Johnny Depp in some fucking contemporary Shakespearean tragedy, going to get the girl and get to live?"

"You're right," agreed Billy with a smile. "Only I would think like that."

"Anyway, the D.A. wants somebody's head on a silver platter-like yesterday. Word is, that head could very well be yours. Detective Agis goes way back with McBride, so we can probably assume she's against us."

"Let me get this straight, we have Fiona Apple and Alannis Morisette, is what you're telling me," was Billy's response. Billy didn't like Apple or her songs. *What experience did she have?* thought Billy. *What makes her an authority on relationships at the ripe old age of 18?* Alannis, on the other hand, was a cool and very successful pop artist. The summer her single, "You Ought to Know" was released, Billy didn't get laid once with the number one song featuring the lyrics, "Does she go down on you in the theater," and "Are you thinking of me when you fuck her?" *They just don't write songs like that anymore,* his train of thought continued. To him, McBride was Fiona, and Agis was Morissette.

"I called around and I think we should retain counsel as soon as we enter the city limits," was Dickie's response.

"I concur. Don't want to be riding into town naked, so to speak."

"I know you're not planning on calling your father for help," said Dickie. "But after the lecture your afraid of getting, it might make your life alot easier."

"And have to listen to I told you so for about the hundredth time?"

"Well, he did tell you so and he's been right for the hundredth time."

"I know, I know," sighed Billy.

"Call him and see if this lawyer, Danny O'Connell, is the right guy. If he is, I already have an appointment lined up for first thing tomorrow morning."

"Will do," said Billy. Dickie could tell that Billy was merely placating him.

To Billy, the reality of the situation was truly just starting to sink in. He swore to himself that he wasn't going to use today, but the more he thought about his whole situation, the more the desire to use grew. He went into the bathroom and did a bag of heroin and a little bit of coke. When he came back up front, Dickie had moved to the back of the bus with the band.

Billy laid his head back on the headrest. The drone of the bus' engine and the wheels turning underneath him felt good, like he was moving on. He closed his eyes and the narcotics once again eased his anxiety just enough for him to relax. Though of course, and he knew this, they'd only cause more anxiety in the long run.

Another jackpot, was Billy's thought. That's where his best thinking had gotten him again. *Where had all the time gone?* And what did he have to show for it? He didn't have a whole hell of a lot but he figured at least he was still in the game. He still had a chance, he kept telling himself. What was it with his generation? He didn't know a lot of happy campers. There were those who had sought financial success and had achieved it, although now that they had it, the money somehow hadn't brought them the piece of mind they had hoped it would. Many were stuck in unhappy marriages, divorced, or still single and disillusioned and there were those who'd chased their dreams at the expense of everything else, as opposed to the almighty dollar, but had also failed to achieve a state of nirvana. It seemed as if those who sought money and material wealth did so solely to please or impress others-never once thinking about themselves and their true desires. "Be careful that the fortune that you seek is the fortune that you need," sang Ben Harper. Billy found it ironic that, by society's definition, the rich were selfish and the artists were selfless. The way he saw it things were exactly the opposite. The rich had in fact sold their souls to please others, while an artist's sole motivation was self preservation and self promotion."

The few friends Billy had who were truly happy had acquired their money and material possessions without trying to keep up with the Jones'. They had realistic expectations when it came to their dreams and those that were happy were more realistic about their limitations but didn't let those limitations stand in their way. Billy and the people he knew who'd been unrealistic about their expectations had ultimately met with disappointment and unhappiness.

Charlie must have been aware that Billy's mind was racing. "Don't beat yourself up over it too bad, or it will eat you alive. You have nothing to be ashamed of. Yeah, you may not have the money your friends do but you have experience, life experience. All the money in the world can't buy the experiences you've been fortunate enough to have had. I don't know what it is-human nature or religion-that forces us to constantly focus on our shortcomings. "Never count my blessing only dwell on my disasters," as Ray Lamontagne would croon. We never seem to give ourselves credit for the good we've accomplished, particularly for ourselves.

Billy marveled at how both Charlie and Dickie could read his mind. Then again, this wasn't their first rodeo, they'd been doing it for a long time. He was thinking, *I've had drinks with Mick and the boys, alot of good looking women, and partied in Amsterdam!* He knew these weren't the type of positive experiences Charlie was referring to in his lecture. "But in reality, Charlie, I may have a lifetime of experience but I'm still left with nothing but an empty feeling in my gut."

"Some people have everything and still feel as if they have nothing. It's all perspective."

"Yeah, I can see that, Charlie."

"Now that you realize it, it's up to you to do something about it. Get the fuck off this bus and get yourself a life and a good woman. Then if you want to, get back on the bus. There are people who enjoy what you do-people who depend on what you do to help them emotionally. However, you'd be doing everyone and yourself a favor if you did this because you wanted to, not because you had to. So what, you didn't turn out to be Mick Jagger. But guess what pal? Only one person did. And we both know he's no day at the beach. Take the good things you've done from this point, forget about the shit and build from there. Don't sweat the losses. Let them go. Throw them out where the tall grass grows."

"James McMurtry, you drive to him, too?" Billy interrupted.

Charlie continued without answering. "Another thing, you can't give a shit about what other people say, think, or do. We all do it, but it's just negative energy. With that, I'm done pontificating."

As the bus rolled west on the Mass Pike, the sun was beginning to set. There was a clear space between the horizon and the purple and orange remains of the sunset. Whenever Billy was on tour and the bus was headed west, he wished the bus could slip through that open space between the colored clouds and the horizon and disappear into the night. He chased and he chased, but the bus never made it before the darkness enveloped both the sky and the bus.

He liked believing in the idea that he was chasing a dream. Whether he was chasing the ultimate performance, composing the ultimate song, reaching the ultimate high, or finding the ultimate relationship, but he wasn't chasing anything, he was constantly running. He was running as fast as he could but he was simply staying in place. Constantly running from his father, his mistakes, his relationships; he knew he was running from anything and everything. His reality was that after running all this time he wasn't any closer to anything he loved and not a single, fucking inch further from the part of him he was running from. *"This running ain't no freedom." Maybe David Gray was right* Billy thought.

Chapter 27

LAST DAY—By line Margie Markowitz, New York—District Attorney McBride held a news conference late yesterday. McBride said an arrest in the murder of Belinda Caruso is imminent. The Post believes, but has been unable to officially confirm, that the suspect is Billy Sunday. Billy Sunday and his band DROWN are expected to play the Acme Lounge in New York's Greenwich Village this evening. Above the front-page story were two pictures. The first was of Billy Sunday, looking a little disheveled and a little worse for wear. The press, always pursuing its own agenda, was trying to add a slant to the story. Next to Billy's picture was DA McBride's official headshot.

It was no wonder Jimmy had slept until 8:00 am, he thought as he read Markowitz' story. McBride never woke Kelly up when it was good news. He'd intended on getting up early but the pace of the investigation combined with his age had him feeling a little run down.

Late last night back at the squad room, they received a call from Danny O'Connell who informed them that he represented Billy Sunday. He let them know that Billy was willing to come in voluntarily for questioning. O'Connell was an up and comer in New York City's criminal defense community and he'd worked for one of the big Law firms, where it was all about billable hours and becoming partner as fast as possible, after graduating from Suffolk Law School. He'd defended white-collar crimes, bank and securities fraud and a couple of bank robbery cases. He had some limited success which may not seem like much on the surface, but given the fact that all his clients were guilty, limited success was tremendously successful in his business. Danny had a certain swagger that the press loved and in a case like Billy Sunday's they'd eat it right up.

Jimmy was hoping to keep McBride out of the loop in relation to Billy's initial questioning. Kelly was against informal questioning from the beginning but O'Connell wanted to make a deal. Billy would come in voluntarily for questioning and then be released in O'Connell's custody so he could play the Acme Lounge gig that night. If he was to be arrested, O'Connell would surrender him within twenty-four hours of being notified by the NYPD. Jimmy knew that to make a deal like that would require the DA's approval.

McBride initially said no to the deal. If, after the questioning, there was enough to hold him she wasn't about to let him go. O'Connell's response was to take a walk because in his opinion there wasn't enough evidence for even a warrant. After the New York gig, Billy would be on his way to the next city and would then have to be tracked down and extradited. McBride reluctantly agreed to the questioning outlined by O'Donell when presented with this scenario and Jimmy gave his word to O'Connell that they had a deal and were in agreement on how Billy's surrender was to go down. Jimmy knew McBride had no intention of keeping her word but he had every intention of keeping his end of the bargain.

Billy jumped at the knock at the door. He had no idea what time it was or for that matter where he was. *Knock, knock, knock, that incessant, fucking knocking,* he thought as the hollow sound reverberated through his brain.

"Billy, get up. We have to go meet O'Connell," Dickie's voice echoed through the door. He was hoping somebody had the wrong room. "Yeah, yeah, yeah," moaned Billy as he rolled over and began to fumble around looking for some sweat pants. He quickly glance around to see if anyone was with him. *Good,* He thought, *nobody else here. Bad, couldn't find any sweat pants—Ying and Yang, good and bad, that's my life.*

"Listen, tell her to hurry up and put her clothes on," said Dickie.

"I'm coming, Dickie, hold your horses. Don't go get your pee all hot." As Billy began moving toward the door, out of the corner of his eye he glanced a line of something and a rolled up dollar bill on the hotel room desk.

"Fuck," he said to himself. He changed direction, tightened the bill's roll as bent over and snorted the powder. Snapping his head back, *Good*, he thought, *at least some coke in there*. He swiped the top of the desk clean with his fingertips then licked them on his way to the door.

"All right, all right", he barked, opening the door. Dickie's first response was to burst out laughing, but soon realized there wasn't anything funny about what he was looking at. Billy was standing in the doorway wearing only boxer shorts with the Rolling Stones infamous tongue printed at the fly. His skin was pasty white, he had dark circles under his eyes and his hair was a tussled mess that ran amok atop his head.

"You look hung-over to the bejesus!" Dickie said, incredulously.

"Wasn't looking too good, but I was feeling real well," quoting Keith Richards.

"Keith tell you that?" Dickie asked, smirking. "Could be worse, I guess. Keith looks like that all the time."

"Blasphemy against God himself and so early in the morning," retorted Billy. "You going to give me that?" asked Billy, pointing to the big teacup in Dickie's hand.

"Fuck you, go out to the bus and make your own," was Dickie's reply. Billy grabbed the cup out of his hand and took a sip. The warm elixir felt good as it worked its way through his body. "Jasmine, too," said Billy, smiling and blowing over the rim of the cup.

"Listen, I don't even bring tea to the woman I'm screwing, never mind you, it's definitely not in my contract."

"Dickie, you're a gentleman and a scholar, thanks," as he rooted around for something to wear that wasn't wrinkled.

"For the tea, don't mention it, C'mon, get ready, already."

"Give me fifteen minutes," said Billy, "I'll meet you in the lobby."

As Billy stood under the hot water steaming out of the shower, he wished he'd taken Dickie's advice the night before. He should have stayed in the hotel room all night. As it was, he stayed until 10:00 pm. "Billy could resist everything but temptation." Was one of his father's favorite quotes. At ten o'clock he took a taxi down to the village. Like a lot of almost famous people, he was seldom recognized outside the context of his profession, but right now he was probably as famous as he was ever was going to be, at least for being a musician, given the New York Post's front page's media attention. Being a Monday night, Billy knew his friend Candicita was bartending at a little joint called The Bowery. Candicita's friend's called her Candi. Billy thought she looked and tasted as sweet as candy, which is what kept him coming back whenever he was in town. As he walked through the front door, he was faced with a small rectangular bar. Candi was serving a customer at the other end of the bar which gave him a perfect view of her backside. Her blonde hair flowed down just below her shoulders. A black cotton V-neck T-shirt was stretched tight across her chest and she wore a pair of lime green leather pants that rode low across her hips and tight across her perfect, taut ass. Her black leather, high heeled cowboy boots made her appear taller than she actually was. She was up on her tiptoes serving the customer across the bar. Billy was going to have to remember that position for later, if there was a later. Behind Candi and the customer she was serving was a small well-worn, wooden dance floor which led to a small bandstand where there were instruments, *but thankfully no band* thought Billy.

When Candi turned away from the far end of the bar with the customer's cash in hand, she did a double take. At the other end of the bar, Billy was dressed in his ripped, faded blue jeans, a black Pooka Stew T-shirt, blue, hand tooled leather cowboy boots and a Red Sox cap pulled low as he gave her a wink. She sauntered right past the cash register, right up to the edge of the bar and as she lifted herself on her tiptoes she lifted his cap and gave him a tender kiss on the forehead. He gently took her face in his hands. She had high cheekbones, a cute button nose and soft lips that outlined her perfect mouth but it was her emerald green, bedroom eyes that got Billy every time. "How you doing, beautiful?"

"Lousy," Candi replied, pouting her lips.

"Tell me, what's up?" Billy asked.

"Last week I had a date with this guy and we ended up at my place and I thought we really got along."

"Did you sleep with him?" Billy interrupted.

"Oh yeah, If you want to call that sleeping," murmured Candi, narrowing those bedroom eyes.

"*You don't need Viagra with a girl like Candi,*" Billy thought.

"So what happened?" asked Billy.

"Well, he promised he'd call, but the next night he left with another woman who he wrote this really pretty song for, but of course he may have murdered her, so...," Candi said, trying not to smile. "Now, a week later, he's infamous and he's forgotten all about me."

"Ah, another sad story in the big city," said Billy. "Why don't you knock off early and let me make it all better?"

"Fuck you," she snapped, no longer role playing but still laughing. "I thought you were getting into town tomorrow night? You've become quite the celebrity around these parts."

"I came in early to try and avoid the media. I've also got an appointment to speak with the DA tomorrow." he answered.

"Sounds like fun," she replied. "Don't get me involved, Billy, it was bad enough when that bitch made her little scene at the showcase the other night. When I heard she was dead, I said to myself, couldn't happen to a nicer girl."

"Don't worry," said Billy, "there's no reason for you to be involved. Seriously, what time do you get out of here?"

"My boyfriend's in town, Billy."

"Boyfriend? Boyfriend!? I don't remember you mentioning a boyfriend when the three of us were going at it last week."

"Yeah, well, he wasn't around." she said.

"What's this guy do that suddenly you're the faithful sit at home type?" asked Billy.

"You're such an asshole, Billy. He's an investment banker. They're the new rock stars and they make a ton of money which they actually manage to hold onto for the most part. Besides, when they leave, they actually come back when they say they will and act like they're still in love with you."

"What a novel concept," Billy said sarcastically. "Where's the excitement in that?"

"Oh, I don't know Billy, a little stability and sanity may not be all that exciting but it's a lot less stressful."

"I bet he's not very good in bed, is he?" At this point, he was ready to go down fighting, Candi just looked too good. The way things were going it may be the last piece of ass, female ass that is, that he would have for a while.

"Maybe not as good as you, Billy. You happy? I said it, Asshole. You guys are all the same, measuring everything by the size of your dicks!"

Billy smiled wide, "Yes, I am happy you said it. Let's get out of here."

"Got your own hotel room?" she asked.

"Yep, I'm a big rock star, don't forget."

"Got any drugs?"

"C'mon, look who you're talking to," he said with his arms outstretched.

"Give me an hour and I'll have this place closed up," she replied. "I'm too easy."

"No, you're just horny."

"I must be to put up with you. Just you and me tonight, though, all right?"

"Wouldn't have it any other way." He grinned.

"For Christ sakes, how long does it take for a guy to get a drink around here?"

Unnoticed by Billy and Candi, the patron she had been serving when Billy arrived had left his barstoool and walked over at the pay phone. After calling information first, he put fifty cents in the pay phone and after three rings, a male voice answered, "Page six, Margie Markowitz' line."

"Yeah, hi, I'm at The Bowery Bar down in the village."

"Yes?"

"Billy Sunday just walked in and is going at it hot and heavy with the blonde bartender."

"Thank you very much," said the male voice, just before hanging up the phone.

Billy began sipping the Heineken Candi had slipped him as she began to give the few hardcore customers left last call. The gentleman who'd made the call returned from the phone and sat down next to Billy. "How you doing?" he asked Billy. The man was small and thin and dressed in jeans and a navy blue sweatshirt, he wasn't unkempt in appearance, but from his spotty complexion and drawn features he appeared to be no stranger to alcohol. From his droopy eyes to his slow, interrupted speech, he seemed to have been at the Bowery for a while. *Maybe since about 1982,* was Billy's thought as he almost laughed out loud.

"Not bad for an overweight, washed up Irish kid. You?"

"Fine, just fine," the man replied. "Say, ah, you're ah, that musician, Billy Sunday."

Billy assumed that if the guy was someone he should be watching out for Candi would have warned him. She simply smiled at Billy as she continued the process of cleaning up the bar.

"Yeah, that's right, I'm him," Billy thought for a moment about denying it, but that would only make him look guilty since the guy obviously recognized him. Billy figured that if you were at a point in life where you had to start denying who or what you were, you might as well be dead, for all practical purposes.

"Listen, hey, my sons in a band, you know, and I was wondering if you could fill me in on the business side of things, you know, like how a record deal works, you know?"

Internally Billy breathed a sigh of relief. He was figuring the guy for either a member of the fifth estate staking him out, or some closet wannabe serial murderer looking for camaraderie. Buoyed by the fact that all the guy wanted was a little insight on the music business, he was more than happy to oblige. "Okay," he started. "Let's say you get a major record deal." The bar patron was listening intently. "First, you'll get an advance. Let's say one million, for the sake of argument."

"Dollars?" the stranger asked, rhetorically. "So, you're an instant millionaire."

"Not exactly," he continued. "Here's how it goes. Right off the top, your manager gets twenty percent or two hundred grand."

"For what?" the man asked.

"Never really figured that out," said Billy, "they just do."

"So, you're down to eight hundred thou."

"Eight hundred G, that's right," said Billy. "Now, the lawyers get say fifty G for you know, lawyer stuff," he kept on, trying to anticipate the guy's next question. "That leaves seven hundred and fifty thousand. Out of that, you need to pay, say, two hundred and fifty thousand for the record album. Which leaves you with five hundred grand. Then, if you do a video, which nobody will probably ever see, that will run you about one hundred grand, so now, what are we down to?"

"Four hundred grand," was the man's reply.

"Yeah, that's about right, four hundred G. Now, say the band needs equipment, clothes, you know, shit like that. You're looking at another hundred grand, easy. If there's five guys in the band and they get sixty grand a piece which leaves them forty grand after taxes."

"For how long?" the man inquired. "You know, until you get your next check?"

"For how long? How about forever? In most cases there is no other next check!"

"Huh?"

"This is actually the best part," he continued, really into it now. "That original one million is recoupable from royalties." He could see right away that he had lost the guy. "You want another beer?" Billy waved his empty bottle in the air towards Candi and with his other hand, he signaled two. This kept the guys attention, at least. "Where was I? Oh yeah, recoupable. That means if the album sells, you have to pay back the one million."

"But if it doesn't sell, you don't have to pay the money back?" said the man wiping the top of the fresh beer bottle with a bar napkin.

"That's right," said Billy, "recoupable, not returnable. And the royalty rate is usually around a buck."

"One dollar?"

"One dollar per record sold."

"You're shitting me? Right?" the man said with uncertainty.

"And it only gets better," replied Billy. "If the artist recoups at a dollar a record, he'd have to sell a million records."

"CD's?" the man interrupted.

"Yeah, CD's. The industry still uses the term records but that includes CD's," explained Billy. "So, you'd have to sell one million records just to break even. But the record company grosses ten bucks a CD, so they would only have to sell one hundred thousand to gross a million bucks. The final capper is that out of a thousand or more albums released last year only about a dozen made it to platinum. Of those dozen, probably ten were by established artists."

"So, a measly forty G, huh?" Billy's new friend pondered between swigs.

"There are some publishing royalties for the songwriter that's paid differently, but that's basically it," surmised Billy.

"So let me see if I get this straight," said the man, trying to focus his eyes on Billy. "The manager makes money. The lawyer makes money. The studio makes money. And the label makes money. So as long as you're not the musician, it's a pretty good racket."

"Huh?" said Billy, not sure he heard the man correctly.

"I mean, so long as your not the artist, you know, the guy who creates the stuff, it's a pretty good business."

"I guess that's about right. I knew I was getting screwed, but I never really looked at it that way," said Billy.

"So you're basically broke?"

"Yeah, basically."

"What about the forty large? Long gone?"

"Long gone. You know the story, fast women and slow horses, a bad combination."

"Well, thanks for the info." The man stood up, polished what was left of his beer and made his way out the door.

"You all right?" asked Candi, seeing Billy alone.

"Yeah, yeah, fine. Are we out of here?"

Around midnight, Billy and Candi grabbed a taxi out in front of The Bowery. Billy knew he'd pay tomorrow for this decision, but he figured, *Hey, might as well go out with your boots on-or off, as it were.* As they rode back up to Times Square, Candi snuggled over to him in the back seat of the cab. "What happened to Belinda?"

"You've been dying to ask that, haven't you?"

"Yeah, well, I know you didn't do it, Billy."

"Maybe you're sitting here thinking-I'm going to show you a real good time, maybe for the last time."

"Oh, you're going to show me a real good time," said Candi, as she moved her hand casually across his crotch. "And if anyone's going to die tonight, it ain't going to be me," she whispered softly into his ear. Her teasing had its desired effect. In an attempt to get a little cool air, Billy rolled down the window as Candi laughed. After a moment, she turned serious again.

"You weren't in love with her, were you?"

"Yeah, in a way I was, I guess. Or maybe I loved her at one time and pushed her away."

"I know what that feels like."

Billy pretended to ignore her response. "By the end it was like an old sweater. Torn and frayed but still comfortable and warm when you put it on. She just wanted to control things all the time. I don't know, I just couldn't deal anymore."

"Can I give you a woman's point of view even though I know you don't want to hear it? Guys never want to hear it because it hits too close to home."

Billy knew her opinion was coming anyway, *why fight it?* He thought, "Shoot."

"She didn't want to control you. She loved you and just wanted you to love her back. You're one of those guys, Billy, that women fall for over time. When we fall, we fall hard, it just sneaks up on us." The plural reference wasn't lost on him.

"You're cute. Your kind and creative and your definitely funny, you're also pretty good in bed."

"Just pretty good?" This time, Candi pretended to ignore him.

"And when we finally give in and fall in love with you, you leave or you push us away. Then we grow to resent you and end up hating you for it. But you're one of those guys who it's virtually impossible to hate, which aggravates us even more." By now, the taxi had pulled up in front of the Embassy Suites in Times Square.

Candi's gentle diatribe, combined with his own thoughts on the bus ride down, had his mind working on overload. It was true that he'd run away from every relationship at the first sign that things were getting serious, or worse, the curse word of all curse words: commitment. After her dead on analysis he figured she wasn't going to come up to the room but she surprised him, kissing him softly on the cheek, her lips warm and damp and said, "C'mon baby, I know your hurtin' so let me heal it." With that, she took his hand and led him out of the taxi. Once they were through the lobby and in the elevator she fell against him, pushing her body up against his as she opened her mouth and kissed him passionately—on the lips first, then his ears, and down his neck which she began biting lightly. She rubbed her hands up and down the sides of his legs and then slowly placed her hands between them and with one hand she massaged him while with the other hand she massaged herself. When the elevator stopped at his floor they spilled out into the hall and walked each other to the door. As he fumbled for the passkey she remained draped all over him and once the door was opened they tumbled right into the bedroom, disrobing each other in the process. Candi's skin felt soft and smooth against his body and it was as if her skin held an electrical charge as his body grew more alive with each touch. She slowly began kissing her way down his chest and the hairline that traveled down to the place between his hips where she took him gently into her mouth while he ran his fingers roughly through her hair.

After a few minutes, he said softly, "Climb on top of me, baby." Once she was on top they rocked back and forth together until Candi began whispering in his ear. "That's it baby, right there. Don't stop, don't stop, oh baby, I'm gonna come, come with me baby, come with me." And he did.

She collapsed on his chest, breathing heavy but still kissing his neck softly. As soon as they finished he started to think how nice it would be to have this with her every night: meaningful conversation, meaningful sex and with a person who actually meant something to him. Why couldn't he bring himself around to making it happen? Clearly, from the way she spoke in the taxi, she was interested as well. Again, the inclination to leave began to stir. Maybe those initial thoughts were because he knew a relationship with Candi, at this point in time, was impossible. Before he could give it another thought she slipped back down his body and they continued to make love until about 5:00 am and then did a few lines. *Nothing like narcotics after great sex*, they were both thinking. Billy must have fallen asleep because the next thing he knew Dickie was banging on the door.

He came out of the shower a little more awake and on the pillow was a note on the hotel stationary: *Thanks for a great night. Love you. Good luck tonight and hope to see you after the show, XXX Candi,* he smiled. A night of great sex could always compensate for a lack of sleep. He dressed, whistling The Grateful Dead's, "Ripple", "If I knew the way I would take you home," Jerry Garcia sang softly in his head, as he left the hotel room.

Chapter 28

Billy was going over last Wednesday's chain of events with Danny O'Connell in his uptown law office. Danny was dressed in a sharp, navy blue pinstriped suit, red suspenders, matching red silk tie and a white button down shirt. Dickie was also there dressed in tan slacks, tan, Cole Hahn loafers and a maroon cotton shirt. Billy had on new blue jeans, black and white python cowboy boots, and a Hause of Howe, "Hang the Rich t-shirt. Dickie noticed that today Billy had a little bounce in his step and that his spirits were higher than they had been yesterday. He'd been down in the hotel lobby at 5:00 am, as he was an early riser, and noticed Candi leaving the hotel. Christ, she could put a bounce in his step just thinking about having her in his bed. He liked Candi because she seemed to actually care about Billy, unlike the rest of his groupies of which Dickie considered Belinda one, record company president or not.

Danny, Dickie, and Billy were walking down 5th Avenue together toward mid-town and as they approached the police station an unmarked cruiser pulled up along side of them. Behind the wheel was Jimmy Gerard. He rolled down the passenger window and said, "Get in and hurry."

Being closest to the curb Billy opened the black sedan's rear passenger door and the three of them got into the backseat.

"We haven't formally met, I'm Detective Jimmy Gerard," said Jimmy as he glanced back in his rear view mirror. "And you're the infamous Billy Sunday, I take it?" Jimmy couldn't help but notice the dark circles under his eyes and that his pupils were slightly constricted. *Not stoned totally, but he's had a little something to take the edge off,* Jimmy thought. He didn't blame him. He would have wanted to do the same thing if he was in his position.

Danny and Dickie said, "Hello." Billy simply nodded.

"Do you mind if I ask what's up?" asked Danny.

"Somebody tipped off the press that you and your client were coming in," replied Jimmy.

"Any idea who?" inquired Dickie.

"Take a guess," responded Jimmy.

"The bitchstrict attorney," said Danny.

Jimmy was actually a little taken aback with his own use of the adjective for McBride since he wasn't aware his nickname for the D.A. had made it to the street. That meant it had probably made its way back to McBride. *Who gives a shit?* thought Jimmy. The way McBride was handling this investigation only confirmed what he knew all along. McBride was about as bright as a nightlight.

As they came within a block of the station they saw the media trucks were everywhere. It was similar to the scene in front of the Paradise two nights ago but being New York City, the scene was bigger like surreal. After making a right and continuing halfway down the block he made a left into the alley where he stopped in front of an automatic garage door. The four of them sat in silence as the garage door slowly opened and the car eased into the motor pool that was located below the station house. He pulled the sedan close to a fire door that lead inside the station house. He opened his door and everyone else followed suit as he motioned them through the fire door. They crossed a hallway and gathered in the waiting elevator. There was an uncomfortable silence as the elevator doors closed in front of them. Dickie broke the tension by saying, "Detective Gerard, thank you for sparing us from the ambush."

"Yeah, well, I gave Danny my word and I intend to keep it. This is looking more and more like my last stand and I intend to go out the way I came in," was his response.

"With a little honor and dignity?" asked Danny, finishing his statement.

"Yeah, something like that, something just like that," said Jimmy. "But actually I was also thinking upright under my own power."

"That was particularly generous gesture in light of the reception you received up in Boston. Which, if I must admit, was mostly my doing," informed Dickie.

"No problem. Dickie, is it? As far as Boston goes, you were just being loyal to your boy here. Loyalty being the most valuable of all qualities," continued Jimmy. "Love is stronger, but love is a fickle emotion that can't be controlled. Loyalty, now that's a conscience decision every time. There's no greater quality in a person than blind loyalty. The BPD are good guys and protecting one of their own is their job. It was a game of cat and mouse and I would have been highly surprised if we actually got any face time. That being said, I wasn't happy with the way things went down but I can respect why it was done. That's kind of why I picked you up, like I said, I gave Mr. O'Connell my word, no media, and I want to keep my word."

As the elevator made its way up through the stationhouse, Billy began getting nervous, though anxious was a better description of how he was feeling. The elevator door opened on the third floor and as Jimmy held the elevator door open with his hand he motioned for the three occupants to exit. He opened the squad room door next and waved his small entourage through where they stopped and waited. *Even when they come in willingly, they come grudgingly*, Jimmy thought. He stepped purposefully on and the three followed past the four metal desks to the back of the squad room where he opened another gray door to a square room approximately ten by fourteen feet where a gray metal table sat in the center surrounded by four chairs. Kelly Agis was seated in one of the chairs furthest from the door and she was dressed in a tailored, black pinstripe business suit. She rose from her seat as they entered the room.

Billy couldn't help but sneak a glance at her as he walked into the room. Not every girl was attracted to him but the ones who were usually gave him a certain look that he had come to know. He couldn't really describe the look, but he felt the familiar feeling from Kelly as she looked at him for just a split second. Once she was before him he couldn't stop his eyes from taking a walk all over her. He noticed how her black heels accentuated her athletic thighs which brought him to her thin waist and fit upper body and then to her pretty face framed by her flowing red hair.

For an instant, he wondered if she was wearing a garter belt and he liked the image he created of her in one. *Some are sicker than others,* he thought. Since he'd initially entered with his head down she hadn't noticed his wandering eyes. She had been doing the same thing to Billy which made her feel like a nervous schoolgirl. Behind her was a one-way glass window and the room resembled the interrogation room seen weekly on the television show Law & Order.

Danny O'Connell knew Beth McBride was behind the one-way glass and that by now she was fuming that they had somehow thwarted her planned media coup. She'd really be bullshit when she found out it was Gerard who'd circumvented her plans. Gerard, however, was the only cop who wasn't afraid of McBride. Gerard went back out of the interrogation to get another chair for Dickie which he placed in the corner of the room.

As they were all seating themselves with McBride observing she asked, "Who's the guy in the corner?"

The uniformed captain next to her answered, "I believe that's his road manager."

"He is the one responsible for fucking us up in Boston?" She didn't wait for an answer. Her initial instinct was to have him removed but thought, *Fuck it. We'll show him how things are done in the big city. Turnabout is fair play.*

Once they were all seated O'Connell immediately went over the previously agreed upon guidelines. His strategy was risky, particularly in light of what Billy had revealed to him earlier in his office but word had been passed down to him through the grapevine that McBride was going to arrest and indict someone soon. Furthermore, that someone was going to be his client, Billy Sunday. While Billy didn't have an alibi and was going to voluntarily put himself at the scene O'Connell figured they'd take a shot at agreeing to the interview and maybe Billy would be able to raise some inconsistencies in another suspect's story, thereby, shifting the focus off of him. What did Billy have to lose? If they were planning on arresting him, they were going to arrest him, regardless of what he had to say.

"Okay, we are going on the record with questions limited to Mr.

Sunday and his relationship with the deceased Belinda Caruso," O'Connell began. Kelly hit the tape recorder that was sitting in the center of the table. She and Jimmy decided beforehand, as a tactical maneuver, to allow her to handle the interview figuring that Billy would be more comfortable talking to a woman.

"Good morning. I'm Detective Agis here with Detective Jimmy Gerard. Today is the eleventh of April. Interview with William McCarthy, Jr., also known as Billy Sunday. Also present are Mr. Sunday's attorney, Daniel O'Connell and his business associate William Poole. All right, Mr. Sunday, did you know the deceased, Belinda Caruso and if so, could you please tell us how you became acquainted?"

Billy told the story of how he and Belinda had met and about their on again, off again relationship.

"How would you describe your relationship with Belinda?" Kelly asked.

"Fucked up," said Billy in an attempt at humor. He managed to get a smile out of Kelly but O'Connell's glance indicated he wasn't as amused by his glib response. In fact, O'Connell was downright bullshit. At that moment, the severity of the situation finally began to sink in for Billy. "No, seriously? We were friendly and through everything we'd been through together we remained friends. As far as our business relationship, that always remained professional."

"Moving on to last Wednesday, April fifth, strike that," said Kelly. "Were you in New York last week, Mr. Sunday?"

"Yes." Taking Danny's advice, he kept his answers as brief as possible.

"When did you get to New York?"

"Last Tuesday afternoon, a week ago, I guess."

"I don't want you to guess, Mr. Sunday."

"Last Tuesday."

At this point, all the parties knew that this was going to be slow going. Kelly and Jimmy had expected as much. Billy was pretty well educated and had very competent counsel. Kelly continued. "What did you do when you arrived in New York?"

Danny interjected. "Let's keep it specific to Belinda Caruso, Detective. This isn't supposed to be a fishing exhibition."

"Did you see Belinda Caruso last Tuesday after you arrived in New York?"

Danny interrupted again. "I'll let my client answer, but please keep the questions specific, Detective." With that, he motioned for Billy to answer.

"No, I did not see Belinda on Tuesday."

"Were you still in New York on Wednesday, Mr. Sunday?"

"Yes."

Jimmy rubbed his face in his hands. This was going to be a long morning.

"Did you speak with Belinda Caruso last Wednesday?"

"Yes."

"What did you discuss?"

"Well, I had a showcase scheduled that night for Belinda's record label. She wanted to make sure everything was all set and she told me she was going to bring some Indies to the show, so she wanted to be sure that we played all the radio tracks." After answering, he looked over at Jimmy. Jimmy's facial impression gave him the impression that he might as well have answered the question in a foreign language. Kelly, on the other hand, seemed to have some understanding as to what he was talking about. He decided to clarify things. "Indies are independent record promoters. Belinda said she would see me at the show."

"Did you see her at the show?" Kelly continued.

"I first saw her when I was on stage. We didn't get a chance to talk before the show."

"Did you get a chance to speak to her after the show?"

"Yes."

"What did you talk to her about?"

"How she thought the show went. Who was present from the Industry. Stuff like that."

"Did you and Belinda discuss anything in private?"

"No, not really." Because of the way Belinda had him cornered at the time of the argument, Billy didn't see Little Stevie eavesdropping on the conversation. His lie to both O'Connell and the police about his confrontation with Belinda, he figured, was only by omission and therefore not a real lie.

"Did you leave the club with Belinda?"

"No."

"Do you happen to know who she left with?"

"No idea."

"Did you see her again?"

"Yes."

"When?"

"Later that night."

"Wednesday night?"

"Wednesday night."

"What time?"

"Around midnight," Billy wasn't giving it up easy.

"Where?"

"At her office on the Upper East Side."

"What happened?"

Danny had warned Billy to tread lightly around this question. Any admission of illicit drug use could be enough to detain him.

"We talked for a little while."

Kelly pushed forward. "Did you have sex with her?"

"Yes." The question and answer had made it seem so cold, so emotionless. *That was almost how it had felt.* Was Billy's thought. The way Belinda had demanded sex made it an act void of passion, though still pleasurable; the opposite of the way he had felt last night with Candi.

"Did she perform oral sex?"

Billy hesitated. O'Connell nodded for him to answer.

"Yes."

"Did you ejaculate?"

"During oral sex?" He couldn't hide his surprise by the question.

"During oral sex, yes, did you ejaculate?"

"No," said Billy. He began shifting uncomfortably in his seat. The grouping of the questions, the subject matter, and the weakening of the narcotics had begun to make him antsy. He realized his body language undoubtedly would make him look guilty to some police shrink observing through the one-way glass. He was partially right. Agis, Gerard and McBride had all begun to take note of his physical reaction to the questioning. Luckily for him, so had O'Connell.

"Let's go off," said Danny.

O'Connell leaned over and whispered to Billy. "Are you all right?"

"No, I need a break," He responded with mental exhaustion weighing on him

"The bathroom is out the door to the left," Gerard offered.

Billy left the room and walked into the bathroom with the atmosphere of the interrogation room enveloped around him. He pulled a mustard colored pill from his pocket and licked the coating off the pill, dried it with a paper towel, broke the pill in half, placed it in a bill, crushed it with a credit card, poured the powder onto the sink and snorted the line with the bill. Using in a police station. This was most likely on one of those checklists used to determine if you have a problem with drugs. The checklists say that if you answer yes to one or more question-you have a drug problem. Billy could answer yes to all of them and began wondering if the police station had cameras installed in the bathrooms.

Fuck it, He thought. Getting high was probably the least of his problems and a possession charge would be a blessing since he may be going down for murder. He washed his hands and face while avoiding the mirror in front of him. He'd worked his way out of jackpots before, but this one looked pretty bleak and was more than just a jackpot. How was he going to prove he was innocent to someone else when he'd had sex with Belinda shortly before her demise? He eventually looked in the mirror noticing his face looked drawn, pale and that there were dark circles under his eyes. He'd lost enough weight that it was visible in his face. He was looking like a junkie, again. *Fuck it*, he thought for the second time. I'm paying O'Connell to come up with a reasonable doubt. This was supposed to be the farewell tour that he'd spent the last two years working so hard toward. He wanted to show everyone that he had persevered, that he had overcome all the odds and succeeded where others had failed. Maybe he had really pursued this life because it fueled his addiction and allowed him to run from everyone and everything. What was it about him that he continued to run from something and not to something? Constantly running yet never getting anywhere. The answer, as much as he didn't like it, was that he was running from himself. He'd been running from his thoughts and feelings as long as he could remember. *Enough self-*

abuse, he decided. Now wasn't the time or the place. He exited the bathroom and re-entered the interrogation room.

No one had moved or spoken in his absence.

"Can we get back on record?" asked Kelly, all business. O'Connell nodded and she pressed the tape recorder. Before the interview started, Jimmy took note that Billy had returned with a little more color and his eyes a little glassier and appeared to be a little calmer and less fidgety. He was moving as if he were in slow motion. There was no question he was on something and he made a mental note to see if he could somehow tie Billy to the drugs at the murder scene and then maybe connect the murder to the drugs, somehow. *I should take another look at the autopsy,* Jimmy thought.

"All right. Did you have intercourse with Mrs. Caruso?"

"Yes."

"Did you have anal intercourse?"

"Yes."

"Did you ejaculate during intercourse?"

"Yes."

"Inside her?"

"Yes."

"Was Mrs. Caruso tied up?"

"What?" this question stopped him in his tracks and he appeared genuinely surprised.

"Was she tied up?" repeated Kelly.

"To what?" he asked.

At this point, O'Connell stepped in. "I believe the answer is no. Correct, Billy?"

"Correct. Belinda was not tied up to anything."

"What happened after you had sex?"

"You know, we hung out for a while and then I left. I told her I was headed back to Boston in the morning to rehearse for the WXKL show."

"Was Belinda upset about that?"

"No, she knows that I have to work."

"Was she alive when you left?"

"Of course she was fucking alive when I left. Are we done?" He'd had enough.

Sensing any further answers would only be counterproductive given his client's present temperament, O'Connell said, "We're done, Billy. We're done."

O'Connell half expected the two detectives to read Billy his rights, then and there, but no one moved. Apparently, they didn't feel they had quite enough or that there was still some conflicting evidence and/or testimony, which for Billy, was good. Or at least it was better than the alternative. O'Connell asked Billy and Dickie to step outside. Understanding Billy's uneasiness, Dickie said they would meet O'Connell down in the motor pool, if that was acceptable. Gerard said that was fine, knowing this would piss off McBride even further since she would have preferred to see Billy in handcuffs where she could parade him out in front of the media. Alternatively, she could deal with him leaving a free man, so long as he walked the media gauntlet just outside the front door. The back door wasn't acceptable and the motor pool entrance was out of the question.

As far as Gerard was concerned, Billy going out the front door wasn't part of the deal he'd made with O'Connell.

After Billy and Dickie left the room O'Connell turned to Agis and Gerard and asked, point blank. "Where do we stand?"

Jimmy took over. "Your client is still our primary suspect. He didn't give us anything that would clear him and further implicated himself by admitting to being at the scene just prior to the time of death. He gave conflicting testimony that we need to check into." Danny took this for what it was. They thought Billy was lying about something.

"Fair enough," said Danny, unclear about what Jimmy was talking about with regard to conflicting testimony. "All right, I'd like to reach some agreement in the event you decide to arrest my client." These types of arrangements weren't unusual when an attorney knew his client was about to be arrested or indicted by a grand jury. He would try and iron out plans with the authorities for the client's peaceful surrender.

"What do you have in mind?" asked Gerard.

"Knowing that the DA would prefer an arrest on national television, I'd prefer pretty much any alternative," said O'Connell.

"So would I," agreed Gerard.

"Well, seeing how we don't know at this point if we're even going to arrest your client, I think it may be premature to make such an arrangement," Kelly interjected, reluctantly carrying the DA's water on the issue. Jimmy didn't mind. In fact, he respected her for doing her job.

"Let's hope that's the case since after all, my client is innocent," declared O'Connell.

"Look, Counselor, your client may not be guilty, but he's far from innocent. For all our sake I hope if he is tried for this crime, the jury doesn't convict him for those crimes for which he is guilty," said Jimmy.

"Well, since we're all here, why don't we make a contingency plan in the event he is arrested," said Danny.

"Fine," said Kelly. Having put up her token resistance to appease McBride, she could now agree with what was the right thing to do.

"As I'm sure you're aware, his band has a show tonight in the village. He's not going anywhere before then. If you decide you want to hold him I'll surrender him after the show. Just call my cell phone anytime. Also, I'd prefer he be held overnight somewhere in solitary, as opposed to being incarcerated with New York's rank and file arrested," he requested.

"Agreed," said Kelly.

"Agreed," Gerard chimed in.

O'Connell rose and thanked them both. "I'll show myself out. Give me regards to the District Attorney if you happent to see her." He exited the squad room and entered the waiting elevator then disappeared behind the closing doors.

When the doors opened at the motor pool, before O'Connell could step out, he was intercepted by Billy. "Well, how did it go?" Billy asked as he stood in font of the opening at elevator doors.

"Well, you told the truth as far as I know but I don't think they believed you, to be honest. They implied you lied about a few things," responded Danny.

Shit, Billy thought, *had somebody seen the argument? They never asked him if anyone else was there.* The waning narcotic high was beginning to turn to paranoia.

"If I were you," said Danny, "I wouldn't buy any green bananas today." He was attempting to make light of the situation but given his clients present state of mind it hit Billy hard. Suddenly, the exhilaration from the night with Candi that had fueled him up to this point was totally gone. So too, was the anger he'd felt while being questioned. The mellow high was rapidly dissipating while the only thing he was left feeling was an overwhelming sense of dread and gloom.

While he and his attorney were conversing downstairs, McBride strutted into the interrogation room just as Jimmy and Kelly were about to leave. Dressed in a gray business suit and a powder blue blouse with her blonde hair and make-up she was picture perfect, *she looked press conference ready*, thought Jimmy.

"I want him picked up on-stage tonight. I'll have the media outside the club when you take him out," Declared McBride.

"Are you fucking crazy?" replied Jimmy. "You know that's not the deal we just made."

"Listen," said McBride, staring angrily at Jimmy, "thanks primarily to you, I've been reacting to the media this whole investigation and it's about time I get proactive. He lied about the fight at the club, lied about tying her up, and I think he lied about killing her. If you two don't want the collar, I'll get a couple of detectives who'd like the biggest arrest of the year." With that, she spun around on her heels and headed out the door.

"Fucking…, began Jimmy.

"Don't start," Kelly interrupted. "Let's figure out how we're going to handle this arrest."

Chapter 29

Billy sat in the back of the bus with the other guys and he was pretty lit. The tour book showed they had two hours until set time with the bus parked in front of The Lions Den, another music club in the village. The media had commandeered the street where the Acme Lounge was located so the Drown tour bus was perfectly camouflaged for the time being, just another tour bus idling in front of another music club. Billy was thinking that Dickie was quite proficient at this cloak and dagger thing. *Maybe he was some sort of spy in his past life? Or maybe he was a road manager guru able to adapt and handle any situation thrown at his precious cargo; the band.* Billy was trying and succeeding at numbing himself to the cold, harsh realities surrounding him. Dickie was more than a little concerned because Billy wasn't looking good physically and he worried he might be over-doing it, not intentionally but unintentionally on purpose.

With an hour to go, Dickie left the guys on the bus and headed over to the club, trying to avoiding the media as best he could, which was a difficult task as the reporters were everywhere. The Acme Lounge had a red door that was centered between two picture windows. The ground floor, which was actually on an upper level, was a long narrow restaurant. The butcher-block tables were relatively full for a Tuesday night as Dickie walked through the restaurant. The white walls were adorned with modern art; strange shapes and photos containing bright colors. Dickie didn't care much for the art. The bar was located in the rear right corner of the restaurant with barstools that were full with twenty-somethings, but there was no one standing. Dickie glanced at his watch and noted it was 10:00 pm. He handed over the band's guest list to the bartender and asked that he give it to the manager then made his way back toward the front of the establishment. Just before arriving at the entrance door he made a right and he went down two narrow flights of wooden stairs. There was a small table staffed with a ticket taker at the bottom and Dickie flashed his laminated badge from around his neck before making a quick right and passing through a small hall/ante room and made a left. There was a small bar on his left and on his right was a sound booth where Techie was sitting comfortably nursing a Heineken. Dickie put up one forefinger letting Techie know they had one hour until show time. He wasn't aware of Detectives Agis and Gerard's presence as they were partially concealed in the narrow hallway behind the ticket taker. The hallway bypassed the actual room and led to the left of the stage. Even though he didn't physically see the two detectives, he knew they would be around or would be showing up shortly. With no backstage and no rear entrance, he had no idea how he was going to get Billy in and out of the room and he was running out of options. It was really Billy who was out of options. Getting Billy out may not be Dickie's problem according to Danny, via a cell phone call Dickie received before leaving the bus. As yet, there was no word from NYPD which Danny was taking as a bad sign. Gerard was a stand up guy but he wasn't the one who was calling the shots. After saving Billy's ass earlier in the day, McBride was surely going to see that Gerard was kept out of the loop from this point forward or at a minimum to follow her orders or end up behind a desk for the rest of eternity.

Back on the bus, Billy was bouncing on the balls of his feet, wired for sound. The lack of sleep over the past couple of weeks was catching up to him and his nervous energy was only being enhanced by the drugs he was taking. "Tonight, I want to rock from beginning to end, all right, guys?" Billy dictated. Normally, he liked Drown's sets to ebb and flow with each song floating into the next. He liked to allow the highs and lows and the rise and fall of each song to gradually build into a crescendo with the climax reached in the set's last song. The set would then be followed by an encore which would bring the audience back down gently. To him, the set was what he imagined drowning might be like in the beginning-a building concern then a burst of frantic energy and finally peace as one succumbs. This was his philosophy on how to perform live. But tonight, he wanted to put the petal to the metal and rock right through.

With a half an hour to go, Dickie was back on the bus and handing Billy a ticket to his own concert. Charlie opened the bus door and Billy, dressed in jeans with both knees ripped out, including the crotch and patches with skull and crossbones sewn in, a black Delta Spirit T-shirt and a Red Sox cap, hopped off the bus. As he hit the sidewalk, Charlie eased the bus away from the curb and the diesel exhaust consumed him as he crossed the street in the bus' wake. As he turned the corner to the street where the Acme Lounge was located, Charlie was parking the bus across the street from the club's entrance. The media horde did a one hundred and eighty degree turn from the club's entrance and began to lunge forward as soon as the bus came to a complete stop. As Billy walked down the deserted sidewalk he pulled the brim of his hat down and entered the club. Walking in the door he handed the doorman his ticket and ID and entered the building unnoticed by all. He bounded down the two sets of stairs and instead of taking a right at the bottom as Dickie had earlier in the evening, he proceeded straight past the ticket taker. The girl in ticket booth recognized him from the soundcheck the band had completed earlier in the afternoon and she smiled shyly toward him. *Cute, but not my type*, he thought, as he gave her a wink. Heading down the narrow hall he stopped dead in his tracks. Twenty feet in front of him he saw Kelly and Jimmy talking. He made a quick U-turn before they noticed him. Kelly threw a quick glance up the hallway as he disappeared around the corner. She'd caught a figure moving in her peripheral vision but couldn't sure if it had been Billy. Jimmy grabbed her arm as she began to move up the hallway. "After," Jimmy said, "We'll get him after." This enabled Billy to move into the gathering crowd.

Unbeknownst to Billy, the D.A. McBride had begun holding an impromptu press conference on the sidewalk in front of the Acme. The media flock left the bus and returned to their original position in front of the sidewalk listening to McBride, wearing the same outfit she had worn at the interrogation earlier in the day, announcing the imminent arrest of

Billy Sunday in the murder of Belinda Caruso. She was awaiting the suspect's arrival in NYPD custody, "at any moment."

Danny O'Connell was still at his office watching New York's all news channel, Channel 1, when the anchor went live to the Acme Lounge. When he saw McBride he went ballistic. He should have known better than to trust that bitch. Anyone who'd made the mistake of trusting any prosecutor these days got burned. *What could I have possibly been thinking?* He thought. He should have been at the club protecting his client. He grabbed his suit coat from one of the office chairs and headed for the Acme Lounge.

Back at the Acme, Billy wasn't coming through the doors in custody, he was actually making his way through the crowd toward the candle lit stage. A roadie handed him his guitar and a blue beer cup as he hopped the three-foot riser. Coming up from the crowd he had surprised everyone and almost before the crowd knew it, he was seated on his amp and had begun strumming on his guitar. His guitar was loud enough that it could be heard through the open doors upstairs and the sound of his guitar surprised McBride. Initially startled by the sound of music, she quickly composed herself, turned and made a b-line for the door where she ran down the stairs and at the bottom was stopped by one of the club's bouncers.

"Sorry, Ma'am. Filled to capacity. No admittance per the Fire Marshall."

McBride flashed her credentials. "I'm the District Attorney of New York and I have a murder suspect in there."

"Ma'am, I don't care if you're the Queen of England. There's already NYPD in there. If anyone's going to get arrested, I'm sure they can handle it."

"That's the problem," she said out loud but to herself, as she could see it was going to be of no use to protest further.

The bouncer knew who McBride was and why she wanted to go in the club. His obligation, the way he saw it, was to the musicians and not the fucking cops and certainly not the DA's office.

At about the time same McBride was headed back up the stairs the band was making their way to the stage. Once settled they immediately went into the Grateful Dead's version of the country blues tune, Mexacali Blues. Knowing Margie Markowitz was sure to be close by Billy modified the lyrics. "It's three days ride from Boston and I don't know why I came, I guess I came to keep from paying dues, so instead I grab a bottle and a girl who's just fourteen and an empty case of the New York blues, Said her name was Belinda and she was fresh in town, I didn't know a stage line ran from hell, she took me into her room whispered in my ear, go on my friend do anything you choose, now I'm paying for those happy hours I spent there in her arms with a lifetime sentence of the New York blues, Is there anything a man don't stand to lose when he let's a woman hold him in her hands, you just might find yourself out there on horseback in the dark, riding and running across those desert sands."

He couldn't help but notice Kelly and Jimmy as they were standing near the stage to his right. He wondered when they were going to pounce. Despite the fact that she was here to arrest him, he also couldn't help but notice how attractive Kelly looked. Figuring this could be his last performance for a while, maybe ever, he rocked and delivered. The band closed the set with Dylan's "Tonight I'll Be Staying Here With You." Jimmy could have sworn Billy gave him a wink during the chorus. The encore was another new, as yet untitled song, written for the occasion:

> "Judge and jury came back before I left the dock
> With a guilty verdict and a plank they wanted me to walk
> The forewoman brought back the verdict you all wanted to see
> Don't need no trial of my peers to know I'm guilty

(Chorus)
> "If you see me coming, Katie bar the door
> Cause all you'll find with me on your kitchen floor
> Is pimps, pushers, needles and whores
> So far gone don't know right from wrong anymore

> "Hangman says I murdered a friend of mine
> Way down in New York City,
> But death ain't no greater sentence than the one

189

Already imposed on me
Lines and lines of brown colored bars
All my mind can see

(Chorus)   "If you see me coming, Katie bar the door
Cause all you'll find with me on your kitchen floor
Is pimps, pushers, needles and whores
So far gone don't know right from wrong anymore

"I'm so pale, you people have bled me to death
Can't sentence me to nothing I didn't already catch
The scars are there to remind me of the things I done
If you can find room for one more go ahead and have
your fun.

With the closing of the song, the set was over. As the stage and room went black Billy sensed someone moving toward him in the darkness. He prayed it was a roadie as he reached into his pocket and swallowed whatever pills were there-in the event it wasn't someone who worked for him. Then he heard Jimmy say those fateful words: "Billy Sunday, you have the right to remain silent."

Even though he'd heard those words a million times on TV, in movies and even in person on a few occasions, Jimmy's reading of his Miranda rights seemed surreal.

He felt Kelly gently grab his arms and gather them behind his back. He then felt the cold metal on his wrists. Unfortunately, it wasn't a totally foreign feeling for him, however, it was still a feeling you never got used to. Then he heard the *click*.

Outside of the club O'Connell had encountered McBride on her way back out. He was bullshit. "This wasn't the deal we made. What the fuck is going on here? Where's my client?" He had his back to the street but McBride could see the media approaching with their cameras rolling.

"Excuse me, Counselor." McBride brushed Danny off. He decided he better find his client and let McBride pass.

Jimmy and Kelly didn't know exactly what to do with Billy now that he was in their custody. The few reporters who'd made their way into the show could see through the darkness that Billy had been arrested and given the small size of the room they were quickly converging on the stage. They hustled him into the hallway that was adjacent to the room with Billy cooperating. He was pretty wasted, so they danced him around like a rag doll. "I thought you were supposed to call my lawyer?" managed Billy.

"We were kid, but the DA overruled us," replied Jimmy. He heard Billy mumble two names he'd never heard of, Fiona Apple and Alannis Morissette. To Jimmy, Billy seemed particularly upset with Fiona Apple, *whoever the fuck that was.* He thought. Whatever Billy was rambling about seemed to bring a smile to Kelly's face.

"All right, Billy, if you cooperate we'll try and get you out of here as quick as possible, but we need to move now," said Kelly, still holding Billy by the arm. Billy could sense the pressure closing in around him and the lack of sleep combined with the booze, powders and the stress of the arrest were conspiring to shut his whole thought process down. He felt his knees start to buckle.

"Jimmy, he's getting awfully pale," observed Kelly. "We need to get him out of here."

"Uncuff him, but make sure you hold onto him," said Jimmy.

Billy felt dizzy as they pushed and prodded him up the narrow hall.

"When we get to the top of the stairs we're going to make a right and then another right, all right Billy?" said Jimmy. "They'll be an unmarked cruiser and we're going to put you in the back." They formed a single file line, sticking close together-Jimmy in front, Billy in the middle and Kelly bringing up the rear. They exited the club in the middle of a pack of people and quickly ducked right. Most of the reporters were to their left and focused solely on McBride. As Billy made the second right he stumbled forward as they were having difficulty holding him steady.

"Breathe. That's it, easy," said Kelly.

"Fuck me," exclaimed Jimmy.

Billy looked up after hearing Jimmy. Along with a photographer, sitting on the hood of the unmarked cruiser, was Margie Markowitz. Kelly tried to take off the blazer she was wearing and throw it over Billy's head but she was too late. The photographer's flash was already popping with the repeating light providing a strobe like effect as Jimmy and Kelly hurried Billy into the back of the car with Jimmy slamming the sedan door closed.

"All right, Margie, you got what you wanted, now please let us do our job." Jimmy wasn't really that upset and he had to give Margie credit. She knew Jimmy wasn't one for press and photo ops but she'd found a way of circumventing their plan.

"Okay Jimmy, any comment?"

"No, not really. What does Rod Stewart say? Every picture tells a story."

"You and Detective Agis want your picture on the front page of tomorrow's Post?"

"No thanks," They said in unison.

With that, Margie and the cameraman jumped off the hood and took off down the street.

Jimmy and Kelly entered the front seat of the sedan and Jimmy started the car and pulled away from the curb. They left in a wake of a cacophony of sound and light exploding on the street in front of the Acme. The car eased into traffic with Billy in the back seat and his head tilted back as he stared up at the ceiling, feeling nauseous. He caught a chill as the sweat from the stage was drying on his body in the cool night air. He shivered briefly with his mind unable to focus. Kelly turned in her seat toward him.

"You okay?" she asked gingerly.

"Yeah, just peachy, all things considered. I feel like I've just been named Captain of the Titanic after it hit the iceberg," he responded. Kelly laughed. She took a hard look at Billy with his head back and his eyes closed. He didn't look capable of murder. To her, he looked like a regular guy trying to make his way through life, on his terms. *However misguided they may be*, she thought. To her, like most women in Billy's life, she defended him by maintaining he was probably just misunderstood. Then again, in her line of work, she had seen some fine men do some cruel things. What was that saying: "The surgeon operates to save your life, but deep down there's a part of him or her that enjoys the cut." *Maybe a part of Billy really enjoyed the cutting. Or maybe he enjoyed rough sex that went to far? Or maybe Belinda had threatened to take away his dream? Or maybe he made a deal with the devil, Phil Caruso in return for his dream, or maybe in the end it was just the rivalry between him and Vell over Belinda.* Men had killed for a lot less, as the cliché went. *Who knows?* She continued to think, turning back to face the front. Her thoughts made her realize that McBride may not have much evidence against Billy but she had a whole lot of motive. In any case, whatever happened or didn't happened, why or why not, it was a waste; a waste of one life and now with an arrest, a waste of another life.

Jimmy glanced first at Kelly and then in the rearview mirror. He didn't bother with all that analysis because his intuition told him that Billy wasn't the guy. The problem for him was that even though he didn't believe Billy was the guy, he had no idea who was the guy. The bad luck for Billy was that with McBride calling the shots Jimmy and Kelly were going to do everything possible to make him look like the guy.

Having outwitted the media at the club, Jimmy pulled into the motor pool and parked with the station house being relatively quiet. Just as he'd done a few hours earlier, Billy made his way from the motor pool to the elevator. This time, however, he was going a little less willingly. Booking was on the station house's first floor and Jimmy knew it was only a matter of time before the media figured out to where Billy had absconded. Because of this they'd prepared to have him booked, fingerprinted and photographed on the third floor. In the elevator he removed the cuffs for the second time and Billy rubbed his wrists where the cuffs had been. Subconsciously, he was trying to erase the memory, wanting desperately to be anywhere else. He thought of something Dickie used to say, "All you had to do was click your heels three times, Dorothy." He thought of trying it just for kicks but instinctively knew it was probably a little too late for that. It was going to take a lot more than magic slippers to get him out of this jackpot. Immediately upon their arrival at the squad room he was fingerprinted, photographed and then placed in the interrogation room.

At midnight, DA McBride walked in.

Just what I fucking don't need, Fiona Apple, Billy thought.

"Mr. Sunday, as you are aware, you've been charged with first degree murder in connection with the death of Belinda Caruso," McBride began.

"I want my lawyer," was all Billy would say.

Fortunately, the pills he'd swallowed at the club were jettisoning through his bloodstream and despite being under the influence, he continued to grow physically and mentally tired of the whole charade.

"Why don't we make this easy on everyone," McBride began again. "Why don't you tell me how it happened. Was it an accident? A crime of passion, maybe?"

"Fuck you, Fiona," He answered. McBride gave him a quizzical look.

Maybe I should cut a deal? He was thinking. He was guilty of using drugs, which in turn had impaired his judgment, which had led to the problems at Belinda's. *Maybe the sex they had, had been too much? Maybe it would be easier to confess and get it over with once and for all? Live out his days at Riker's Island. Christ he had had more experiences that most men could ever even dream of possibly having. Spending the rest of his life in prison was not an ending that he had ever ruled out, actually.*

"Jails, institutions and death," Dickie had said to Billy at one time or another. That was all drinking and drugs promised you in the end. It looked like he was now destined for all three, neglecting to realize he was already in jail. He began to wonder if New York was a death penalty state and he was pretty sure murder was a capital offense in New York. He figured, *Even so, with a crime of passion the death penalty would be unlikely, wouldn't it?* McBride shoved a pad, a pen and paper toward him. Billy shoved it back. He figured this might make him look guilty but what the fuck? He felt guilty.

Just then, O'Connell burst through the squad room door. Sitting outside the interrogation room door, Kelly and Jimmy jumped up. They didn't try and stop O'Connell. Jimmy figured McBride had broken the deal so they left her on her own with O'Connell.

"What the fuck, McBride!?" He screamed so loud Jimmy thought they might have another murder on their hands. "Billy, you didn't say anything did you?" One quick look at Billy told Danny he wasn't in much of a condition to do anything. "Listen, McBride, you fucked me. You fucked me with the arrest when you knew he'd surrender. Now, you're interrogating when you know he's lawyered up. This bullshit ends now." McBride brushed Danny off with a wave of her hand, further infuriating both Danny and Billy.

"Your client is being arraigned in Court Room 1 at 9:00 am tomorrow. See you then, boys." With that, she opened the interrogation room door and waltzed out of the squad room.

Chapter 30

DROWN(ING) MAN was the headline on the front page of Wednesday's New York Post. Underneath the headline was a picture of Billy hunched over and being led to the squad car. The by-line was *Margie Markowitz, New York—Like a wife beater/murderer that attends the deceased spouse's funeral, Billy Sunday eulogized his alleged victim and friend, Belinda Caruso, from the stage of his last two performances. After the second performance, he was arrested by New York Detectives Jimmy Gerard and Kelly Agis and charged with Mrs. Caruso's murder in an apparent sex tryst that went bad.*

Bad town to have a PR problem, m'boy Billy," Jimmy was thinking, while reading the morning paper in his apartment. Billy Sunday looked to be guilty in everyone's eyes despite the fact they hadn't heard a single shred of evidence. In Jimmy's opinion, there wasn't much more than a single shred and this rush to a judgment of guilty seemed to be the case for every murder defendant since that travesty called O.J. Jimmy pulled on his gray suit jacket over his white button down, he adjusted his gray and maroon tie, checked his court outfit in the mirror and headed out the door to the arraignment.

The New York Supreme Court was located in mid-town and the court was housed in an old gray, granite three-story structure which couldn't be mistaken for anything other than a courthouse. He and Kelly drove to the back of the courthouse with Billy in the back. In the face of all the events of the preceding two weeks and the preceding day in particular, Billy had actually slept in his cell. Lying on his bunk he remembered his mind racing and he thought for sure he'd be awake all night but his body must have been past the point of exhaustion and simply gave out. The sleep had felt good-maybe because it was unexpected. Maybe because in some ways he had reached the end of the race, no more running. And Jimmy and Kelly had been kind enough to leave him by himself in a holding cell at the station.

After arriving at the courthouse, Kelly and Jimmy released Billy into the custody of Danny O'Connell so he could wash up and make himself look presentable. This was unusual for a first-degree murder defendant, however, given the media attention the case had already drawn, they had been willing to make an exception in their treatment of Billy. He wasn't going to get too far with Margie Markowitz lurking around every corner and Jimmy felt he owed Danny O'Connell one after the clusterfuck at the Acme Lounge. They knew Billy wasn't going anywhere as he could have run when they uncuffed him last night. Finally, O'Connell was ethically bound to produce Billy. Danny whisked Billy into the first floor men's room that he had made sure was deserted before they entered.

"You look horrible," assessed Danny.

"Haven't had a lot of sleep or peace of mind lately, Counselor, you know?" he answered. Danny handed Billy a razor.

"Shave it all-even the goatee."

"Really?" asked Billy.

"Really."

Although he remained pale and drawn, Billy actually cleaned up pretty well. He still had black circles under his eyes and his pupils were still tiny pin points from the previous night's medication the visible effects of opiates lasting up to seventy-two hours. He put on the pressed blue suit and shirt O'Connell had brought him.

"All right, we're going to head into court," began Danny. "I'll waive the reading of the charges to spare us the drama. The judge will ask you how you plead. You'll say, not guilty. Then we'll get into bail. As you can imagine, I haven't had an opportunity to discuss bail with the lovely DA. Have you given any thought to bail?"

"No," said Billy. "I haven't given any thought as to how I'm going to pay you." Not what a high priced defense counsel wants to hear on the morning of an arraignment.

"Well, Fiona Orange," continued Danny.

"Apple. Apple, Fiona Apple," Billy corrected. They both broke into nervous laughter.

"Christ," said Danny, "the bitchstrict attorney, Fiona Apple, does anybody call this broad by her real name? Anyway, she'll be looking for a high bail."

"Yeah, well, I'll deal with it somehow," Billy had no idea how he was going to make bail. A bail that could easily be seven figures, high seven figures if there is such a thing. The thought of asking his father was not something he was willing to even consider since his father might just say hold him until trial. Then another thought suddenly crossed his mind. *What if the judge denies bail altogether?* He broke into a cold sweat. As he walked out of the rest room, Jimmy and Kelly ushered him back into custody. Now that he was clean cut and dressed in a custom tailored navy blue suit, white oxford, red silk tie and black penny loafers, he looked like a new man.

My type of man, creative but classy when he has to be, Kelly was thinking. This only served to remind her that it had been a long time since she had been intimate with a man. She re-cuffed Billy and brought him back outside. The three of them walked past a loading dock and stopped in front of another door.

"There's only one cell in there for all of the custody cases, so why don't we hold him here?" suggested Kelly.

"Yeah, that's fine. He'll probably be first on the list. Want a cigarette?" Jimmy asked Billy.

"No thanks, don't smoke," said Billy, "only vice I never acquired."

"Good, neither do I," replied Jimmy. "I was just making conversation."

A prolonged silence settled between the three strangers, now drawn intimately together by their intertwined fates. Billy rocked nervously back and forth on his feet while he kept trying to steal glances at Kelly. She was aware when men where eyeing her as it happened often. This time with Billy, however, she didn't mind and in fact, she liked his attention.

Abruptly, Jimmy corralled her and Billy and pushed them through the door.

"Fucking Markowitz, 3:00 o'clock," Jimmy blurted, explaining his sudden aggression. He and Kelly fell into the door way, Kelly lost her balance and threw her arms around Billy as she crashed into him. Being handcuffed, his center of gravity was off and he in turn fell against the wall. Her lithe body leaned hard into his and he felt her hesitate just slightly before pushing herself off him. She felt good and tight against him. Jimmy turned around, saw what was happening and rolled his eyes at both of them. They all laughed.

"You know, maybe under different circumstances, we could have had a nice life together," Billy said provocatively

"Isn't it pretty to think so?" Kelly answered without hesitation.

"Any girl who can quote Hemingway has to be all right," he pointed out.

"Hey, lover boy, give it a rest. Don't you Casanovas ever quit? And as for you, Detective, that's quite enough." Jimmy queried, interrupting the tender moment.

A door opening at the far end of the hall halted Jimmy's lecture.

"State vs. Sunday, Sunday a custody, Sunday here," bellowed the Court Officer.

Jimmy undid Billy's cuffs and grabbed him firmly by the arm.

"Show time," said Jimmy, as he escorted Billy into the courtroom.

"Not exactly the stage I'm used to, or the time of day, Christ, what time is it? 9:00 am? Middle of the fucking night to me, should have listened to my father after all and become an early riser" said Billy. Jimmy let him go at the doorway and he entered the courtroom on his own.

The courtroom was typical of most big city courtrooms; dark wood paneling traveled halfway up the walls with murals depicting courtroom scenes covering the walls up to the ceiling. The oak wood floor was polished to a shine, but well worn. The judge's bench was the same dark wood as the wall paneling with the bench rising to six feet above the floor. To the right of the judge's bench, if one were facing the bench, was the witness stand which was three quarters the height of the judge's perch. Across from the bench were two dark wood tables with two black leather chairs behind each. At the left hand table was McBride and she was dressed in a maroon, knee length designer business suit, accented by black heels and sheer stockings, topped by a conservative fitted, black blouse. She wore a set of pearls around her neck. Billy entered through a door on the right hand side of the courtroom. It looked to Billy like McBride had a new haircut. He was right. She had a file open and was calmly discussing its contents with an associate who looked like her lap dog. *She isn't half-bad looking,* he was thinking. But to him her personality only accentuated her deficiencies. *Maybe that's why everybody saw her as such an ugly person,* his thinking continued. There had to be a song in there. She pretended not to notice Billy approaching and when he was close enough to touch her she looked up briefly but wouldn't acknowledge his presence-at least not to him, anyway.

To McBride's left and Billy's right was the defense counsel's table. There, in his finest Armani black, double-breasted suit, stood Danny O'Connell. The collars of Danny's starched white shirt were so crisp they looked sharp enough to cut. His midnight blue tie was holding up the collar with a perfect knot. Danny motioned with his hand for Billy to come over.

This guy is my last line of defense, Billy couldn't help thinking. The severity of the situation had sunk all the way in.

"How are you holding up?" inquired Danny, while giving him a firm confident handshake.

"All right, considering," was his reply with no amount of conviction.

"McBride refuses to talk to me about bail, so I can assume she's going to aim high, and I mean, real high," stated O'Connell.

"Whatever it is, I'm not sure how I'm going to pay it anyway."

"Have you spoken to your father yet?" Danny asked with a note of anticipation.

"No."

"You don't look half bad, considering," Danny pointed out.

"Considering what?" Billy replied. "Considering I'm national news for murdering an ex-girlfriend when all I did was get laid?"

"Shhh," whispered Danny. "Don't get cocky. Don't you realize where you are?"

"You're right, you're right. Sorry Danny," said Billy, trying to pull himself together. The Court Officer interrupted them.

"Hear ye, hear ye, this honorable court is now in session, Justice Howard Mills presiding."

Justice Mills, all five foot, five inches of him, was draped in a black robe as he stepped up to the bench. He had salt and pepper neatly trimmed hair and wire rim glasses adorned his tan, weathered face. He look learned; sort of a stereotypical justice. He banged his gavel once.

"Good morning, Counsel." Mills nodded first in the direction of McBride and then in Billy and Danny's direction.

"Why don't we begin," he said. "Miss McBride, I'd like to say it's an unexpected pleasure, but given the sensationalism you've orchestrated around this case, I figured I might be seeing you this morning, so please begin."

McBride mistakenly took that as a compliment and began in a clear, concise voice. "Your honor, this is the State of New York vs. Billy Sunday. The charge is murder in the first degree, your honor." Just as she was about to begin reading the charges, O'Connell interjected.

"Your honor, the defendant waives the reading." This was a common practice. The arraignment was the first phase of the criminal court proceeding. After the arrest-usually the next day, or next morning to be exact-the defendant is brought to court where he is arraigned or formerly charged with the crime for which he was arrested. At the arraignment, the clerk normally reads the charges and the defendant enters a plea. The defendant often waives the reading, as Billy had done, because the prosecutor may use the reading to embellish the state's case. McBride was disappointed, but she knew she'd get another shot at disclosing the facts during the bail argument.

"How does the defendant plead?" commanded Justice Mills.

Danny touched Billy's arm lightly. Billy, who was already standing, moved forward slightly and bumped into defense counsel's table. "Not guilty," He returned in a strong firm voice.

"Miss McBride, I assume you would like to be heard *briefly* on bail?" Mills was anticipating an opening argument in the form of a self serving monologue from McBride at some point this morning but he intended to keep the proceedings orderly and compliant with the rules of law. He wasn't about to let the hearing deteriorate into a Court TV reality show.

"Your honor," McBride began, "this was a brutal and pre-meditated homicide."

O'Connell sprang to his feet. "Objection, your honor."

Objections during bail arguments were unusual. Mills could see right away that nothing about this case was going to be ordinary—the District Attorney was personally trying this case which was highly unusual. Mills addressed both attorneys, "Counsel, please approach the bench." Conversations solely between the judge and attorneys were called a bench conference; also very unusual during bail hearings. Mills swiveled around to his right, as McBride and O'Connell approached the bench. They stepped up on a small podium and simultaneously leaned their heads toward him. Almost as second nature, the judge covered his microphone with his left hand and began addressing the two solicitors in a hushed tone.

"All right, Miss McBride, for whatever reason, you've staked your political future on this case. I will not allow this courtroom to be a campaign stop on your way to the senate or wherever you think you may be headed. I expect you to follow the rules of evidence and law. I will not tolerate the slightest bit of grandstanding. Are we clear?"

"Yes, your honor," she answered. Mill's lecturing McBride had brought a smile to Danny's face. His satisfaction turned out to be premature. Judges dispense justice equally. Mills then turned his sights on O'Connell.

"As for you and your client, Mr. O'Connell, the defendant is accused of a very serious charge. As such, I intend to hear and allow the jury all the evidence the law permits. When I say evidence, I mean evidence. I don't want myself or the jury to be distracted by gamesmanship by you on behalf of your client. At this point, we don't know whether your client is guilty of this charge. However, I do know that most of these so-called rock and rollers who end up before me are no angels. So let's all straighten up and fly right. Step back, please."

McBride and O'Connell resumed their respective spots behind their tables. O'Connell, with his back to the judge, winked at Billy. He assumed this meant they'd won the initial round of what was sure to be a long and drawn out battle.

"District Attorney, please continue," Judge Mills instructed.

"Thank you, your honor." McBride decided she'd better tone it down a notch. "This murder was particularly egregious, your honor. The victim was tied up and then strangled and left for dead. The defendant here before us is a musician who has spent the last two years traveling throughout the country and abroad. As such, he has the means and contacts to flee this jurisdiction and the country, for that matter. Also, the defendant has no permanent address and no ties to this community. We request bail in the amount of two million dollars."

Without any reaction, Judge Mills turned to defense counsel. "What are your thoughts on the subject of bail, Mr. O'Connell?"

The combination of McBride's request and the lack of reaction from the judge had Billy's head swimming.

"Your honor, at the moment there are very few facts that implicate my client in the victims death. The evidence is circumstantial at best. The evidence in this case indicates that Mrs. Caruso's death may have been self inflicted, accidental, and at the most a crime of passion committed by any number or paramours. While it is true my client has no permanent address, he is presently on tour in support of his latest record release. At present he possesses a very public persona. With the amount of media attention focused on this case, and my client in particular, I believe his whereabouts will be self-evident at all times. His appearance for court, which is the purpose of bail is assured. I ask that my client be released on personal recognizance, your honor."

Mills covered his mouth and turned his head as he coughed twice. This pause, although unintentional, only added to the drama. McBride, O'Connell, and Billy stood silently awaiting the judge's response. "I can't say I understand today's youth," Mills began. Both O'Connell and Billy thought this was a bad start.

"How can a person in today's society have no permanent address? I thought gypsies were extinct. The issue of home confinement is mute since the defendant is, in effect, homeless." This remark evoked nervous laughter from the gallery seated directly behind both counsel tables.

"Given that," Mills continued, "The Defendant does not have a history of violence and furthermore, he doesn't pose a risk of flight since by his nature he appears to be in perpetual flight." More chuckles from the gallery. "I do, however, agree with part of the defense counsel's argument. Given the press' attention to this matter, Mr. Sunday should not be hard to find. I will also add, Miss McBride, that you brought this upon yourself, in part, since it's my understanding that your office has been stoking the so called media flame. Notwithstanding these facts, it is still the most serious of charges any defendant before me faces. I am setting bail at one-hundred thousand dollars cash." Without missing a beat he slammed down the gavel. "Next."

Two court officers approached Billy from each side while lightly grabbing an arm and escorted him back through the side door which he had entered. Both attorneys appeared unhappy with the judge's decision which usually meant it was a pretty good decision. This was the nature of the legal profession-nobody was ever happy; not the judges, not the victims not the lawyers and especially not the defendants. The judicial process had become one big compromise. While this was the status quo, none of the parties completely resigned themselves to this reality. The combination of the politics in the DA's office had Danny wondering whether his life's pursuit, trial practice, was still a worthwhile endeavor for a stand up guy. He'd known the answer for a while, given the ever-decreasing moral standards of opposing counsel but this case was making the answer crystal clear and things had barely begun.

Billy was returned to the holding cell. Given the fact that all court sessions had just begun, the cell was empty and he found himself all alone and once again feeling sick and exhausted. The proceedings had kept his mind busy and his adrenaline running high but now that it was over, he could feel his body physically and mentally crashing on him-big time. He was surprised his body had made it this far. Looking back over the past week alone, he'd traveled back and forth between Boston and New York, he'd done three showcases in five days, he'd used everyday—not to mention sex with four different women, including twice with two at the same time in the last five days, one of whom was now dead. Running the movie over in his head had mentally, as well as physically, exhausted him.

It wasn't lack of sleep that made him tired, he felt depleted down to the marrow of his bone and he knew that even a week of sleep wouldn't make a difference.

This wasn't in the brochure, he was thinking.

The way he'd lived his life up until now, there was a pretty good chance things would end badly; a jealous husband, and/or a jealous girlfriend, a drug overdose, an accident. When you lived on the edge like he did, you could see everyone around you falling over that edge. But like everyone else, he never thought it would happen to him until ultimately one misstep and gravity had taken control. *The ironic part is that when it did happen, it became crystal clear that it was inevitable. What had Belinda done to him? Or was it what had someone else done to him?* Was all he could think to ask himself. He showed up and slept with her, per her request. By the time he arrived at her apartment just after midnight he was exhausted and as high as a lab rat. The sex was nothing but a psychedelic blur and had been animalistic as they were both still angry at each other over their argument earlier in the evening. The fact that Belinda had insisted on a threesome normally a turn on to Billy made little difference. Animated sexual words had turned to physically charged gropes, rambunctious pushing and pulling. He remembered the other woman lying on the bed beneath Belinda inserting the sex toy she was wearing around her waist into her. With Belinda riding the woman she reached over and greased Billy with her hand. Billy then forced himself into her from behind. She asked him to grab her throat; to almost suffocate her until she reached orgasm from the double penetration. This was a technique that they were both aware of because it was reported to be extremely satisfying. Had he actually suffocated her. *But she was alive when he left,* he pointed out to himself. Belinda came so hard her screams had to have awoken the neighbors. Billy couldn't recall what exactly happened after that, but he remembered climaxing. He remembered the other woman asking for the same thing but Billy got dressed and left shortly thereafter. He wasn't sure who she was but he had seen her somewhere. She seemed pretty well acquainted with Belinda by the way she moved around her body. Plus those two had been well into it by the time Billie arrived. All the toys, lubes, and ropes were already out and in use. The sex was great but in the end the whole episode had left him feeling empty. Had someone set him up? The who and why was easy. Phil Caruso had mentioned to him at the showcase that Belinda was becoming a problem and that her taking a much needed vacation would benefit both Phil and Billy. But Billy thought Phil was referring to rehab. And there was Vell had his dislike, jealousy and egocentrism really led him to murder Belinda to rid him of his rival?

His knee-jerk reaction was to go back to Boston in search of Nacy. Looking back now he realized Nacy didn't exist for him anymore. It was a fictional relationship created solely in his mind. A panacea for all of Billy's self-created problems. He now understood his fear of commitment had always won over his desire for stability. He was thinking, *Look where doing what I wanted, when I wanted, combined with a fear of all things has put me. I'm incarcerated and on trial for murder! Whatever had been done, for the first time he was willing to admit he had done to himself.*

Billy's mind rewound back to the night in question. *Maybe she'd had a heart attack after I left, in which case would I still be guilty?* He was leaning against the dirty white cinder block wall of the cell, sliding down until seated on the cold steel bench bracketed to the wall. His elevator was headed to the ground floor.

"Rock fucking bottom," he said out loud.

Just thinking of calling his father for bail money only escalated his depression. He and his father had never been on the same page and he knew without a doubt that his father was done paying his way out as he had said as much, more than once. It was time for him to pay for his own mistakes. He decided that if he was going to have to go it alone, then there was no reason he should subject himself to further abuse from his father. He loved his father and he knew his father loved him, which only made the fact they couldn't resolve their differences more frustrating. "We always did feel the same we just saw it from a different point of view," as Dylan had sung. No, he didn't need his father's aggravation, especially now.

Just as he was coming to the realization that without his father he had no chance of making bail, Jimmy Gerard came back down the corridor.

"Let's go, William, you made bail," said Jimmy. As Jimmy drove him from the courthouse back to the station house Billy almost jumped out of the car when Jimmy told him who posted the bail.

Chapter 31

Phil Caruso stood at the desk in the lobby of the station house. Heading down the stairs from the squad room, Billy almost tripped when he saw his boss, the late Belinda's husband, waiting for him. Jimmy had told him Phil was responsible for posting the one-hundred thousand dollar cash bail, but he figured it was just some sort of sick joke.

"Hey, Billy, there you are. C'mon, my car's waiting outside," Phil announced in a warm, friendly tone. Kelly, Jimmy, and the rest of the squad house stood looking on in total disbelief.

"C'mon, kid, move it. The tour bus is over at the label. You need to move your ass if you don't want to miss any tour dates," Phil continued. "Detectives, thank you for your assistance in expediting the release of my artist. We at Artiste stand behind our artists." With that, Caruso grabbed Billy's arm and whisked him out the door.

Most of the reporters were still at the Courthouse where McBride was conducting yet another press conference. Fortunately for Billy, nobody had tipped the media to Caruso being the one to post bail. There were a few reporters from the tabloids who snapped photos of Billy and Phil, side by side, as they left the precinct and entered the waiting limousine.

Inside the limo Billy sat in silence, stunned by the turn of events. Phil picked up a folder off of the leather seat that stretched around the limo's interior. "How you doing, Kid?" Phil asked, with genuine concern.

"All right, I guess," managed Billy. In spite of the fact he'd been physically intimate with Phil's wife throughout their marriage, he couldn't bring himself to thank him.

"Listen, I'd like to get our story straight, so to speak," said Phil. "I know you'll find this hard to believe, but I didn't bail you out from of the goodness of my heart." He handed Billy some papers. "This week's Soundscan, you know how to read it?"

"I know how," he said, rather abruptly. He studied the first page and then quickly glanced through the remaining pages.

"Fifty-five thousand and some odd units the first week," commented Phil. "That's without much airplay, which is rapidly changing, due to your recent legal problems."

Phil sat smiling like a little kid.

You sick prick, Billy couldn't help thinking. He knew the stories about going to any length, but this was ridiculous.

"I've staged protests in each of your next five tour stops and I'm having the publicity department work with the media which should further enhance the Soundscan." Phil didn't like the look he was getting from Billy, "All on the QT, of course."

"You people are scavengers; Belinda was a friend of mine, not to mention your wife."

"Don't give me that shit Billy," Phil replied angrily. "You saved my ass and now I'm returning the favor by saving yours. You should be grateful. Plus we both know what she was about, let's not pretend now that she's gone she was something else."

"Grateful, you cold prick? I didn't go there to save our asses," said Billy. "Which I might point out, my ass is only saved temporarily. What happens if I get convicted? You most likely have life insurance you're collecting. Let me out."

"The trial ain't my problem," said Phil. "I'm just paying your legal fees."

"All recoupable out of my royalties," Billy interjected.

"Hey, I'm a businessman. I'm not the red fucking cross," Phil replied. "But either way, you'd be rotting in a jail cell with a shitty public defender if it wasn't for me,"

"If it wasn't for you, I wouldn't be in this mess. Let me out, let me out, let me the fuck out," Billy screamed. He opened the car door, as if he was going to jump so Phil signaled for the driver to pull over.

"Go fuck yourself, Caruso," said Billy, jumping out of the limo as it slowed to a stop. In a show of emotion he slammed the limo door after he had exited.

He'll come around, Phil thought. Either way Phil was covered. He had an airtight alibi, the life insurance had increased the plus side of the ledger substantially and the red ink in the form of Belinda had stopped bleeding—no pun intended. Also Billy was right about one thing, for the time being he had saved Phil's ass. The DROWN record sales could very well save his job. He couldn't have planned it any better.

Billy wasn't the only one surprised by the turn of events. "Looks like your boy just jumped out of the limo about ten blocks from here," Jimmy relayed to Kelly.

"My boy? He's not my boy," Kelly insisted.

"I saw how the two of you look at each other. I don't know what the fuck you're thinking, but hey, love is blind I guess." Jimmy countered.

"How do you know he jumped out of the limo?" asked Kelly.

"I had them followed. Wanted to see how badly we fucked up not following through on connection between Billy and the grieving husband." He watched as Kelly's spirits sank.

"Don't worry. Billy almost jumped out while the limo was moving. Maybe he and Caruso aren't that cozy after all."

"We need to get a look at them-like now," said Kelly.

"I agree. Caruso just hit the lottery, his wife won't be spending any more and he has a couple million dollars in life insurance coming his way."

The unmarked cruiser wasn't the only car following Caruso's limo. No sooner had Billy exited the limo when a taxi stopped a block ahead. Dickie waited as the cruiser continued to follow the limo. Once they were gone, he yelled, "Hey, Sunday!"

Billy initially thought a tabloid reporter was trying to ambush him. He was pleasantly surprised when Dickie walked up to him and grabbed his arm.

"C'mon kid, you've had enough excitement for one day." He guided Billy, who was now on autopilot, into the waiting taxi.

"The reporters have been swarming the hotel where we were staying so we'll meet the bus in Harlem on our way out of town," informed Dickie. "What did Caruso want with you?"

Billy filled Dickie in on what had transpired. They were stopped at a traffic light and could see the bus sitting idle a couple of blocks ahead.

"Listen, this is against my better judgment, but I picked up some detox meds," said Dickie. "You really need to straighten yourself out, Billy."

"I know, I know," said Billy automatically.

"Not just because of you're legal trouble, but because you can't keep going the route you've been traveling. You look like you're on death's door. I'm going to give you a couple of sleep meds when we get on the bus and I want you to sleep. We're off until tomorrow night in Philadelphia. I want you to sleep until the show, all right? I'll have the Russian sound check your gear."

"Fine," said Billy, too tired and worn out to disagree. He was grateful for Dickie's adopted motto, "The show must go on!" Never once had Dickie mentioned quitting.

As he boarded the bus, Billy popped the sleeping pills. Charlie swung the bus doors closed and headed southwest towards Philly. Looking out the window he saw the familiar space between the horizon and the dark clouds. He fell asleep before the bus could slip through the opening into the twilight.

And that's how it went. Billy and the band toured, records continued to sell, Kelly and Jimmy investigated-both doing their jobs while the wheels of justice continued to turn.

Chapter 32

"We have good news and bad news on the DNA," informed Kelly, holding a plastic baggie containing the beer cup from The Paradise show. She and Jimmy were in the squad room. Jimmy was dressed in light colored cotton slacks and a blue button down dress shirt. Kelly was attired in a short yellow skirt and a white sleeveless top. Memorial Day had come and gone and hints of the oppressing city heat were starting to radiate.

"Let me guess," said Jimmy. "Sunday's sperm is a match for intercourse, but not for what was found orally."

"How did you know?"

"Because that's what he told us when we interviewed him."

"And you believed him then?"

"Not until just now," Jimmy smiled.

"Now what?" asked Kelly.

"Well, Detective, the way I see it, we can put Sunday at the scene somewhere near the time of death but we haven't been able to make the connection between Caruso and Sunday."

"That doesn't mean it isn't there," Kelly replied.

"I know, but Caruso paid Sunday's bail and legal fees out of an Artiste Records account. There's no way the Board would allow anything funny, particularly murder. I'm assuming that as long as Drown is selling records they'll continue advancing him his own money. There are rumors about protests being staged to generate publicity but we can't confirm that, either. It's hard to believe Caruso would stoop that low."

"Don't be," said Kelly, "From my limited experience, a staged protest is a high point in the promotion of anything. Even if we can confirm its true, it doesn't help our investigation."

"That's why we haven't spent much time pursuing it," said Jimmy.

"In any event, we need to identify the unknown fingerprint and the sperm found in the victim's stomach," said Kelly.

"And we need to do it before the upcoming evidentiary hearing on the admissibility of the DNA from the cup-in the event the cup gets thrown out," said Jimmy. "We had Brill's fingerprints on record and there was no match. Caruso didn't know the apartment existed so I doubt they're his fingerprints."

"That leaves Vell,"

"Have you spoken to McGregor again?" asked Jimmy.

"A couple of times, he still saying no immunity, no Vell."

"Just like he stated up in Boston."

"Right,"

"Well, Brill's statement is that he left before Vell did," noted Jimmy. "If Vell did have sex with her, it was after Brill left."

"So Vell was lying?" asked Kelly. "The interview was off the record so he didn't perjure himself."

"No, but maybe we can shake him up a bit," said Jimmy. "Convince McGregor he's a suspect. Get him to come down."

"McGregor will still want immunity," she continued.

"Call McBride, see if she'll grant Vell limited immunity."

"Immunity, unless we can reasonably show Vell did it, or something like that?"

"Yeah, I mean, were pretty sure Vell didn't do it. He was back in Boston at the time of her death," said Jimmy. "In addition to lack of opportunity he lacks the means and motive. Although we've heard he and Sunday have had a blood feud going for a while, we don't know if the feud was enough to drive Vell to set up Sunday for the murder. Quite frankly, Vell doesn't seem smart enough. Let's get him down here and maybe he can shed some light on Sunday's motives. If he was that close to Belinda, maybe she talked to him about Billy?"

"All right, I need to talk to Beth about the evidentiary hearing anyway." Kelly picked up the phone, "The District Attorney, please, Detective Kelly Agis calling." After a few minutes of waiting for McBride to pick up, Kelly continued, "Hi, Beth. Good. Yes, things are developing. Yeah, you saw the DNA results. Jimmy and I were just-okay, all right, I'll tell him. I'll see you at the Courthouse at around 8:00 am, thanks, Beth. Goodbye." Kelly hung up and looked at Jimmy. "She doesn't want to give Vell any immunity yet. She wants to wait until the evidentiary hearing is over. She thinks Mills will allow the cup as evidence. She figures we don't need Vell. If Mills throws the cup out, then she'll grant Vell immunity."

"Risky strategy," said Jimmy. "Because at that point, we'll have to grant Vell total immunity and McGregor will know it."

"You just said you were pretty sure Vell didn't do it?" said Kelly.

"Yes, but I still have no idea who did and until then I don't like granting anyone immunity," answered Jimmy.

The next day, Justice Mills, DA McBride and Danny O'Connell all assumed their respective places in the courtroom. As it was a motion hearing, Billy's appearance had not been necessary.

"What do we have, Counselors?" Mills asked after banging his gavel and bringing the court to order.

Standing behind the defense counsel's table, O'Connell looked up. He was dressed in one of his designer suits, underneath was a white starched shirt and a gold power tie. "Good morning, your honor. This hearing is in connection with defense counsel's motion to suppress evidence. In particular, DNA resulting from the seizure of a beer cup from The Paradise Rock Club in Boston," Danny began.

"Both parties ready?" Mills asked.

"Yes. Yes, your honor," was the simultaneous reply.

"Proceed please, Mr. O'Connell."

"Thank you, your honor. May it please the court? The facts in this matter are relatively straightforward, your honor. Without a warrant and without reasonable suspicion, Detective Kelly Agis of the NYPD illegally seized a beer cup my client had been drinking from during his performance. At the time, my client was not a suspect in this case. The cup was on a stage where my client had just finished performing. As the stage is limited to performers only, my client had a reasonable expectation of privacy that his personal belongings on said stage would not be subject to police search and seizure. I ask that the cup and DNA resulting from said cup be suppressed as evidence against my client. In the alternative, your honor, I would argue that if the seizure of the cup is allowed, the cup and resulting DNA be suppressed on the grounds that the chain of custody was broken in removing the cup from the stage in Boston and delivering the cup to a lab in New Jersey for testing. Thank you, your honor."

In general terms under the law, when the police seize evidence they must account for the whereabouts of the evidence at all times while it remains in their custody. In addition to accounting for the evidence's whereabouts, the state must show that the evidence could not have become tainted.

"Miss McBride, may we have your thoughts on the subject?" asked Justice Mills.

"Thank you, your honor. The State would like to call Detective Kelly Agis."

Kelly approached from the gallery and walked up to the witness stand. Justice Mills swore her in as a witness.

"Miss Agis, do you swear the testimony you are about to give is the whole truth and nothing but the truth, so help you God?"

"I do."

"Good morning, Miss Agis," Beth began.

"Good Morning," Kelly replied.

"Miss Agis, could you take us through the events of the Sunday in April when you seized the cup in question?"

"Sure. My partner, Jimmy Gerard and I, were investigating the homicide of Belinda Caruso. We had information that two individuals who were in Boston had been seen with Mrs. Caruso on the day and evening of her murder. The first, Mr. Vell, had agreed to meet with us along with his lawyer. After meeting with Mr. Vell, we proceeded to the Paradise Rock Club. Mr. Sunday was performing there that evening. We made numerous attempts to meet with Mr. Sunday, but were unable to do so. Detective Gerard and I attended the performance. After the performance, I noticed a cup that Mr. Sunday had been drinking out of was left on stage. I approached the stage, took the cup and transported it back to New York. Upon my return, I sent the cup to the lab for DNA testing."

"Thank you, Miss Agis. Nothing further, your honor," said McBride.

"Your witness, Mr. O'Connell," said Justice Mills.

"Thank you, your honor," Danny began. "Good morning, Miss Agis."

"Good Morning."

"At the time you were in Boston, was my client, Mr. Sunday, a suspect?"

"Yes."

"He was a suspect? You had a warrant?"

"No, we did not, at the time, have enough evidence for a warrant. However, we did have an eyewitness who placed him at the murder scene around the time of death."

"And you spoke with Mr. Sunday that night and that conversation further indicated to you that he was a suspect?"

"No, we never had the opportunity to speak with Mr. Sunday."

"So, if I understand you correctly, you grabbed the cup without knowing if in fact my client was a suspect?"

"No, I told you we had reason to believe Mr. Sunday was a suspect." This was a stretch and Kelly and McBride both knew it. Was this enough to convince Mills?

"After you grabbed the cup, you bagged it in evidence and marked it for identification according to NYPD procedure?" Danny turned his back to Kelly and began walking back to the defense table after he finished the question.

"No."

"No?" Danny turned back toward Kelly while exaggerating his surprise.

"No," said Kelly. "I didn't have any evidence bags with me."

"So, how did you get the cup back to New York?"

"I put the cup in my purse," answered Kelly, knowing that any attempt at disguising the truth would not appeal to Justice Mills, no matter how painful the truth was in this case.

"In your purse? You at least emptied your purse out, right?"

"No," replied Kelly.

"Nothing further, your honor," said Danny.

"Closings," said Mills, moving the matter right along.

Defense went first. "Your honor, it is clear from the facts presented today and Ms. Agis' testimony that at the time she went to Boston this investigation was at the preliminary stage. My client, Mr. Sunday, was not a suspect at that time. This is clear since there was no warrant for his arrest. Furthermore, Ms. Agis was not prepared to gather evidence in the event that she did speak with my client. Finally, the chain of custody was broken when Ms. Agis placed the cup in her purse along with her personal objects. I would ask that the Court suppress the cup and any evidence resulting from said cup."

"Thank you, Counselor, Miss McBride?" said Justice Mills.

"Your honor, case law clearly states that a suspect who leaves evidence in a public place should have a reasonable expectation that the evidence can and will be lawfully seized. The stage at The Paradise is a public area where anyone can pass, as Miss Agis did. As further evidence that this was a public place, nobody attempted to stop Miss Agis as she approached the stage and ultimately took the cup. Second, your honor, it was not reasonable for the two detectives to carry evidence bags to Boston on a preliminary investigation of a suspect. Had the detectives been required to gather evidence, they could request assistance from the Boston Police. Miss Agis acted reasonably in both seizing the cup and bringing it back to New York in her purse. Had she awaited the assistance of the Boston Police, it is likely that an employee cleaning the club would have taken the cup and the evidence would have been lost. Under the prevailing law, the cup and the evidence resulting from the seizure of said cup, should be admitted. Thank you, your honor."

Mills glanced at some papers the clerk had handed him at the beginning of the proceedings. Presumably, they were the briefs the attorneys had filed, respectively, in support of their positions.

"Hhhhhmmm," Justice Mills cleared his throat. "Normally, I would prefer to wait on ruling in this type of hearing, but given both the media attention and the evidence I am inclined to rule now. The seizure of the cup is border-line. Case law does provide that items left in a public place by a suspect do carry a reasonable expectation of being subject to seizure.

The issue, for me, is whether Mr. Sunday was a suspect at the time he left the cup. There was no warrant. However, it is not reasonable to expect to obtain warrants immediately upon deciding an individual is a suspect. The key word here being suspect. Weighing in the defense's favor is that at no time was Mr. Sunday informed that he was a suspect. The question there then becomes whether the NYPD had a reasonable opportunity to inform Mr. Sunday that he was a suspect and, thereby, alerting Mr. Sunday to the fact that items left in public by him could be subject to search and seizure. The NYPD had no problem informing Mr. Vell he was a suspect and he was in Boston, thereby, Mr. Sunday should have had the same expectation of being informed that he was a suspect since the circumstances were similar. Fortunately, I do not have to decide that issue. Therefore, the transportation of the cup back to New York does not satisfy case law in connection with maintaining the chain of custody in connection with evidence that has been lawfully seized."

Danny broke into a smile. McBride simply looked down at the table. Justice Mills banged the gavel. "There is case law that supports law enforcement using reasonable efforts where normal procedures and regulations cannot be followed. That was not the case here. Boston Police were present at the scene. Miss Agis knew or should have known that they could assist her in obtaining evidence in the proper and legal manner. It is true that the cup could have been retrieved by anyone in the interim, while Ms. Agis awaited the Boston Police Department's assistance. However, the cup being in a public place the police should have had the reasonable expectation that its owner or someone else may retrieve the cup. The opportunity for tainted evidence in the way the cup was transported back to the lab is far too great in this case. The cup and all the evidence connected thereto are hereby suppressed and inadmissible."

Murmurs quickly grew into excited voices. Mills banged the gavel.

"We now have another matter related to this case before the Court, I believe?" asked Justice Mills. "I have before me a motion from defense counsel requesting an expedited trial date in this matter. Miss McBride, does the state have any objection?"

"No, your honor, the state has no objection."

"Fine, this matter is then set for trial a week from today. I'll see you then, Counselors."

BANG! With the final fall of the gavel, Justice Mills signaled the end of the proceeding and immediately retreated to his lobby. Obviously pleased, O"Connell had no one with whom to share his victory so he made his way to the Court Officer, presumably seeking a back way out to avoid the media.

McBride turned from the table and with her eyes she searched the courtroom until they landed upon Kelly and Jimmy who were at the back of the gallery. She motioned with her hand for them to approach. The reporters were perched at the bar that separated the gallery from the floor of the court. As long as McBride stayed within the confines of the actual courtroom, she was safe.

"Not exactly a surprise," McBride said to both Kelly and Jimmy once they'd reached her.

"Sorry, Beth," said Kelly.

"Don't worry about it. I don't think we had enough to show he reached the level of suspect." said Beth.

"We discussed that at the time," Jimmy interjected.

"Hey, you guys took a shot. It just didn't go our way," said McBride. Jimmy was surprised she was taking this initial defeat so well.

"Where are we at now?"

"Well, we still have Billy's admission that he had sex with Belinda, but if he doesn't take the stand we may have a tough time getting it in. We need to explain the remnants of oral sex since Billy denied that," said Jimmy. "If we don't explain it, O'Connell will use it to show reasonable doubt and he'll be able to show that someone else was there having sex with Caruso and that someone else could have murdered her.

"We can use the coroner," said McBride. "The semen in her stomach was partially digested, so it had been hours prior to the time of death-unlike the semen found in the anal cavity. Who do we think she had oral sex with?"

"Vell," Kelly replied.

"All right, ferret out the facts. We need to explain it."

"What about?" began Jimmy.

"We'll have to give him full immunity. I know, Gerard, you told me so. I'm not worried about Vell and his sins. I want Sunday to hang for the murder." With that, McBride picked up her briefcase, approached the bar and faced the waiting media.

Chapter 33

The second of July was a warm and pleasant summer day in New York City. The outside of the courthouse was surrounded on three sides with satellite television trucks as the talking heads battled for sidewalk space. All were live from New York on the first day of the trial.

This time, Billy entered the courthouse through the front door. At 8:30 am he and Danny appeared out of nowhere with Billy looking fit and healthy; he'd lost weight and he no longer had an ashen complexion or gaunt look. His navy blue suit looked loose on him where it once strained at the seams. His white button-down shirt and sky blue tie brought out the blue of his now clear eyes. He exuded a confident and relaxed demeanor. By his side, Danny was wearing a navy blue pin-striped, seersucker suit. They were smiling brightly as they strode up the courthouse steps, ignoring the questions being shouted out at them by the multitude of reporters lining the steps and sidewalk.

Shortly after they had entered the courthouse, McBride arrived in a Lincoln Town car. She was dressed conservatively in gray business suit with a white silk blouse underneath. Her black heels were practical and a silver chain rested around her neck with a crucifix nestled in her cleavage. The two male assistant DA's that flanked her were dressed like Senators with their eyes focused straight ahead and their hair cut short and gelled to perfection. After exiting the vehicle McBride paused, waiting for the reporters to swarm her as they formed a half moon around her and her two assistants. Boom mikes, hand mikes and cameras were being thrust at her from every direction.

"The State is confident in our case against Billy Sunday and fully anticipates that he will be brought to justice for the murder of Belinda Caruso. Thank you." Short and sweet, McBride turned her back on the media and made her way up the steps and into the courthouse.

Justice Mills began the proceedings as Court TV began rolling live and the trial of the decade began like most over-hyped media events-uneventfully.

The first order of business was to pick a jury; voir dire, as the process is defined in legal terms. The jury was picked fairly quickly with only a few people actually claiming they hadn't heard or read anything in regards to the trial before them. The media attention leading up to the trial had been so intense that even if you lived under a rock in New York City, a reporter would have unearthed the rock. Of the numerous polls on the subject, fifty-one percent believed Billy innocent (seventy percent being women) while twenty percent had better things to think about. Since his arrest, there had been no new wars, no presidential scandals, and no upcoming elections. It had been a slow summer as far as current events was concerned, just the usual run of the mill murder, rapes and pillaging that go on in New York. *The Music Biz Murder*, as it was now being dubbed, stayed front-page tabloid news. The jury consisted of eight men-six white, one black and one of Spanish decent along with four women—two white, one black, and one Spanish. Neither McBride nor O'Connell could really tell whom the jury would favor but both sides figured that as long as the jury arrived at the truth, each side would have its interests served.

"Good afternoon, ladies and gentlemen of the jury," McBride greeted and the trial was underway. "I am the District Attorney for the City of New York. My name is Beth McBride and I will be prosecuting this case on behalf of the people of New York City. The defendant in this matter is William McCarthy, best known as the rock and roll musician, Billy Sunday. The state intends to show that Mr. Sunday did, with malice aforethought, commit the homicide of Mrs. Belinda Caruso. This is to say he planned to and succeeded in carrying out the murder of the victim, Belinda Caruso. The state will show that Mr. Sunday had the opportunity to kill Mrs. Caruso. Through forensic evidence, the state will show that Mr. Sunday was present in the apartment immediately prior to her death. The state will also show that Mr. Sunday had the means to kill Mrs. Caruso and that Mr. Sunday engaged in a pattern of violent sex with the victim and that sex ultimately and intentionally resulted in the victim's death. Finally, the state intends to prove that Mr. Sunday had the motive to commit this crime. Mrs. Caruso owned the record company which Billy and his band DROWN recorded. Mrs. Caruso thereby had control over his career. The one thing Mr. Sunday wanted out of life, the one thing Mr. Sunday continually pursued at the expense of everything else, was fame and fortune as a recording artist. And when the one person who could make that dream become a reality, Belinda Caruso, threatened to take that dream away because of the defendant's promiscuity, Mr. Sunday killed her. He killed her in an effort to keep his dream alive. And for a while, he's been enjoying his dream. The publicity that's been generated as a result of the murder has resulted in more ticket sales and CD sales for Mr. Sunday. In closing, the state will show through the evidence and testimony from witnesses that Mr. Sunday is guilty of the murder of Belinda Caruso. The state will then ask you to put an end, once and for all, to Mr. Sundays dream and turn his reality into the nightmare which he so richly deserves. Thank you."

Danny slowly rose from the defense counsel table and with each hand he grabbed the lapels of his suit coat. His feet were planted firmly beneath him so that his weight was distributed evenly and he was standing straight and tall in front of the jury. He smiled coyly just before he started speaking. "Good afternoon, ladies and gentlemen. My name is Danny O'Connell and I represent the defendant before you, Mr. Billy Sunday. Mr. Sunday is a musician." Danny motioned with his hand towards Billy, who was sitting up straight and attentive at the defense table. "Now, you may not like rock and roll or his music in particular," Danny continued. "And I must add that I've heard it and I don't particularly care for it." This brought smiles from all the jurors and a slight scowl from Mills. Danny rocked up slightly on the balls of his feet and began to slowly pace in front of the jury box. "You may not care for his music or his lifestyle." Danny had decided it was strategically best to put the issue about his reputation on the table right away. "You may think that he has a low set of morals, however, that does not mean that he has no morals. And even if he had no morals ladies and gentlemen that is neither a crime nor why we are here today. Billy comes from a good solid upbringing and a stable home. He has a college degree. He has no legal record or a history of violent behavior. He has no police record, which means the state will not be able to show a single instance of violence committed by Billy in his whole life. Yet, the District Attorney would have you believe that this non-violent, mild mannered musician, one night suddenly became a calculating, cold-blooded murderer. I'm not implying that it's impossible for a man with a mild temperament to lose his temper. But I am saying that this is not what happened in this case." Danny, now standing dead center in front of the jury box, continued. "Billy and Belinda Caruso were lovers and as lovers they participated in consensual sex. They had a friendship that transpired over a number of years and like any friendship that endures over a long period of time, they had their share of arguments and disagreements. But like any true friendship they always managed to resolve their differences. And that, ladies and gentlemen, is what Billy went to do that Wednesday night on the Upper East Side. Billy and Belinda had a disagreement earlier in the evening and Billy wanted to set things straight before he left New York and continued on his tour. He went to Belinda's apartment at her request. He didn't rush over there in a rage. And the reason Billy wanted to set things straight was not only to maintain their friendship, which he valued, but also because Belinda was in fact Billy's boss. Belinda ran the record company that had exclusive rights to Billy's band, DROWN. The D.A. would have you believe that Belinda was going to take Billy's dream away and that this was the motive for the murder of Mrs. Caruso. Without Belinda, Billy had no dream. Belinda was the sole person who believed in him and had taken a large financial gamble on Billy because she felt it was a worthwhile endeavor. No other record companies were knocking on Billy's door. Billy had no incentive and no motive to have a disagreement with the only person in his life that believed he could achieve his dream. Billy's record had already been released, the single had been being playing on the radio and the wheels were already in motion, so to speak. For the D.A. to try and convince you otherwise, is insincere at best. Now, I'm not saying the publicity surrounding Mrs. Caruso's death and this subsequent trial didn't help my client sell tickets or records. But ultimately, it's the DA and the state who are driving that publicity. My client has not sought to benefit from the unfortunate demise of his friend. He hasn't given a single interview to the press, radio, or the television stations. He has declined hundreds of opportunities.

Now, the DA has also failed to mention to you that there were other suspects who all had motive, means and opportunity to commit this crime. There is her husband, Mr. Phil Caruso. Mrs. Caruso was a woman who pursued adultery as a hobby and spending Mr. Caruso's money, as a habit. The defense will show that in addition to motive, Mr. Caruso also had means and opportunity. In addition to Mr. Caruso, the defense will show that the state's key witness, Johnny Vell, also had motive, means and opportunity. The defense will show that the state rushed to give Mr. Vell immunity before clearing him as a suspect. This is because, as the defense will show, Mr. Vell ultimately could not have been cleared as a suspect. After all the evidence and testimony, the defense will present to you that not only has the state not proven beyond a reasonable doubt that Billy Sunday is guilty of the murder of Belinda Caruso, the defense will show you that to convict Billy Sunday of this murder is simply not reasonable. Thank You."

McBride began putting in the State's case. The first witness was the coroner, Steve Simkins

"Good afternoon, Mr. Simpkins," Beth McBride began. She then guided Simpkins through his education and work history, concluding with his appointment as coroner for New York City.

"Mr. Simpkins, did you conduct an autopsy on the victim, Belinda Caruso?" McBride asked.

"Yes," he replied.

"Is this the autopsy report?" asked McBride, as she handed him a black notebook.

"Yes."

"Using this report, I would like to ask you a few questions about the death of the victim. Could you identify any toxins found in the deceased bloodstream?"

"Yes, I found a number of foreign toxins. Along with alcohol there were narcotics—specifically oxycontin, heroin, and cocaine."

"Based on what you found, do you know when these chemicals would have been ingested?"

"By the quantities present, I would say shortly prior to the time of death."

"I'll get to the time of death in a minute. In your opinion, could the toxins have caused or contributed in anyway, to the victim's death?"

"No, based on the amounts found and the condition of the victim's vital organs, there is no evidence that her death was the result of an overdose of any of the chemicals or combinations thereof."

"Thank you, Mr. Simpkins," McBride continued. "Now, you mentioned the time of death. What was the established time of death?"

"The victim died sometime between midnight and 2:00 am Thursday morning," Simpkins then explained the medical details as to how he arrived at this conclusion.

"In addition to the time of death, can you tell us what resulted in the cause of death?"

"The cause of death was strangulation."

"Can you explain that further, in detail?" McBride asked.

"The official cause of death was asphyxiation due to strangulation. The means of strangulation is not exactly clear. There was evidence of manual strangulation, namely bruises on the throat and neck that matched hand patterns. There was also evidence of a ligature, for example, indentation lines around the victim's neck. So although the cause can be determined, the exact means, either by hands or ligature, cannot.

"Thank you, Mr. Simpkins. I have just a couple of more questions, if I may? In your autopsy, did you also find evidence of sexual activity?"

"Yes. The autopsy revealed partially digested semen in her stomach and recently ejaculated sperm in her anus. The sex appeared to be consensual as there was no signs of rupture."

"Did semen in the stomach match the other semen found?"

"Objection, your honor!" bellowed O'Connell, jumping to his feet.

"Withdrawn. Nothing further, your honor," McBride said, knowing that O'Connell's objection would be sustained, based on the results of the evidentiary hearing but at least the topic was introduced to the jury.

O'Connell began the coroner's cross-examination dispensing with the pleasantries. "Mr. Simpkins, in addition to the chemical toxins found in the victim's bloodstream, were there any other foreign substances?" O'Connell asked matter of factly.

"Yes, there were other substances, but nothing out of the ordinary and certainly nothing that would have contributed or caused the victims death."

"Did you check for bacteria that could have been present in food?"

"There were common bacteria that would be found in food items."

"Were you aware that the victim had complained of stomach pains earlier in the day, after eating sushi?" O'Connell continued.

"No, I was not made aware of that," Simpkins replied.

"Was there bacteria that could have been carried by raw fish?" O'Connell asked.

"Some."

"Some, but not all?"

"Some, but not all," Simpkins answered by repeating O'Connell.

"Had you been aware that the victim complained of stomach pains after eating sushi, would you have conducted additional tests during the autopsy?"

"Not necessarily. The tests we use detect most common food bacteria's, including those found in raw fish. These tests do not uncover more exotic blood-born illnesses, like those contained in sushi."

"Is it true that some of the exotic bacteria contained in sushi are deadly? Is that correct?" asked O'Connell, baiting the hook.

"Correct," answered Simpkins.

"So, without performing those tests you can't rule out the fact that Belinda Caruso's death may have been the result of toxic food poisoning? Either intentionally or unintentionally?"

Simpkins moved uncomfortably on the witness stand. "That is highly unlikely. Our tests would have uncovered the existence of a foreign substance, if not exactly identifying it."

"Unlikely, but not impossible, is that correct, Mr. Simpkins?"

"Correct," Simpkins replied sheepishly, now realizing he'd been had. "Nothing further, you honor," O'Connell concluded.

"Thank you, Mr. Simpkins, you may step down," Justice Mills said. "This court is in recess until tomorrow morning." Mills brought down the gavel and waited for the jury to leave the courtroom before he exited.

The next morning, Beth McBride called Andy Solomon, who testified to seeing Billy at Belinda's apartment late Wednesday night, early Thursday morning. O'Connell had mentioned Billy's presence at the apartment in the opening so initially he didn't plan to question Solomon. However he thought of one question the answer to which couldn't hurt and could possibly help.

"Did the police ever take your fingerprints?"

"No, why would they do that, I was at home, in bed."

"Thank you. Nothing Further."

McBride, in an attempt to both clarify matters and swing the momentum in favor of the prosecution, called the state's key witness, Johnny Vell. Vell strode into the courtroom dressed head to toe in music business black. His hair was greased back and his complexion was tan and he was trying to appear relaxed, as he took the stand and was sworn in.

"Good morning, Mr. Vell," McBride began. She took Vell through his name, present address, education and job history. She then began questioning him about the events on the Wednesday in question.

Vell recounted the testimony he'd given to the Detectives in his lawyer's office. His testimony matched the initial interview up until the time when Vell and Belinda arrived at her apartment. After that, the similarities to his prior account ended.

"Mr. Vell, what happened once you returned to Mrs. Caruso's apartment?" asked McBride.

"At first, Belinda said she wasn't feeling well and when I asked her why she told me she was upset, you know, stressed out about Billy. She told me that she heard Billy had been in town the night before but that he hadn't called her. Worse, for her, was that he'd been seen in the company of a couple of other women. Belinda explained to me that she and Billy had been romantically involved for some time and that part of the deal with her signing his record to Artiste was that she was going to leave her husband and go on tour with Billy. Billy hadn't mentioned it and the fact that he'd been in New York and hadn't contacted her, had her very upset. She began to cry. In an attempt to comfort her, I hugged her."

"What happened next?" McBride asked.

"One thing led to another and we ended up, well she-I mean, I think she was trying to get back at Billy," Vell began to ramble.

"Did she perform oral sex on you?" McBride asked.

"Yes."

"Did you ejaculate?"

"Yes."

"Then what happened?"

"Well, at that point we were on the bed. We were still ah, how do I say this, ah, intimate, when there was a knock at the door."

"What happened next, Mr. Vell?'

"We dressed quickly. She thought maybe it was Billy."

"Was it?"

"No."

"Then who was it and what happened?"

"Well, it was her nephew who is in a band called The Dead Boys. We listened to some of his music. Then I left."

"Did you see Mrs. Caruso again that night?"

"Yes."

"When was that?"

"Wednesday night. Billy and his band were playing in the village and I bumped into Belinda there. I stayed for a couple of songs and then I took the last shuttle back to Boston. That was the last time I saw Belinda."

With that, McBride concluded her direct examination, "Nothing further, your Honor."

Danny gathered his notes while rising slowly from the defense table. He was dressed in a gray, hand made double-breasted suit. "Good afternoon, Mr. Vell," Danny began. Just like with the coroner, Danny went directly for the throat. "How long have you known my client?"

"A while, I guess. I mean, we've both been in the music business a long time now."

"Yes, a real long time. Isn't it true, Mr. Vell, that you were once in a band with Billy?"

"That was a long, long time ago."

"Is it also true that you were asked to leave that band?"

"I wasn't asked to leave, I mean, I decided to go into the business side of music."

"And do you blame Billy for throwing you out of the band?"

"Billy and I have had our differences, but not because of the band thing."

"Was one of those differences Belinda Caruso?" Danny continued, before Vell could answer. "You had met Belinda in New York and in LA at several music events, is that correct?"

"Well, yes. Belinda was around the scene a lot. I don't see what that has to do with anything?

"You liked Belinda, but Belinda preferred artists, isn't that correct?"

"I wouldn't know." Vell replied, his tone becoming less pleasant toward Danny. At this point, McBride began to glare at Vell. Clearly, he had not revealed this information to her.

"You wouldn't know. You figured that had Billy not kicked you out of the band, Belinda would have been yours and not Billy's? This is the source of your problem with Billy, isn't it?"

"No, that's not true. It was just never convenient for us. We were always seeing other people and then she married Phil. It had nothing to do with Billy. The disagreements between Billy and I stem from, I mean, I guess, I don't really know what they stem from, you'd have to ask him. I mean, I always liked Billy." By this time, Vell was visibly agitated and nervous.

"You told numerous people in your industry that you were going to get Billy; ruin him, swearing that he'll never get a record played, is that correct?"

"Well, yeah, maybe. But that was business and had nothing to do with Belinda."

"So, you tried to set Billy up?"

McBride, who'd been waiting to pounce, had finally been given the opportunity; "Objection, your honor. Defense counsel has no foundation for that question."

"I agree," said Mills, "sustained."

"You figured that if you could get Billy out of the way once and for all, you and Belinda could be together, is that right?"

"Objection."

"Overruled. You're treading on thin ice, Counselor,"

"Withdrawn, nothing further," O'Connell had the last word and was able to show that Vell had motive and opportunity.

"We'll adjourn for the day, 9:00 am tomorrow. *BANG*. Mills lowered the gavel.

A couple of hours later, Billy and Danny were back in Danny's office. By now, the sun was setting and it was getting dark. "How do you think we're doing?" asked Billy.

"So far, so-so," answered Danny. "We've introduced an alternate theory that I'm not sure I can prove but we really don't have to prove it. I just need to raise a legitimate possibility to raise a reasonable doubt. The problem is that they can put you in the apartment with the fingerprints and they can put you there at or around the time of death with Solomon's testimony. The other problem is that I assume this witness tomorrow, the kid from CBGB's, is going to testify about the argument which you lied about to both the police and me. That means McBride will have shown motive, means, and opportunity. That may be enough. It's too close a call to risk putting you on the stand, but you could go down hard either way."

"Huh?" Billy uttered in astonishment.

Danny realized Billy hadn't been listening to one word he'd said.

"Billy, what aren't you telling me?" O'Connell demanded as he leaned forward in his desk chair.

The next morning, McBride began with the testimony from Little Stevie. As he walked into the courtroom, he mouthed the words, "Sorry" in Billy's direction. He was dropping a dime on his peer. However, once he took the stand and noticed the reporters, he forgot all about Billy. He relished telling, in great detail, how he had witnessed and overheard the argument between Belinda and Billy. O'Connell knew Stevie's testimony was dangerous, but he wasn't about to take any chances. O'Connell could tell by the end of his testimony that Stevie was claiming his ten minutes of fame and was playing up to the cameras and making a fool out of himself. O'Connell could not take the chance that Stevie would fabricate something that would only hurt his client further. O'Connell had Little Stevie read the Detectives interview report. Nonetheless, Billy's motive could be somewhat established, if still unclear.

Somehow, it had happened again; something both McBride and Gerard had sworn would never happen again. The case appeared to pivot on Gerard's testimony. McBride called Jimmy Gerard to the stand. He began by taking the members of courtroom through the discovery of the crime scene and the condition the body was in when he and Kelly had arrived. Through Gerard, McBride was able to introduce several photographs of the crime scene, showing Belinda tied to the bed and the bruises on her neck. "Were there forensics done in connection with the bruises on the victim's neck?" McBride asked.

"Yes."

"What were the results of those tests?"

"The results indicated that the victim was strangled by a pair of male hands along with a ligature of some type which appears to have been the victims left stocking."

"Were you able to match the defendant's hands to the bruises on the victim's neck?" McBride continued.

"No, we were not able to produce a match. However, we were not able to rule them out, either. The tests were inconclusive."

"Were the defendant's fingerprints found in the apartment?"

"They were all over the apartment."

"Were they found on the victim's left stocking?"

"The defendant's fingerprints?" Gerard inquired, making sure he was giving McBride what she wanted.

"Yes, were the defendant's fingerprints found on the victims left stocking, Detective?"

"Yes, the defendant's fingerprints were present on the fabric."

"I have nothing further, your honor," McBride concluded.

Danny O'Connell rose to cross-examine Jimmy. He decided to take a different approach in the cross-examination of Gerard than the approach he'd taken with the former witnesses.

"Good morning, Detective. There were a number of prints at the scene, were there not?" asked Danny.

"Yes, there were."

"Both full and partial prints, correct?"

"The majority were partial prints. I believe the only full prints found were the suspects, Mr. Sunday's, Mr. Brill's, and Mr. Vell's."

"That's all?" Danny pressed.

"I believe so."

"No other prints?" Danny asked. McBride looked up. Jimmy shifted in his seat as McBride looked fiercely in Jimmy's direction.

How the hell? Jimmy thought to himself, *Do they know about the fourth print? Was it in one of the reports or was O'Connell bluffing?*

"Mr. Gerard, was there a full fourth print? An unidentified fingerprint?"

"Yes, yes there was," said Jimmy. McBride's enthusiasm vanished.

"So there was a fourth print. Was this print ever identified?" Danny continued with his line of questioning.

"No, we were never able to identify the fourth print."

"Where was the print found?"

"On the front door knob, the stocking and the headboard where Ms. Caruso had been tied."

"Do you know when the print was left in the apartment?"

"No, there is no way of knowing when it was left."

"Is it possible that the print was left the night Belinda died?"

"Sure, I guess it's possible."

"Is it possible there was a third person in the room the night Belinda died?"

"Sure, I mean, anything's possible."

"So, another possibility is that someone else was in the apartment with Belinda after my client left?"

"Yes."

"Did you or your partner examine this possibility when you were investigating?"

"No, we did not," said Jimmy firmly.

"Thank you Detective, nothing further, your Honor."

The case was delivered to the jury with both sides believing they had a chance but neither totally confident in the outcome. McBride had shown motive, means and opportunity but her whole case was circumstantial. O'Connell had introduced a few alternate theories in an attempt to create reasonable doubt, the essence of his job. The first theory being that Belinda had been food poisoned, the second that Vell set up Billy for revenge and the third theory being that some mysterious third party had done it either before during or after Billy had left. All three theories were a little far fetched, but O'Connell hoped that they were not out of the realm of possibility and thereby would cause enough reasonable doubt for the jury to hang its hat on.

In either case, Danny had raised enough reasonable doubt to convince at least one juror; just enough that after two weeks the jury came back hung. The twelve jurors could not unanimously agree on whether to acquit or convict Billy. The judge in an attempt to break the impasse gave a final jury instruction. It was never clear whether the jury had bought any of the alternate theories. Some columnists concluded that the rushed and shoddy police work simply confused the jury. In the end it didn't matter as after three weeks of deliberating to a stalemate the judge released the jury and declared a mistrial.

Chapter 34

The hung jury only fueled speculation as to who was responsible for the murder. While nobody was found responsible, in a sort of karmic retribution all the players involved suffered. Phil Caruso, in his infinite wisdom and fearing the worst, had shorted Artiste stock on margin after Belinda's body had been discovered. Drown's album went platinum, driving Artiste's stock up in price. Phil lost the life insurance proceeds and then some. He also lost his job. Vell was further tarnished by the trial, but since he had little in the way of a good personal reputation to begin with the damage was incremental. His final ruination came when two media conglomerate's finished purchasing any and every commercial radio station in the country which left room for only two independent promoters, and Vell wasn't one of them.

Kelly Agis resigned from the NYPD and left to parts unknown. McBride had gambled and hadn't exactly lost, but she hadn't won, either. For a while she went on a media crusade trying to convict Billy in the press which also didn't work. Shortly after the trial, everyone had moved on to other scandals and it appeared her political career had topped out as New York City's District Attorney. Jimmy Gerard retired. He had enough time logged in for his benefits and he didn't have the energy or the desire to break in a new partner. Word on the street was that McBride had blamed Jimmy for the unfavorable outcome of the trial with McBride also saying that O'Connell's question about the fourth fingerprint had merely been a fishing expedition. Had Jimmy lied and claimed no knowledge of a fourth fingerprint, no one would have known about it and she believed she could have secured a conviction. Jimmy had had enough.

On a balmy fall evening Jimmy was at home flipping through the channels and waiting for the Yankee/Red Sox game to start. It was September and the pennant race was on. As he was channel surfing he caught a glimpse of someone he vaguely recognized. He flipped back through the channels till he came upon Billy Sunday. Here he was, finally granting an exclusive interview on one of those hour-long TV news programs, about both his career and the case.

Hey, more power to him, Jimmy thought. He'd always kind of liked Billy. He certainly felt no animosity toward him. As he continued to flip through the channels he started thinking, *What a waste, not only of time, money and reputations, but of a beautiful woman's life. Maybe she hadn't been the most saintly person in the world but she didn't deserve to die. In the end no one cared about Belinda.* Jimmy hadn't thought about the case in awhile, but the fact that he and Kelly were never able to ultimately solve her murder continued to bother him on occasion. He couldn't wrap his head around O'Connell's poisoned sushi theory, though he did seek out the chef Charlie, to no avail. The identity of the mysterious fingerprint turned out to be an even longer shot. Once again, he tried to put the unsolved case out of his mind, but there was a nagging doubt that kept running around and just wouldn't dissipate. It was like calculus he knew the answer was there but somehow just couldn't put the equation in the right order. Once the answer was known it would seem that it had been obvious all along. The thought was not unlike the song title on the tip of your tongue that you couldn't put your finger on; when you can't remember the name but the melody sticks in your head until you finally come up with the name, sometime days later, at the most random time. "Holy Mother of God," Jimmy said out loud, "Jackpot!" He dropped the remote and reached for the phone.

"Margie Markowitz."

"Hey," blurted Jimmy as he tried to still his beating heart.

"I don't believe it. You always said you'd call. I just didn't know you were going to wait thirty years."

"We need to talk," said Jimmy.

"Like now?" asked Margie, inquisitively.

"Now."

"Can I ask what this is about?"

"Billy Sunday."

"Oh, did you happen to catch his interview? I've seen a preview, not much new," said Margie.

"Maybe not, but I have something new," said Jimmy.

"You do? Like what?" Margie inquired.

"I think you know who did it," Jimmy answered.

"What was that? Never mind, I'll be right over." After hanging up she left her apartment and immediately headed for Jimmy's.

Jimmy and Margie were sitting on the couch with the TV on low. Jimmy wasn't too surprised with the speedy arrival of Margie banging on his door.

"Who was your source on all things Billy Sunday?"

"You know I'm not going to tell you that."

"Let me guess, was it a woman?"

"Yeah." She spoke with no inflection in her voice.

"A young woman?" continued Jimmy. He was looking for her to provide him with enough affirmation to convince him he was barking up the right tree.

"Yeah, how did you come to that revelation?"

"She was there," deadpanned Jimmy.

"What are you talking about?" asked Margie, confused.

"Your source was there the night Belinda was murdered," said Jimmy.

"What makes you think that, and now, after all this time?"

"I remember thinking at the time that the information you were getting was as if the person was there. Then the photo you produced of Belinda tied up," pointed out Jimmy.

"The one that ran on the front page?" asked Margie.

"Yeah. Originally, I thought it had been taken from the doorway. I figured maybe some reporter made it past the uniforms and managed to snap a picture. But I bet if you look at again, you'll be able to tell the photo could have only been taken from inside the room," said Jimmy.

"The fourth fingerprint," realized Margie.

"The Godforsaken fourth fingerprint," reiterated Jimmy.

"I never knew the girl's name," said Margie. "She used an alias and I tried looking her up."

"Which was?" asked Jimmy.

"Heroine," Margie replied.

"Like the drug?" Jimmy asked, quizzically.

"No like the savior, h-e-r-o-i-n-e," Margie answered. "That's what she implied she was to Billy, she said she was his savior. She was going to save him. She ranted that Belinda was just using Billy and she got what she deserved in the end. She swore that she didn't kill Belinda, had nothing to do with it but she wasn't upset Belinda was dead. She wanted me to know that Belinda just wanted a good time and didn't care whether it came from Billy or anyone else-man or woman. Went on and on about Belinda having a good time for the last time and that even if Billy had to go to jail for a while he was better off."

"Did you ever ask was she there when Belinda was killed?" asked Jimmy.

"Never thought of that," answered Margie.

"You never printed any of that," Jimmy said, with the dawning realization that Margie had more insight into the case than the prosecution or defense.

"She sounded like a strung-out rambling lunatic," Margie answered in her defense, "but the information she gave me was solid, so I listened to her nonsensical diatribes. Then she just stopped calling after Billy was arrested."

"Do you have a phone number, address or any way to contact her?" Jimmy asked, sounding hopeful. Why hadn't this woman surfaced during their investigation? Why didn't Margie see the connection?

"I've got nothing on her. She used an alias and insisted she contact me. I checked the caller ID and the numbers were all pay phones on the Upper East Side, but like I said, she just stopped calling."

They sat in silence.

"Did you ever interview any strippers at the clubs Billy was known to frequent?" Margie asked, after sitting there contemplating what Jimmy was inferring.

"No, we concentrated on the men in Belinda's inner circle. Why?" asked Jimmy, wondering what else he had missed.

"Well, when I received the promotional snippet for Billy's interview tonight I decided to take another look at the case for the hell of it. I came across a message. An anonymous tip from somebody in a bar said Billy was in there the night before he was arrested, supposedly, he was hitting on the bartender. I didn't think much of it. I sent someone down there but by the time they made it to the village Billy was gone and the bar was closed. For the hell of it, I called down to the bar when I rediscovered the message and I spoke to a woman but she wouldn't give me her name."

"Was it your source?" asked Jimmy, again hopeful.

"No, I thought of that, too. I asked her, even though it didn't sound like her. She swore to me she wasn't my source and I believed her. Anyway, I got to talking to her after assuring her that I was done writing about the case. She told me that she was the girl with Billy on the night that Belinda gave him the ultimatum at CBGB's," Margie could see by the confused look on his face that he couldn't figure out where all this was going.

"Stick with me, Jimmy," Margie continued, "She said she was the girl with whom Billy had a threesome the night before. That was the threesome that Belinda was so upset about. She said to get revenge Belinda wanted a threesome with Billy and another woman that night. I asked her if Billy ever mentioned who the third girl was and she said no but it was probably an escort or a stripper. She told me that she heard later that the girl's boyfriend walked in just after Billy left and flipped out on her and Belinda, like violent. I asked if Billy if he knew or heard anything like that but he said no. He did say that he had to change his cell phone number and that she was practically stalking him saying her boyfriend was going to get him next if he mentioned a word. I heard her stage name but I didn't write it down, something like Justice or Beverly Hills, you know, one of those typical stripper names." Margie stopped and stared at Jimmy. He was smiling. "What?" Margie asked with anticipation but no clue.

"Holy shit! I don't believe it. North or south?" Jimmy asked Margie.

"North or south, what?" Margie asked in return.

"Dakota, motherfucking Dakota," Jimmy said, almost to himself.

"We interviewed a Dakota who was a couple of doors down the next morning. She seemed enamored with Billy. Her boyfriend on the other hand didn't seem to care for either Jimmy or Belinda as much.

Now Jimmy finally knew why O'Connell had asked Andy had he been fingerprinted. Because had he been fingerprinted the NYU Law student would have found himself past the courtroom bar but in the Defendant's seat and not the counselor's chair.

"This Dakota was there and kept feeding me Billy to protect Andy. Having already killed Belinda it was probably a reasonable conclusion that she was next if she didn't help take the focus of both her and Andy," said Margie.

"And it actually fucking worked son of a bitch those two kids weren't as dumb as they looked."

Billy Sunday was on the TV screen. He was sitting in the back of his tour bus being interviewed by a female news reporter. He looked good, he was physically fit, his eyes were a clear, deep water blue and the dark circles were gone. He was dressed in his favorite black Beatle boots, jeans and a faded long sleeve, black T-shirt with the Grateful Dead Steal Your Face logo embroidered on the left breast. They turned up the sound to the TV.

"So Billy, where do we begin? It's been quite a year for you," the woman asked.

"I certainly can't deny that it's been quite a year. Cathartic though, cleansing in a lot of ways," said Billy.

"How so?" the woman asked.

"Well, the horrible tragedy of Belinda's death, who despite our differences was still a very important person in my life. Then the witch hunt to convict me of her murder, followed by the jury's failure to acquit me," said Billy.

"What do you mean, the jury's failure?"" the reporter asked.

"Well, I'm not sure if failure is the right word, but I think most people know by now that I did not kill her."

"How has that been cathartic, though?"

"Well, the album she believed in has sold over a million copies," stated Billy, "Without her, the record would have never been released."

"Are you also referring to your decision to stop using drugs?"

"I really don't want to talk about that," said Billy, trying not to sound defensive.

"Then are you still using drugs?"

"Not talking about that," said Billy, firmly.

"Heroin?"

"Why? You got any?" Billy asked, giving both of them a laugh. "All I'll say is I haven't used drugs today. How's that?"

"That's fine," the woman replied. "What about your love life?"

"No comment," Billy said, laughing.

"Kelly Agis, the detective in the Caruso case, is she a friend or more than a friend?" the woman asked.

"No comment," said Billy, beginning to shift nervously in the back seat of the bus.

"She works for you, though, is that correct?" the woman asked, pressing for an answer.

"Yes, Kelly works for me. Oh, she'll kill me, how should I say it, she's Drown's head of security-although mine may be in jeopardy when she sees this," said Billy, smiling and then laughing. "Next question?"

"Rolling Stone Magazine said and I quote, 'Through it all, Drown's Billy Sunday has learned to swim and rise above it all.' Were you drowning?"

"Yes, I think many of us who look for answers outside of ourselves are drowning. I don't know whether society or the media teaches us to do that, or whether it's just our natural instinct. That is to say if you buy the right car, you'll feel better about yourself. Or find the right man or woman and you'll be all right. Or take this drink or pill and you'll feel better, at least for a while anyway. ? Or money-money cures just about everything, right? If a drink or a pill or a car or a person or a couple of bucks makes you feel better shouldn't it occur to you that there is something wrong in the first place Ultimately, we realize too late that we're in over our heads-drowning, if you will, in stuff we don't really need. I realize now that inner peace can only come from within."

"So then, have you learned to swim?"

"Not swim, no. I think I've learned to tread water and just let the current either wash over me or guide me, and I think that's the best any of us can do. They say sooner or later, every river gets to the sea. I guess the trick for me was in finally finding the river."